FELL

When Annette Clifford returns to her childhood home on the edge of Morecambe Bay, she despairs: the long-empty house is disintegrating, undermined by two voracious sycamores. What she doesn't realise is that her arrival has woken the spirits of her parents, who anxiously watch over her, longing to make amends. Where did they go wrong? As the past comes back to life, Jack and Netty begin to see the summer of 1963 clearly: that distant year when Netty was desperately ill and a stranger moved in — charismatic, mercurial Timothy Richardson, with his seemingly miraculous powers of healing, who absorbed all their attention. Now they must try to draw another stranger towards their daughter, this time one who might rescue her . . .

JENN ASHWORTH

FELL

Complete and Unabridged

CHARNWOOD
Leicester

First published in Great Britain in 2016 by
Sceptre
an imprint of Hodder & Stoughton
London

First Charnwood Edition
published 2017
by arrangement with
Hodder & Stoughton
An Hachette UK company
London

A catalogue record for this book is available
from the British Library.

ISBN 978–1–4448–3423–9

Published by
F. A. Thorpe (Publishing)
Anstey, Leicestershire

Set by Words & Graphics Ltd.
Anstey, Leicestershire
Printed and bound in Great Britain by
T. J. International Ltd., Padstow, Cornwall

This book is printed on acid-free paper

For Skye

As God of the high road and the market-place Hermes was perhaps above all the patron of commerce and the fat purse: as a corollary, he was the special protector of the travelling sales-man. As a spokesman for the Gods, he not only brought peace on earth (even occasionally the peace of death) but his silver-tongued eloquence could always make the worse appear the better course. From this latter point of view, would not his symbol be suitable for certain congressmen, all medical quacks, book agents and purveyors of vacuum cleaners, rather than for the straight-thinking, straight-speaking therapeutist? As a conductor of the dead to their subterranean abode, his emblem would seem more appropriate on a hearse than on a physician's car.

Stuart L. Tyson, 'The Caduceus',
Scientific Monthly 34, 1932

Not farre fro thence there is a poole which
    rather
Had bene dry ground inhabited. But now it is a
    meare
And Moorecocks, Cootes, and Cormorants doo
    breede and nestle there.

Lelex tells of Baucis and Philemon —
Ovid's *Metamorphosis*,
Book VIII, translated by Arthur Golding

FIRST

Her key in the lock wakes us. It wakes the starlings too: they rise chattering out of the trees in the front garden and hurl themselves into the sky. They don't fly far; before the door is open they have landed, disgruntled, on the roof ridge. We flutter at each other like leaves, finding the words for things, laughing, stiff as bark, too wooden to grab and hold on tight.

Our?

Our names.

Yes. We are. We are. Dazed as newborns! The proprietors of this place. A respectable house. Netty. Jack. That's what they called us.

She opens the front door. It's stiff, and she has to push hard against the tide of free newspapers and old letters to get in, and when she does, she gasps, and looks around her at the old hallway, which is not as she remembered, its green-and-white-striped paper faded and hanging off the walls, and all the pictures gone. She closes the door behind her and stands, not moving, her breath making clouds around her face. It must be cold. Must be winter time.

This is our house. And here is our daughter and the words for all our objects start to come back to us now, and with the words come the objects themselves: the house and the garden, and the town around it which unrolls like a map, right down to the salt marsh, and it is all ours

3

and this is all we wanted and all we would have wished for if anyone had asked. To stay. To have it all back. To have stopcocks and light switches and — what are they called? plugholes — and sticking plasters and skirting boards and feather dusters. To have ourselves back. To be restored.

She kicks through the old letters, looking up at the damp patches on the ceiling and the strings of cobwebs around the light fitting. The glass shade furred with dust. We have the words for everything now. Lampshade. Light bulb. Doors. There's one on each side of the hallway for the dining room and the sitting room, and at the back, one for the little kitchen, which has its own door that leads into the garden. And we see ourselves, too, the way we were before. Jack stringing Christmas lights around a plastic tree and digging in the garden and painting the dining-room walls, doing battle against the damp. Netty with her dustpan and brush in the hallway, putting lipstick on in the hall mirror, kissing Jack in the kitchen, dancing to the Light Programme in the dining room when the lodgers have gone to work, sitting in her pink armchair doing accounts with a spare pencil behind her ear. A black-and-yellow-striped pencil, vivid as a bee, with a pink eraser fastened to its tip, a bit chewed. And a hole in her tights that is bothering her toe and the smell of flounder — not unpleasant — in the kitchen, and a thought about the doctor, and aspirin, and one more fag before putting the books away and going to bed. The lodgers — our boys, we call them — are laughing on the upstairs landing. When was this? No matter — it's all

4

happening now. As if we were never away.

The boys?

There. Look.

They're traipsing in through the hall right past our daughter, who's all grown up now, though she does not see them, and the house fills up with these young men in hats and ties and jackets, good boys, their rooms chock full with card games and cigarette smoke and Radio Luxembourg. The amount they eat! Constant trips back and forth to May's, and the bill from the milkman has to be seen to be believed. It comes back: aftershave and soap bags and women being snuck in and Jack, helping himself to the Christmas whiskey, turning a blind eye towards the girls because he was young once too and what's the harm in it now and again on a Friday night so long as they don't use up all the hot water or give the house a bad name?

This is what boys will be like.

Will be boys?

Yes. That's it. There it is.

Our daughter (Annette, we called her, and we'd know her anywhere — we never forgot her) wipes the dust from the hall mirror and stares at herself, then examines the glass in the front door, a little cracked but still there. She notices a leaflet from the town council half poking through the letterbox and she pulls it out and looks around again, then lets it fall to the floor with the others. She has a rucksack and a carrier bag and a sleeping bag with her and she puts them down at the bottom of the stairs and goes into the dining room.

The house empties again. Empties slowly, this house of ours, the overcoats and cardboard suitcases disappearing along the garden path and through the creaky gate and onto the street and off, until it's just Jack and little Annette, eating Candy's reheated stew and not speaking. Time passes, or it doesn't. Now there's just Jack, drunk in the daytime and smoking in front of the horseracing with the dishes not done. That's My Lady's Slipper very nicely turned out and up on her toes today looking a real treat in the paddock and here comes . . . but now the race is over and there's nobody left at all. Just the damp and the trees and the leaks and the dust. The wallpaper falls off the walls and one of the little windows in the kitchen shatters. Time works differently now.

We hear Annette coughing in the dining room. We were proud of the three-piece dining set. Table, chairs and sideboard, which we spent a year saving up for. When we finally got the set we realised it was all a bit too big and a bit too grand for the room, and either the table was out or the floor was, because it always wobbled. But having it was important, to give the right impression. To signal to the boys what kind of house we ran. Annette takes off her coat and puts it on the back of one of the chairs. The tablecloth is gone but the table only needs a proper scrub and it will be as good as new. She sees the little pink chair in the bay window. Not as pink as it was, but it could be rescued. She does not sit in it, but stares at it, frowning. She puts her hand against her throat, against her cheek. Rubs her eyes. But this is what the years do.

We expected her to come home to us eventually but we never thought it would take her so long. We never thought at all, if we're really being honest. It was a no-time, a dark-time, until the key in the lock jangled us back to the trees. But there she is, breathing in the stale air. She touches the walls, shakes her head. What did she think would happen? Time has not been kind — we know that — and we know there were things that should have been done in the house that were not done. Repairs and improvements should have been made that were not made. Things have declined somewhat. But what could we do?

She tries the light switch once, twice, and yes, it works, she must have made arrangements. She's taking in the ripped nets, yellow and sagging on their wires, and the black mould that has crept along the folds in the curtains. She covers her mouth and nose with one hand and pulls them open with the other. The light comes in. She sighs. She takes a notebook out of her pocket and starts a list — filler and paint, things to do, things to buy. She has plans. This is good. After a while she stops writing things in the notebook and takes a little silver box out of her pocket. She strokes it with her finger then holds it to her ear and starts to speak. A telephone? One that works without wires — her voice travelling silently through the air to someone else, someone far away. Of course things have changed but this, the sleek shiny box swallowing up her words and sending them elsewhere, this is . . . but what does it matter?

Her voice.
Her voice is.
We're lost for.
Well, the fact is, we have not heard her speak
for a long time.

NEXT

1

For the past two weeks Annette has been cleaning and sorting and moving furniture. She's bought a new mop and arranged for a skip to come. We've been watching her. We know now that the envelope from the people dealing with Candy's things was forwarded through a succession of Annette's old addresses, frequently languishing, undelivered, at out of town sorting offices. We know that it zigzagged around the country for two months and finally found Annette between jobs, stuck with the rent, annoyed with her neighbours. She took the keys out from the envelope, signed some papers and came home. Her family is gone — even Candy — so the house belongs to her. There's no work so what choice did she have, really? This is a cold house full of dust and the damp is making her cough but it's in a nice area, not the best but nicer than anywhere else she's lived and it should be worth something, she thinks, while she's sweeping.

See how it works? Sometimes we can hear what she thinks before she speaks.

She's busy sweeping leaves from the hall when someone knocks at the door. She uses the brush to push the leaves into the old sitting room. Closes the door on them and the ancient Rexine settee, too heavy to move by herself, split and disgorging its foam innards like guts. She hides the brush. She's done her best to prepare the house. She's picked up the piles of old post and free newspapers and she has opened the windows and aired the rooms and bought tea and biscuits. She has wiped out the kitchen cupboards and has taken meter readings. She has done what she could with the mould but if she is being honest, it is not what she'd hoped for, this homecoming. She opens the door and smiles. The woman standing there is a tree surgeon and she's got one foot in the house, the other on the pale front step. She doesn't come in, but half turns, eyes the sycamore trees, and whistles.

'They're big enough, aren't they?'

'They've grown,' Annette says. She sounds stupid. Corrects herself. 'Since I've been away. They've got bigger. Come in. Have a look.'

She hands over her list and takes the woman on a tour. The doors and windows that won't close, or refuse to open at all. The cracks and fissures zigzagging alarmingly from the edges of door frames. Gaps between skirting boards and floors yawning wide enough to fit your thumb into. The wallpaper, where it remains, rippling and puckering as if it is the surface of a lake disturbed by the wind.

'The walls are moving,' she says, 'I know they are. I'm worried the place is going to fall down on me before I can get shut of it.'

They stand together on the upstairs landing, still for a moment, trying to catch the house floating and juddering around them. We could have told them: it doesn't work like that; it waits until your back is turned.

'There's a lot of repair work that needs doing, but you're right to get me in first. Deal with the roots of the problem.' The tree surgeon laughs and Annette does not. 'Once we've dealt with the trees, you'll have to get builders in. Plasterers. The place needs gutting. A rewire. It could take months.'

'Months?'

'If you want it done quicker than that, you're going to have to pay through the nose for it. You're staying here?'

'Just for now.'

Annette describes the apartment in the attic that's a little better, slightly more liveable. But Christ, even up there the damp is so severe that a paperback left out for a day or two grows its own lacy wreaths of mildew that knot and web between the pages and obliterate the text. Her sleeping bag is dewy in the morning. But it isn't going to be forever. The tree surgeon follows her back down the stairs and the doors drift closed behind them.

The boys used to hang about on the upstairs landing but they'd never come up the second flight to the attic. The rules were the rules. That was our place: the family quarters. They respected that. There they are, leaning over the banisters in their shirtsleeves, making plans for the weekend. Nothing to do here, of course, but they could take the bus to Morecambe or pile into someone's car and zip off to the Roxy. They found things to entertain themselves. We locked up at eleven but it was only a small kindness to leave a key under the front doormat and on

Friday nights we did, so long as they didn't take advantage.

The tree surgeon — her name is Eve — is looking at the warped floorboards in the old dining room at the front of the house. She eyes the crazily cracked plaster on the bare walls and the ghostly shadows of damp blooming in the corners. And although her thoughts should be her own, we can hear her too. Is this an invasion on our part? Can she feel us? We can't help it, we can't help anything, and too shocked to speak, even if we could, we only listen: *The woman actually lives here*, she thinks. *It takes all sorts, fair enough. But still.*

'I'm going to have to get going, love.' She calls through the open door. 'I'll send a quote through the post. All the details. Better to have it in writing, you know, for insurers and that. Miss Clifford?'

Annette appears with a tray from the dark hall, too suddenly in the room. She loads up Eve's tea with sugar. Her hands are shaking.

'I don't understand why you can't just do it tomorrow. Take them out. Get rid of them.'

Eve sighs. If only it were that simple. The sycamores are much too close to the house and they have grown far too big. They're mature specimens now. One hundred and thirty years old, or more, is her best reckoning, judging by a one-eye-closed guesstimate of the trunk circumference and the width of their canopies. (Earlier, she'd paced out the length of their root-run in the garden and finished in the street.) The roots are all snarled up under the foundations, mucking up the drains, sucking the water out of the subsoil, shrinking it, pulling the ground out from under the house.

'They're taking in two thousand litres of water a day, each,' she says. No response. 'Look. You're right, when it comes down to it, getting the trees out is a fairly straightforward job.'

'So you can start right away?'

She's like a child, this woman, in her insistence. She dips into her handbag and takes out a chequebook.

'It's more complicated than that. There's all sorts to — '

Annette doesn't hear — she's talking too quickly about deposits and payment plans and the essential task of keeping the house upright.

'How much do you need to get going? Tomorrow, if possible.'

Eve will wonder about this woman later, as she stands in the twilight with the cool of the fuel trigger against her palm and puts petrol into the van. She'll remember her skittish, pleading eyes and be glad she's out of the place. The house was cold, colder even than outside. The mortar was crumbling; the bricks were holding the damp. Ivy had forced its way in through one of the upstairs windows and spread in green and brown tributaries over the ceiling, stems as thick as a child's wrist. The name of the place — The Sycamores — is the worst kind of joke. She'll get back into the warmth of the van, the heaters blowing hot air out like nobody's business, and she will try to put it all out of her mind. But now she is duty bound to say, 'It's not as easy as that,' even as

Annette is waving her chequebook frantically between them.

There are cowboy outfits who'd rush into the
job, but she isn't running one of them. Fair
enough, the money is tempting. The woman
could be one of these rich eccentrics, the ones
who keep all their newspapers in piles and breed
packs of feral cats in the garden and live on three
pounds a week. Die with millions in the bank
and a cellar full of tree roots and out-of-date
cartons of milk. The school fees are due next
month. But no. She's got professional obliga-
tions. She sips the tea gingerly — certain, now
she's thinking about it, that the milk this woman
used has soured — and starts again, more slowly
this time.

'I can take the pair of them out. I can bring
the stump grinder and make a nice clean job of
it. Subject to there being no tree preservation
order on them. No need to check for nests at this
time of year. All being good with the council, we
could just get on with it. But I have to tell you: if
you get rid of the trees there's a chance the
ground will fill up with water. The drains will
almost certainly be shot. The roots will have got
into them. The house might, best-case scenario,
pop upright again. The walls will spit all those
buckets of filler that someone's spooned into the
cracks right back out at you. Subsidence can
resolve itself like that, once the culprits are taken
out. But more likely, if the drains really are
knackered, and they will be, you're opening up a
whole new can of worms. You risk getting one
good rainstorm and — whoosh!'

16

She chops her hand through the air and looks at the ceiling, the way the plaster bubbles and sags like the surface of a pudding. This is a wet place. There is nowhere to go in this town that will take you away from the smell of the bay and the wet slap of the damp Lakeland air against your cheeks. She puts the mug down and zips up her body warmer. Tugs at the cuffs of her shirt.

'The worst-case scenario is, you might not have any house left. You need a proper survey, Miss Clifford. What you need is a structural engineer. Someone to get a camera rod down those drains and see the state of play. You might be looking at underpinning, but I can't advise you on that. Shall I recommend someone for you?'

'How long?'

'Depends who you ask.'

'I want to sell the place. As quickly as I can. I need to get shut of it.'

The woman is getting worked up. On the brink of panic. Eve shrugs.

'You'll get a better price if you get this sorted first. Even if you do have to wait a while.'

'I don't want to wait a while.'

There's that tone again. Petulant. Childish. And Eve does not have time to argue the toss any longer. She needs to be in the van, right now, or she'll be late to pick up Tom and if Maddy has to down tools early to collect him herself Eve's life will not be worth living.

'All right. I'll put a quote through your door. Next couple of days — definitely before Christmas.'

17

What harm can a quote do, in the great scheme of things? She goes.

★ ★ ★

Sell the place? We wait at the bottom of the stairs and test our voices in front of the mirror.

No. This is a family house.

Nothing comes: it is like calling for someone underwater. Our throats are clogged, our lungs filled with seawater, the air is heavy and pushes our sounds back at us. How can we have everything returned to us but our own voices? We cram ourselves onto the kitchen windowsill and wait, feet dangling, as she sits at the table and frowns.

We can hear her again. Every hour more clearly. She thinks of what Eve said — the house, spitting. Horrible. As far as she knows there's no insurance and only the slimmest possibility of borrowing funds — against this badly listing building? With a credit history like hers? — so saving the place might be impossible. How has she become so enmeshed in the fate of this house, and so quickly? She's not set foot in it for decades.

Her father, Jack, died six years ago. *Comfortably in hospital.* The ties that bound them to each other had always been loose, but she had tried to come home. She'd made it for the funeral and stayed in a bed and breakfast. Candy had organised the wake and the pub was crammed with old people Annette didn't know and she felt suddenly shy and teenaged, even though she was well into her fifties. Ther[e] been a terrible, embarrassing moment Candy, her skin sagging, the circles under her eyes larded with make-up that settled into the creases on her face, had tried to hold Annette's hands, patted at her hair and clutched her by the shoulders. Before Annette could slip away, Candy had asked her to come home to the bungalow in Ulverston for a few days. That's where Jack and Candy had gone after they'd abandoned The Sycamores.

'At least consider it,' she said. 'You can see if there's anything of your father's you'd like? You know we never sold The Sycamores. Maybe you could . . . ?'

Annette made her excuses gently, kissed Candy on the cheek, and left her in the care of her nephews. Their friends hadn't recognised her — the unreliable prodigal step-daughter — and it had been a relief to leave.

'I'll come and visit,' she'd said, at the door of the pub. Candy had half nodded, smiling sadly, her hair dropping out of her chignon and falling around her face. Neither of them had believed this, and Annette hadn't visited. She'd not asked for anything either, though she could have done with some money, and she'd been surprised — was that the right word? — when six years later the keys to this spare house that nobody wanted to live in had arrived from Candy's solicitor. *Peacefully and after a short illness.* Her nephews were taking care of things. No need to visit, there was only a paper or two to sign. Annette had never called Candy 'Mother'.

To have this house back, though. To think that Candy hadn't sold it. Had saved it for her. Surprised was not the right word, she decides. Puzzled, perhaps, is closer to it. Her only memories of herself here as a child are vague and confused. Her mother was sick. There was a period when her father would arrange days out, special occasions for the three of them. Now she knows with an adult's understanding it was probably because he was trying to make memories for her of them all together.

This is a part of her life she has not thought about in years. Shedding these heavy memories is a benefit of living in big cities where nobody knows or cares about her past, only her ability to turn up on time, to pay her portion of the rent and to take her turn at cleaning the bathroom. She'd considered different kinds of lives. The kinds containing men and children and sets of matching soup bowls. But she had never wanted them badly enough and knew without knowing how she knew that she could love only imperfectly. Her father had told her — sometimes — that she was too erratic. Unpredictable. Not like other girls.

One of those special, memory-making days comes back to her now, though why this particular one, she doesn't know. She'd been little — just a child — when she'd seen her dad talking to a man at a swimming pool. A decent young man, new to the town, in need of help. That's how her parents explained him, later. They had all that empty space. Why not share it? A full house is more fun. That's the story they liked to tell. And this man — he'd hit her father, right there at the pool. The man had curly hair. She knew his first name, remembers the knowing of it, if not the name itself — she must have known it, mustn't she? — but yes, she was too young, so she wasn't allowed to use it. He hit her dad then came to live with them, and she was told to treat him like a cousin. To show respect. To be friendly. And that is when the days out and special occasions stopped.

She's hungry. If the walls are bowing and the roof really is slipping then maybe the pipes are cracked and she shouldn't be using the gas. She turns the knob anyway, lights a match and waits, looking out at the darkening back garden, the bindweed and bramble choking the place where the vegetable plot used to be. She strikes match after match, pinching the flame out with her fingers and thumb, then blowing on the burned out end to light it again. The little flames leap between her fingers and flicker in the ashtray. A party trick. Also unpredictable. The blue reflection of the lit gas under the pan floats on the glass. White sheets hang limply from the line. The water boils and the window slowly clouds over with steam.

2

Our fine house lies on the outskirts of a little town, the grey houses and hotels and hydros huddled on the gentle lower slopes of the fells, tucked between them and the northern edge of Morecambe Bay. Grange-over-Sands looks out across the River Kent right where it leaves the land and disgorges itself into the sea. A perfect place to settle down. Rest for fell walkers, respite for the sick and a perfect place to bring up children. It's what we've always said. We have a duck pond and some nice gardens and all kinds of things for guests. The lovely cast-iron railings saved because the civil munitions people didn't get this far north when they moved across the country stripping towns of iron during the war. It's not late yet, but at this time of year it gets dark early. The narrow, jumbled streets are deserted. The fells are dark. It's the off season, and the promenade is empty. There's the lido, boarded up. No way to get in, but the water's still in the concrete bowl of the place, an old supermarket trolley in the deep end, and the little yachting pool bright green and thickened with algae.

Reminds us of the times we used to come here. The summers, getting in early before the tourists arrived and took the whole place over, leaving no room for anyone else. We could walk there — ten minutes from the house it was, and easy enough to pop back in case something wanted doing. Looking after the boys — a full-time job. Not much time for recreation. And look: the day brightens and the sun comes out and there's Jack. We watch him lie back on his towel. Eyes closed. Nothing but the bloody orange glow of the too-bright sun through his eyelids. It has been nagging at him: the fact Annette hasn't had much of a summer holiday, but he thinks she likes the lido, that it will do for a day out, that it is near enough to home to be all right for Netty. And Netty lies next to him; keeps nudging him with her thigh. Strange to see ourselves like this. But it is what it is.

'Look,' Netty says, but Jack keeps his eyes shut and despite his cigarette burning steadily — its heat glowing between the knuckles of his first and second finger, the whisper of dropped ash on the back of his hand — he lies still. He keeps his brow smooth, his mouth loosely closed, and pretends to be dozing. The sounds of splashing and laughing don't disturb him, but he's about at the end of his tolerance for Netty's wittering.

'You might as well of stayed in if you're only going to lie there and kip.'

He can smell her sun cream. Some pinkish concoction that makes her face shiny and her hair greasy. It gives her spots and he's warned her off of it but she insists on wearing it anyway. She's fair and freckly like he is, with mousy hair that she bleaches blonde. She says the cream helps her get a bit of colour but the stink of it makes Jack's head hurt. There's a splash as someone jumps in, the slop of water over the

23

sides of the lido, the laughing and 'oohs' from the people sitting on the lower terraces — the people here early enough to get seats within spitting distance of the damn pool.

'Whew, that was a good one,' she says, half under her breath. She must know he's not really listening to her running commentary about the jumping and diving, but she can't help talking anyway. The woman never has a thought she doesn't vocalise.

Jack has been lying there thinking happily about the cash gone from the mail train. About the audacity of the thieves and about where that money might be now. Sacks and sacks and sacks of the stuff. More money than one person would ever need in his whole life, probably. Best thing since *The Dam Busters*. He's half smiling with his eyes closed, turning details from the newspapers about HVP carriages and the bridge — what was it called? Bridego? — over in his head. He tries to make a list of things he would do with a great whack of cash like that — the prize for a fearless, decisive act. There'd be no more trips to the lido, that's for sure. They'd have decent holidays, off to Spain for some proper weather, maybe even Cyprus — though he's heard you can't trust the water there, it would probably be all right in a hotel, a really, really good hotel, and they could, in this fantasy life he's creating for the three of them, afford the very best. First, though, would be a proper doctor for Netty. An American one, off Harley Street. That's where all the best ones have their clinics. He'd drive her there himself, in a big

24

posh car — an Aston Martin in gunmetal grey — park where the hell he liked and let the steady, endless flow of his money cure her, and every other aching desire they had. They'd never have to want for anything ever again.

Netty jostles him. In his mind's eye he sees her moving, tugging the front of her strapless swimsuit upwards as she flips over onto her stomach, her frizzy head by his feet. The light is gone, water patters onto his face and chest and finally, he opens his eyes.

Annette. She's already a big girl. 'Solid' is the word he uses when he thinks of her. Cow-like. Netty says she was the same at that age and that the girl will grow into herself once she gets a bit of height and not to worry. He looks at her squat black shape against the sun, shields his eyes with one hand and hoists himself uncomfortably upwards. They were too late to get deck-chairs, and Netty spread their faded bath-towels out on the rock-hard and lumpy cement of the upper level: a 'grand view', perhaps, of the amphitheatre-shaped terraces, the pool itself, lopsided and shaped like a mushroom, and the queues meandering away from both changing wings and the refreshments kiosk, but one without a speck of shade.

'Is it your ears, love?' Netty asks, and Annette nods, spraying more water over Jack.

'For God's sake, girl, get out of it, will you?'

Netty tuts at him, smiling, and leans forward on her knees to rummage around in the straw bag. It's stuffed full. Spare towels and softening chocolate bars, magazines and packets of cigarettes and her knitting, coiled around it all, spilling out of the bag and onto the beach towels. Annette has her finger in her ear, digging about and moving her weight from one foot to the other. She goes over to her mother, leaving a ring of wide blotchy footprints around their towels. No point lying back down again now — he'll never get off to sleep with this racket.

'I thought we were here to relax.'

'Don't be like that, Jack,' Netty says. 'You should have sorted her out before she went in.'

Jack looks at Annette again, her wide doughy face, a strand of brownish seaweed sticking to her shin, the costume pink and white and threadbare; too small for her across the chest. Netty is still emptying out the bag. She's wearing heart-shaped sunglasses, and Jack sees his reflection in them: squinting in the bright sunlight, overheated and bad-tempered.

'Here it is, here it is, love,' she brandishes the packet of cotton-wool balls, 'it was hiding from me, but I've got it now.'

Jack finds another cigarette and lights up. There are shouts and splashes coming from the pool. A group of men, boys really, taking turns at the diving board — doing fancy flips and tricks and risking getting their heads split open just to impress a gaggle of girls sitting along the edge of the shallow end, dangling white feet in the water, all headscarves and hats and blackened eyelids. The boys are drinking too; stubby brown bottles of beer are lined up along the tiled edge under the diving board, waiting for their owners to surface, water streaming from every limb, and claim them. A noisy lot, and spoiling the place for families. Probably trippers come over on the steamer. Lads from out of town. The water is dark and greenish — there's weed and sand in the shallow end, and the surface is a rainbowed slick of sluiced-off suntan lotion and Brylcreem. There's something else in the water too; some shining slips of silver that Jack thinks, just for a second, might be little fishes.

Netty is still fussing over the girl. She mustn't overdo it. She reads his mind and shakes her head, smiling at him.

'Light me a ciggy, will you? And see if we've any more lemonade. I'm gasping.'

Annette sits in front of her mother and tips her head to one side, allows Netty to dip little tufts of cotton wool into a tin of Vaseline and screw them into her ears. Jack looks past her, across the concrete steps and ledges, crowded with women in sundresses and swimming costumes, men like him, shirtless and with their work trousers rolled up, or lying back in deckchairs, their heads hidden under newspapers. The headlines are too blurred for him to read — his eyes have always been useless — but they'll all be about the raid. Over a million pounds, they reckon, though it's still too early to tell.

A million pounds would be just the thing. Get the house sorted out. The sanding and scraping and painting. The leaky pipes and gutters, crumbling with rust. Get help in for Netty — a housekeeper and a cleaner at the very least. Netty working her fingers to the bone and at the beck and call of the lodgers even in the state she's in. She couldn't get out this afternoon without making two trays of butties — one beef, one ham — and a Victoria sponge for their afternoon tea. The plates are waiting on the kitchen table under damp tea towels with a note propped against the teapot. *Help Yourself.* A million pounds would be a very fine start indeed. He smiles briefly and reminds himself to buy a paper on the way home before looking back down into the rocking, dark water of the lido.

One of the boys Netty has been cooing over jogs along the diving board, jumps, hops, feints a dive and then turns back, waving his hand at the crowd. He didn't bottle it; it's a game; he's going to carry on faking hesitation until every eye in the place is on him. People are laughing and waving at him. Someone shouts: 'Get on with it' and the boy laughs, bows (his head a dark wet mass of curls) and then makes a small dive, almost off-hand, as if he can't be bothered to do anything impressive today after all. Except he's gone then, like a hot blade through butter, slipping into the water almost without disturbing its surface.

Jack holds his breath involuntarily as he traces the pale shape of the boy powering through the water. With just two strong kicks of his legs he passes like a sleek white dolphin straight underneath some old dears doing laps. One more kick gets him past some kids messing about with inflatables, then he surfaces at the shallow end, hardly gasping for breath at all. There's a couple of half-hearted claps from the lower terrace, some giggles from the girls, but out of sight means out of mind and most of the people egging him on a minute ago have now forgotten him. He gets out and stands on the edge of the lido, running his hands over his hair, the water trailing down his spine. He's got his back to Jack now, perhaps surveying the queue at the refreshments kiosk, or trying to remember where he left his towel. Water runs down his legs and puddles around his feet on the terracotta red tiles around the lip of the pool. Jack realises he's still holding his breath and blows out a great stream of smoke.

'He's been doing it all afternoon,' Netty says, and taps Annette on the backside, 'Go on, love, you're watertight now. Have a nice time.'

'Who has?'

Jack rolls a bottle over the towel to her and hands her a lit cigarette. Netty sits cross-legged, grips the bottle in the crook of her knee and finds the bottle opener.

'You know full well who,' she laughs, and then points with the opener, 'that one there.' Jack doesn't look. Just some cocky youngster showing off in front of his mates. A nobody, the same as the rest of them: he's just not realised it yet. He massages the bridge of his nose between finger and thumb. Netty has been putting out her cigarette ends in a pop bottle, the half-inch of warm lemonade in the bottom stained yellow with nicotine and the blackened, screwed-up butts floating like dead bluebottles. He flicks his ash in its direction and looks back at the board.

'It looks lovely and cool.' Netty sighs out smoke. 'I might go down in a bit.'

'Don't,' Jack says.

'It'll do me no harm. I feel like a roast ham up here, and I'm going to look like one if I sit on my arse in the sun much longer.'

'Netty,' he touches his thumb to the back of her hand, just so she knows he means business.

'Look,' Netty elbows him, 'there she is.'

Annette is climbing down the ladder into the shallow end of the pool, all jutting elbows and ungainly feet. The water slices her in half and she takes a breath, shivering, before making the final plunge. Netty has tucked the girl's hair and the cotton wool neatly inside the pink swimming cap without him noticing it, using some womanly sleight of hand that makes Jack wonder what else he misses. He's left his spectacles at home — he doesn't like wearing them out of the house, not in any weather, but especially on a day as hot as this — and in no time at all he loses Annette's bobbing head and can't distinguish the fuzzy blob of her cap from the others.

'Did you tell her not to swim under the board?'

'She's not a cretin.' Netty pokes her cigarette into the neck of the bottle. It meets the liquid in the bottom with a short-lived fizz.

'They're big lads. Not always careful about what they're doing. High spirits. They've had a drink. And in this weather.'

'All right.' Netty slips her feet into her shoes — some white, strappy things with pointy heels that she complained were rubbing her all the way here. That's why they'd arrived late, and to top it off he'd had to carry all the bags himself. She

30

stands up, gets ready to click along the terrace, past the pump house and down the steps to the lido.

'No, you wait there. I'll go down. Give me a minute.'

Netty smiles. He wants to reach over and grab her hand but he bends down, dips into the bag, lying on its side with its contents spilled across the towels, and finds his wallet, thumbs out a pound note. 'Do you want a choc-ice? Some chips?'

She's still smiling, looking down at him like he's her child. The sun is straight overhead, a photographer's nightmare. It's harsh on her, showing every bit of sagging skin under her chin, the fresh crop of pimples along her hairline. Her roots are coming through, a shock of ashy hair against her scalp, and every time he notices it he wonders afresh if he should have a look in her address book for the number of the woman who comes to the house to do her hair and leaves that powdery stink of peroxide all through the kitchen. He could telephone her and get her to come, as a surprise, but then he thinks if Netty wanted — what was her name . . . Fiona? — to come, then she'd ring her herself. She might take him calling her the wrong way, as a criticism. He's better leaving it, he decides. Like he always does.

'Go on then,' she says, and he gives her his arm as she sits back down, 'go and tell them. And get Annette a lolly too. A strawberry split, if they've any left.'

He nods and sets off, then hesitates, looking back, but she catches him and waves him away,

31

laughing and — when she thinks he's not looking — putting her hand to her side and wincing as she roots about in the debris from the straw bag for her magazine.

By the time Jack has picked his way through the couples and families on the terraces, the boys have stopped their diving and are leaning against the side of one of the changing wings. From somewhere, perhaps high up on the terrace he's just come from, a child squeals, but he turns his head too late and sees nothing. There's a portable radio going somewhere, and he recognises the song, all the stations have had it on non-stop. Annette likes it, he remembers, and thinks of her singing alone, in her bedroom.

It might have been better for her if they'd had another one — a boy, maybe, though it won't happen now, not with Netty the way she is. He's not sure he'd know what to do with a son anyway. He had no brothers, no sisters. Neither had Netty. It hasn't done them any harm. The child cries out again. He shakes his head as if the sound were water trapped in his ear canal and he could dislodge it that way, like a dog, then gathers himself and strides over to the boys, aware of his wife's eyes on his back, the freckles and peeling red skin on his shoulders. He wishes he'd slipped on his shirt.

'Everything all right, lads?' he asks, feeling naked and foolish. He turns his damp pound note over in his hands and envies the boys their brown bottles of beer, the labels peeling off in the heat. That's what's in the swimming pool, the little silver fishes. Labels, from the beer bottles.

'Nice day for it, eh?'

He laughs at himself, anxious to demonstrate he is a concerned father and husband, a citizen and a reasonable man, not a spoilsport. There are four boys in all; the one who was larking about on the diving board is standing furthest away, towelling off his feet, and the other three are leaning against the wall and pretending not to hear Jack — though they cut their eyes at him and his pound note then glance away, towards the fourth, with looks on their faces that suggest they're trying to suppress laughter.

The fourth looks up, meets Jack's eye and then straightens slowly, swinging the towel over his shoulder and smiling. The boy's smile is so brilliant, so guileless and shining and so, so, clear, as clear as a glass of water, that for a moment Jack is completely refreshed; the stickiness of the day blown away by a stiff cool breeze.

(How strange that was, he'll think later, once the boy has moved into the room they always have trouble letting because of the damp patch on the underside of the bay window and the way the moisture makes the paper peel and the room smell like old sheets, no matter what they try to do about it, how utterly strange and unexpected it is to think of a smile as refreshing, as if a smile is a crisply ironed tablecloth or an opened window on a hot train journey or a fizzy drink with crackling ice-cubes in it.)

'Tim.' The boy puts his hand out and they shake, formally. 'My name's Timothy Richardson.'

A Scottish accent. Something soft and well-bred about it. A gentle voice, with a smirk to

33

it, as Netty might say. The boy has put his tee-shirt back on, but rolled up the sleeves tight under his armpits. He's only wearing his swimming trunks and the tee-shirt and there's something faintly obscene about it, much more than the bare chests of his friends. It's as if (the refreshing sensation fades along with the boy's smile, the heat closing in on him again and giving him trouble marshalling his thoughts properly) he's wearing the shirt to underline the fact that he isn't wearing any trousers. There's a packet of cigarettes tucked into his rolled-up sleeve in some complicated, fashionable way that Jack can't quite make out — his eyes getting worse every day, especially in this blinding light.

'What do you want?'

It isn't as rude as it would be if someone else said it. Just confident. People always would want something, and he may as well get the transaction over with. What does he want? Nothing. Everything. The boys are looking at him expectantly and he's got to say something, so he does.

'My wife,' Jack gestures behind him at the area where he thinks Netty is sitting, though the rest of the lido has diminished, somehow. 'My wife was a little worried about the diving.'

He becomes aware of two things. One: the boy has a tiny tattoo — small as a halfpenny — on his upper arm (it might be the letter J, or an anchor, or perhaps an insect of some sort) and two: Timothy Richardson's friends are laughing at him.

'Come here,' Tim says. Jack steps forward. The

34

light is really terrible now, his eyes and throat dry. The boy's face blurs; a portrait smeared before the paint has dried. A familiar drumbeat starts up at the back of Jack's neck. It makes smart time across his teeth and the fine bones in his nose and around his eyes.

'It's the sun,' Tim says, and grabs Jack's face, roughly. For a brief moment — two or three seconds at the most — Tim's fingers are pressing into his right cheek, his thumb into his left. He can smell the salt water on the boy's skin, feel the coolness of his palm against his nose. The heat and light and the pain in his head subside and a vibration starts in his chest, a little thrum downwards, across his belly and upper thighs. Tim takes his hand away.

'Will that do you?' he grins.

Jack blinks, takes a step backwards and then sits down on a ledge, heavily. The heat of the bare concrete doesn't bother him and he decides he needs to breathe slowly until the last of those vibrations pass along his legs and disappear. Tim squats in front of him but Jack finds himself blushing and quite unable to speak. His vision — can that be right? — is just a notch or two clearer.

'We're done with the diving now, don't you worry.'

Jack takes a while to find his tongue. Better to be at home, locked into the downstairs lavatory and able to inspect himself in the shaving mirror in private. There's no pain at all, not anywhere, but he resists the urge to rub at his face and expects, when he gets back, to see Tim's red handprint across his cheek, a livid imprint, as humiliating as a slap. The other boys are still there, warm and unruffled, as if what has just happened is unremarkable, or as if it didn't happen at all. Jack is at a loss to explain this himself but already he knows he would like it to happen again. He buries that thought and replaces it with another, the one that should have come to him first.

'My wife. She's called Netty. Mrs Clifford. Mrs Clifford has a trouble. The doctor can't do anything for her. You could . . . ' He doesn't dare ask. 'Look. She's sitting up there.' He points.

Netty is waving. What has she seen? What might it have looked like? He wouldn't want her thinking the boy struck him. Nothing like that. They wave back at her, the two of them.

'You might like to come to Sunday dinner. Tomorrow afternoon, about two? That is if you don't already have plans, of course.'

'I'll come, of course I'll come.' Tim rubs his hands together, as if he's warming them up, and Jack writes down his address on the back of a bit of card torn from a cigarette packet, with a pencil provided by one of the boys. That'll wipe the smile off their faces, he thinks, without quite knowing what he means, but feeling quite recovered and pleased with himself. He'd taken some swift decisive action there, in inviting the boy to dinner. Didn't let the opportunity slip though his fingers, but used his noggin for once. Help Yourself. That's more like it. He walks over the terraces, leaping from one level to the next without taking the steps, hopping jauntily over

36

the hot concrete to where Netty and Annette, who is wet through and shivering, are waiting for him.

★   ★   ★

When they get home from the lido Jack scurries off and spends an hour looking at his eyes in the shaving mirror. He tries on his glasses then folds them and puts them away. It doesn't get dark until past nine o'clock, and when the sun begins to go down, he's marvelling at the clarity of the view from the attic windows. Grange is famous for its sunsets. Of course the sun sets everywhere — he's not an idiot — but here it's a local peculiarity. Something to do with the wide, uncluttered horizon, the miles and miles of flat wet sand and some unique quality of the visibility caused by the Gulf Stream and the cold air rolling down to the bay from the fells. He stares at every orange and purple inch of it, waiting until there's not an ounce of light left on the horizon. When the sun has gone, he goes down both flights of stairs and finds Netty watching television in the sitting room. His mind is made up. He asks her to stand next to the hall mirror at the front door. He gives her the newspaper.

'I've things to get on with, Jack.'

He ignores her. 'Just help me with this, will you?'

He walks along the hallway and through the ribbon curtain right to the back of the kitchen.

'What are you playing at?'

'Hold it up. So I can see it.'

Netty huffs and holds up the newspaper against her chest. Jack is eighteen feet away from her, maybe even twenty. He reads. First the headline, then, after a pause, the article beneath. The story is about the water bailiffs fining a man for shrinking his shrimp nets under the regulation size and over-trawling out on the bay.

'So they took his nets off of him and made him pay two pounds, and it serves the daft sod right for getting caught,' Jack says.

'You're playing with me.'

Jack searches her face. She thinks it's a trick; that he's learned the article off by heart and is playing a joke on her. Jack feels the boy's hand on his face again. Smells him. Feels his knees start to buckle. What a thing!

'Try me, love.'

He tells her to pick any page in the newspaper she likes. Any book in the house, in fact. He needs to prove this to her. Needs her to admit that it is real, that something has really happened, before he tells her how. Before he mentions the boy. She purses her mouth at him, goes away and comes back with a knitting pattern. Eyebrows raised.

'Go on, then.'

Jack grins. When he reads its strange nonsense to her, word for word, she finally believes.

'He did it just by touching you?' she asks.

★　★　★

She isn't stupid. Isn't credulous. But she does consider herself open-minded. The year before,

38

she had an operation. After that and the long walks along the sea front for the healthy air, and after the strange diets she put herself on, all the while growing thinner and sicker and further away, after all that had been tried and found wanting, she started to see a woman. Someone who'd come now and again and sit with her in the early afternoons.

This woman is a neighbour: the kind of person who goes to church on Sunday mornings and sits at the back, disagreeing with what is said during the sermon and refusing to sing verses from hymns she finds doctrinally disagreeable. But still she goes. Candy, her name is. She has a reputation for drinking too much and changing her boyfriend as often as she changes her clothes. But people forgive her for that. They smile and ask her how she's getting on when she's out at the shops.

What they can't quite forgive her for is her old-fashionedness. For spitting on her fingers and rubbing the jaw of a little boy with mumps. For answering the door in a red silk kimono, her mascara smeared around her eyes, and coming out in the middle of the night to whisper prayers over a labouring woman who'd waited too long for the midwife to come. When they don't need her, people laugh at her strange ways and Candy never reminds them of that when they call her to make the sign of the cross over their sheep and get rid of their ringworm. She doesn't get invited to the knitting circle and the women's coffee morning, but when the babies won't stop crying, someone will send a message to her flat and she will work a kind of magic with a piece of knotted string and a chain of Hail Marys.

If Annette doesn't dawdle on the way back from school she might catch them together; Candy pouring coins out of an envelope into the cup of her hand, Netty buttoning up her blouse or retying her shoelaces. Netty might describe a version of what they are up to if the little girl ever asks her about it. It would be something to do with taking into your body the good things heaven is sending down to you. It is an attempt at a miracle. But we know that Annette does not ask and Netty and Candy continue to work hard at their miracle a couple of afternoons a week. They step up the pace once the spring gives way to summer.

But, Netty thinks, Candy is one thing. She is local and harmless. People are used to her. This boy is another thing. They've not seen him before. No one knows who he is, where he's come from, what church he goes to. Nothing.

★   ★   ★

'I don't know how he did it,' Jack says.

He is frightened and excited and something else — something he doesn't, and never will, have a name for — but he is still Jack Clifford and that means no matter what his emotions are up to, he still considers the practicalities. In the following days he will make an inspection of the house and write a list. He'll promise he isn't complaining — not looking a gift horse in the mouth — just freshly overwhelmed at all the new

40

things he can see. All the fine detail there is in the world that now requires his attention. Cracks in the plaster, peeling paint, screws missing from guttering, plants sprouting out of the downpipes: the work that needs doing on the place has tripled overnight, he'll say, joyfully.

'You must have some idea what happened,' Netty says. 'You were there, weren't you?'

'He sort of touched me. No, not touched, he grabbed me. And I went . . . funny. It was a bit better straight away, but, I'm not joking, it feels like it's carried on improving. I couldn't have read all that when he first did it. But now,' he looks at his watch, 'four hours on, I can. Who knows what it'll be like tomorrow?'

'And after all you've said about Candy.' She scoffs. She rolls the knitting pattern up. 'You've gone soft. Did he want money?'

'He didn't ask for a thing. Not even change for the fag machine.' He puts his arms around her. Whispers in her ear, because the girl is not supposed to know her mother is sick. 'He's coming for Sunday dinner. He didn't invite himself. I asked him to come.' The thought of the boy in his house, sitting on his chairs — it is enough to make his skin prickle again, but Jack takes a deep breath and steadies himself. 'We're going to see if he can do it for you. We won't push him. Won't make him think we're desperate. He might want us to pay. He might take advantage, if we lay it on too thick. But we'll just ask. All right?'

What does Netty do now? She could wipe her eyes with a corner of her apron, or go into the kitchen to check there is enough food for an extra guest at the table. She could shout at Jack for being so foolish. She could hope.

3

He didn't hit Jack. It wasn't like that. Can we tell Annette that? Explain it to her? Impossible at the time. Our hands were full. Our minds elsewhere. Too much on our plates. But perhaps now . . . ? We follow our daughter as she moves around the house, putting things into boxes then stacking the boxes in the hallway. She's brought a radio with her but she doesn't switch it on this evening. She'll probably ditch the radio too, at some point. She likes to travel light, owning nothing she can't carry alone. And all right, she's upset about the bad news but there's no point getting worked up about it now, she thinks. No point relying on the first person she's asked to take a look at the place either. She needs to use her bloody head, for once. There are lots of tree surgeons. Ten a penny, they must be. Too late to arrange it today, but tomorrow she's going to ask someone else — get a second opinion — get a bank loan and a team of people who will actually do what she wants them to do, and in the meantime, she isn't about to lie down and bawl and give up on the work.

The yellow skip she asked for is in the street outside the house and she goes out the front door and into the garden carrying a cardboard box. It's filled with old things, broken things, useless junk the lot of it, someone should have dealt with it at some point or another — the set of wine glasses we saved tokens for, and a set of kitchen scales with the weights missing, and more magazines. The place is stuffed with them. They all go into the skip, the box breaking on its way in and the crumbling glossies slithering about all over the show. When she's done she stands at the gate, the cold rust of the metal snug against her palms, and just stares at the place. And, strange though it is, even to us, we see Timothy Richardson arrive and he stands in the garden too, on a day too bright and too hot for him to wear his good raincoat but he does. He smartens up and does as he's asked. At least, he does when it suits him.

We watch as he waits in the front garden, not knocking on the door, holding a pair of rabbits by their hind legs. He stares up at the windows and we do too. We understand now that not everything that comes back to us is our own take on things: it's not altogether pleasant, to see our house as he does. A handsome place clad in some sort of grey stone, like the rest of the houses round here, with a steeply pitched tiled roof. A decent enough garden and the street, while not quite the best one in the town, is no address to be ashamed of. The houses are all detached, perched on the low rises of a hill that turns into limestone and scrub and runs upwards to disappear into mist. He smells the salt and mud of the bay, but can't see the sands from here. He looks again towards the tiny attic windows. Maybe they could see the sea from the attic. On a clear day. The houses with a good sea view would be worth more than this one.

Probably a lot more. But still, the place is bigger than he expected.

He couldn't tell much from the woman, some skinny pale hole sitting high up and far away at the lido, but the man himself had looked, if not exactly hard-up, then at least disappointed. He can't be that old, not really — mid-forties at the very latest? — but he looked like he'd been half boiled and put through a mangle. Or like one of the old duffers who'd seen real fighting in the war and come back with the sound of artillery going off in their heads. And how is that possible, when the man owns all this? He resists the urge to whistle as he counts the windows. Makes a guess at the number of bedrooms. Five at least. Then there's the attic. Another two or three up there, maybe another bathroom or kitchenette? Servants' quarters? This house belongs to people who've got pure cash. He's sure of it.

Things are starting to look very promising indeed.

He must tread carefully, though. This is a funny little town, one that can't make up its mind what it's supposed to be. The postcards in the revolving rack in the train station announce part of the town's ambition. Grange-over-Sands: Naples of the North. The place is welcoming enough to tourists if they've got money to spend, right enough, but anxious to maintain that air of respectability: there are no arcades here, no fortune-tellers or burnt-cork artists, no dancing in the street and definitely no shady picture houses. Grange wants to be one of those spa and sanatorium type places too. There are old-fashioned signs advertising the hydros and a couple of grand-looking convalescent homes on the outskirts of town. Tales abound about magic willow water and its healing properties — drinking from the spring soothes teething babies, cheers miserable women and cures horses with the strangles. The air! They never shut up about the air here, as if the inhabitants of the place were responsible for manufacturing it themselves. So a place for healing — a place for sick people to come and rest, to get better. To soak up a bit of the ozone.

Except it isn't only that, is it? This place shares, along with all the other little towns and fishing villages along this part of the coast, facing outwards towards the sea, an obsession with death. He'd not been in Grange five minutes before he'd been portentously warned about the mud and the tides. Told gruesome stories about horses and carts being sucked into the quicksand, decapitated by the ropes meant to rescue them. The lost women and children, swept away into the mist, maybe drowned, maybe just run away. The suicides. The fishermen whose tractors had clapped out before the bore came in, and spent their last minutes wishing they'd stuck to the old ways and the horse and cart. To listen to them talk, the sands were a right bone yard, fully loaded with the wrecks of old vehicles and their lost drivers. Some place for a spa.

The place couldn't make up its mind about itself, but Tim couldn't ever decide what he was either, so perhaps they'd be well suited to each other and he'd end up liking it here a bit better than Morecambe, where his welcome had well and truly been worn out and doors were starting to close against him. It paid to have an open mind to everything. He straightens his tie and twitches at the lapels of the Aquascutum raincoat that cost him a fortune. He should have brought something other than the rabbits. Chocolates for the woman. A bunch of flowers. Maybe he could double back to the municipal beds along the promenade? The flowers are long gone, in this heat, but. Forget it. His mother always said a bit of charm and a smile would get him into any place he wanted, and a lot of places he had no business being. He rings the bell. Let's see, then.

The woman opens the door, pink-cheeked and powdered, her hair like a bubble of yellow candyfloss over her head. She's got sunken grey circles under her eyes and she's tried to paint them out with that greasy yellow stick of make-up girls have in their handbags. Her lips are slick and red, her eyes done up with that black stuff they're always wearing. She looks like death warmed up.

'Hello,' he uses the posh Englishified voice he reserves for mothers and dogs. 'I believe you're expecting me?'

'Of course,' she says, in her own posh voice, smiling far too much. Lipstick on her teeth. 'You're Mr Richardson and we're very pleased to have you here.' She shakes his hand, pulling him gently into the house. Her skin is burning and now Tim knows that Jack has told her everything and made such a song and dance about it that

47

she is expecting him to walk on water before the cheese and biscuits are served. Why does he never learn? He'll have to play this one carefully.

'You must be Mrs Clifford, and I'm grateful for your hospitality.'

'You're very welcome,' she says.

Once the door is closed, Mrs Clifford — obviously nervous and a bit scared of him — opens her mouth and starts blethering.

'I hope you don't mind beef. Jack didn't tell me if you had a preference so I've done a roast with Yorkshire puddings and gravy. It's so hot, but Jack likes a proper roast, even in the summer. Just through there. Most of the lodgers are at their own homes for the weekend — back with their families, that is, for their own Sunday dinners — so we won't be disturbed. Of course there's Annette, say hello Annette, nicely, please.'

He nods at the girl, peering at him from behind her mother's skirts.

'We've got some beer to drink, or tea, if you'd prefer? Tea, is it? Annette, just go in and stir the gravy for me, will you? No lip — off you go! Sorry about that. It's her age. I don't know what to do with her recently. Do you have any sisters, Tim? I've always wondered if a boy would be different. We're all different I know, but boys, I've heard, are much more . . . '

The missus doesn't stop letting rip until her man appears, pulling at the collar of his shirt like he's been caught with his fingers in the jam, and pretending he's utterly forgotten about Tim joining the family for Sunday dinner. He's freshly combed and shaved, the rash on his neck

48

telling Tim the man did a rush-job, in cold water. The missus had sent him upstairs to scrub up, maybe — wanted to make an occasion out of it.

'Are they rabbits?' he asks.

Tim has forgotten he has them with him, and quickly hands them over, glad to be rid of them.

'Fresh as they get, and I can dress them for you before I go, if you like. My mother told me never to arrive for a meal empty-handed, and everyone likes rabbit, don't they?'

Jack looks at them curiously, as if he's about to disagree.

'I'll show you to the dining room. Netty, you'll deal with these, won't you?' he says. The woman takes them and near enough curtseys her thanks before vanishing into the dim bowels of the house. Jack pats his face, looks at his shoes and shuffles past Tim to open a door into the room at the front.

'In here. Make yourself comfortable. We shan't be a moment.' He motions towards a table laid for four, turns his back and leaves him there.

Tim is alone with the smell of boiling potatoes and cabbage and his mouth does not water. Lodgers! The mystery of the house shrinks, and becomes something paltry and disappointing. No need for the airs and graces then. They're no better than he is. He relaxes into the place, disappointed, but more at ease now. It might be no good. But seeing as he's here, he might as well have a meal and see what the potential is. He's kidding himself if he thinks he's got other options: his choices have been dwindling.

He's found himself without a job, again. His own fault. No place to stay, either. He'd managed to bum temporary lodgings with boys whose heads he turned so long as he could buy them drinks and show them a good time. The meat he'd taken with him from the butcher's helped: everyone liked fresh rabbit and sausages. But rabbits or not, he was burning through his money like nobody's business and his great project — to be respectable, to get established in a city, to pack it in with the light shows and party tricks and progress to something more solid, more like what Jack here has — is at risk of capsizing entirely. One door after another has been slammed in his face and this one — Jack and Netty's house — is his only choice now. Better not bugger this up.

There's a pink padded armchair tucked in under the window with a blanket thrown over it. A wee table with a pink and white cloth tucked in beside. A lamp, a pile of magazines, an ashtray with two red-stained butts and a couple of matches. He knows, the way a dog detects fear — by a sense deeper than sight or smell — that this is Mrs Clifford's throne, the place she sits during the day when she's finished cooking and clearing the lodgers' breakfasts and Jack is out doing errands or up on the roof hammering away at slipped tiles. This is her place, where she sits watching . . . what? He crosses the room and sits in the chair, grasping the narrow arms and breathing in sharply.

Through the window he sees . . . well . . . not a lot. The untrimmed hedge; a ragged and loose

50

privet that waves slightly in the breeze, a path and the front lawn. Big trees in the front garden, a couple of leaves caught in the grass. A leaflet or a label or something else, some lost slip of paper, signifying nothing, blowing backwards and forwards on the patch of bare soil under the hedge. This (he notes the old-fashioned wireless tucked into an alcove, the hastily stacked piles of knitting patterns and *Woman's Realms* on top of it) is Netty's little perch, where she can, with the door ajar, listen to the comings and goings of her lodgers through the hall, watch them come up and down the garden path, see Jack trimming the hedge, her daughter with her Dansette and her picnic blanket and her dolls tea party and whathaveyou out on the front lawn.

Tim sits and listens to Jack giving the chunky daughter loud, self-conscious instructions; telling her where to get the napkins, warning her to bring out the Christmas glasses and not the everyday ones — and he carries on sitting and catches the lie of the land very quickly indeed. He looks at his hands. Flexes his fingers a few times, makes fists, shakes them loose. They are ordinary hands, with a couple of nicks across the knuckles and old brown blood caught under the fingernails. He lifts a used match from Netty's ashtray and begins to clean them. So this is Netty's chair and she has placed herself at the centre of all of this, like the hub of a wheel, nursing that sharp and seeping wee pain deep down inside of her and watching it flow along the spokes of her family like tar.

★ ★ ★

Dinner is served. Netty is tense — no, frantic — and sends Jack back to the kitchen for salt, for napkins, for slices of lemon from a jar to put into the water-jug. The wobble on the table that has never bothered her before becomes intolerable and she gets him up again, sends him into the kitchen for a saucer to wedge under one of the legs. Eventually, she'll let him eat. We bite our lips and wring our hands as Tim suppresses a smile.

'And doesn't your mother miss you?' Netty is asking.

'I send her a letter every week, tell her what I'm up to. Send her money when I have it spare. I ring her when I can. It's not cheap, but.' He takes a bite of his beef and chews carefully. 'This is a ball-tip joint, isn't it, Mrs Clifford? You've cooked it very nicely, if you don't mind me saying?'

'How did you know that?' She waves her fork at him. 'You're not going to tell me you're a cook now, are you?'

'No, no.' Tim puts down his knife and fork and pushes back his chair. The girl keeps her head down, working her way through a pile of mashed potatoes and gravy, her hair shielding her face from him. Jack is sawing dutifully at his single slice of grey meat.

'I'm a butcher, Mrs Clifford. A butcher's apprentice, to be exact. I've been there four months and Gregson's not let me do much more than mop the floor and sharpen the knives. But I

52

listen. I serve the customers and I watch. I've picked up a lot that way. I know my chuck from my flank, my London broil from my cross rib,' he laughs comfortably, enjoying the attention he's getting, and Netty, relaxed now, laughs with him.

'Of course. The rabbits. We did wonder, didn't we, Jack? Is your father a butcher too?'

Whether it's the heat in the room (the sun is streaming through the windows, the last of the morning sea-mist is gone) or the steam from the kitchen that has done it, Tim doesn't know, but her hair has deflated a bit, and she keeps pushing it out of her eyes with the back of her hand in an affected gesture Tim speculates is directed at him, rather than her husband. He's got her.

'He isn't. And I couldn't, in all truthfulness, tell you it was my ambition to stay long in the trade either.' Tim stretches out his hands, looks at his fingers. He doesn't want to think about Gregson's rabbits but he is helpless to stop the memory returning: their chattering teeth and darting eyes. (This image will plague him for a long time still.) 'There are unpleasantnesses about it; nothing I'd want to mention at the dinner table.' Netty nods, enraptured. 'I'm waiting on another position opening up. Something more suited to me. I'm planning on going into tailoring. Men's outfitting.'

'Oh yes,' Netty says, 'that sounds much more suitable.'

'I shan't be leaping out of the fire before I've found myself a frying pan though,' Tim says, and when Netty looks confused, elaborates. 'I'm meaning to say, Mrs Clifford, that I've no wish to leave Mr Gregson in the lurch after all he's done for me, and no wish, either, to be without employment. You needn't worry yourself on that score. It's only six pound and nine a week now, but if I stay, it'll go up. And if I move on, it will be for something better.'

It has, somewhere between the thinnish soup and the terrible beef, been accepted that Tim is being fleeced at the boarding house in Morecambe where he is currently lodging and will be moving into The Sycamores early in the week, if not sooner. He has helped this process along by inventing a room with a bouquet of corpse-coloured mushrooms under the window-sill, a drink-soaked landlady who refuses to iron his shirts despite charging him for the same and, as a final flourish and for his amusement only, a hairy fellow lodger called Hans who uses a metal pail of water to wash himself in the garden and who rattles Tim's doorknob in the middle of the night.

'We charge two pound fifteen. That's including breakfast and tea, but you sort your own dinner. By arrangement on the weekends. I usually leave out a bit of an afternoon tea if you're here on a Saturday. One bath in the week. You can use the television set in the sitting room if Jack isn't in there. We don't include the telephone,' Netty looks at Tim's hands again and falters, 'but seeing as you're in the smallest room, I'm sure we could cover a call to your mother. First Sunday of the month. Would that suit?'

'That's very kind of you, Mrs Clifford,' Tim says. 'I can promise you I won't take advantage of your generosity. My mother will be especially grateful.'

'And the immersion heater,' Jack says, 'tell him about the hot water.' It's the first time he's spoken.

Netty reaches for her cigarettes. 'We'll sort that out when the time comes. You two go out and look at the garden. Tim, Jack has some lovely brassicas out there that are coming along nicely. Go and have a look at what you'll be eating come the winter and let me and Annette clear the dishes. We'll call you for the trifle.'

Tim suspects that it's Jack's job to go through the minutiae of the house rules with him now. Women, overnight guests, the evening curfew. Drinking, record players, muddy boots in the hall. Or to ask him about his references. Clear up the matter of his future plans. Matters too delicate and unsociable for the girl's lugholes. They haven't mentioned Netty's sickness at all. Not once. Perhaps they don't talk about it in front of Annette, though Netty's pretty far gone with it and she's bound to have noticed. They'll be waiting for him to broach the topic himself, he expects. Some old-fashioned version of good manners that they subscribe to. Well, they can wait. If all they have to offer is a room and the odd phone call, he'll take it. Beggars can't be choosers.

He takes off his jacket, leaves it hanging on the back of his chair and follows Jack through the kitchen and out into the back garden, wider and longer than the one at the front, and surrounded by more tall green hedges.

'You're welcome to come out here,' Jack says quietly, 'I just ask that the lodgers stay away from my vegetables and shed. And leave Annette and Netty alone if they're out. Otherwise, like I say, you're welcome. Netty always says she wants the boys to feel like part of the family, guests, rather than lodgers. Within limits, of course.'

Tim rolls up the sleeves of his shirt and leans against the back wall of the house. It's been soaking up the heat of the sun all day, and the unpainted bricks are pleasantly warm and rough against his back. Jack sits on a chair he's brought through from the kitchen and they smoke and for a long while, say nothing. Tim will let Jack speak first. It's the man's house, and his job to move things on if he wants to, after all.

'Will you need some help bringing your things over?'

'I don't think so,' Tim says. 'I've not got much in the way of possessions. What I have, I can carry. It's no bother.'

There's another long silence. Tim wants to laugh, because Jack is looking at the loose buds of the Savoys and the helical stalks of tiny sprouts in the shady end of the garden. And it's not mere obedience to Netty, either. This is what Jack believes two men should be speaking about together. Cabbage and sprouts. He's just about stuck for anything else. Tim puts his cigarette out on the patio, notices the way Jack's shirt is stretched tight over his shoulder blades because he's hunched forward so much, and relents.

'I'll be blunt. What is it that's troubling Mrs Clifford, if you don't mind me asking?'

Jack flushes nearly purple.

'If it's delicate . . . ?'

'It's not that. It's a . . . ' he motions towards his stomach, makes a stirring gesture with his finger. 'A growth.'

'I see,' Tim says. The woman's a goner. 'And you want me to help your wife?'

Jack nods. 'She's had all kinds of doctors interfering with her. Operations like you wouldn't believe. There's nothing left inside. They were deciding whether to try her on the radium again. It's been two years of poking, prodding. Nothing's working. And now they've said no more radium.' He stands, draws his chest out. 'Her consultant is throwing in the towel. I don't know what it is you do. If you can't help her,' he says, with great dignity, 'you may as well say so now. There'll be no hard feelings on our part. We'd respect you for it. We haven't assumed anything at all. About what your terms might be. But we would like the truth.'

Tim sees into their bedroom. Jack in his vest and pyjama trousers, Netty exhausted and sunburned. A coral-coloured negligee, stained around the neck with cold cream. They'd have waited for the girl to go to sleep, pulled the bedspread around themselves then whispered together like it was Christmas Eve. Netty asks Jack what it felt like, did it hurt, was he really, really sure? And Jack, holding her as tightly as he dared, swears himself blind that there really is something to this — the boy had some kind of gift (best not question it too closely, in case it fell apart under the scrutiny), he is certain that he'd

57

turn up but it's best for her not to get her hopes up. But it cost them nothing to ask, did it? They might as well just ask.

He sighs deeply. There's no way he's going to get out of this. But it could be — they could be — managed, and there still might be a way he could turn the thing to his advantage. It needn't wreck his plan. It would just be a slight diversion — a stepping stone on a path to bigger and better things.

'It doesn't come to order,' he says. 'It isn't scientific. I can't tell you what's going to happen. But I can try. And if I live here, to be on hand while I'm trying, you mustn't harass me for it. Let me work in my own time.'

Jack walks over to Tim and leans on the wall right next to him, their shoulders not quite touching.

'You'll try it though, won't you? Put your hands on her. Is that how it works? You did . . .' He rubs his eyes, pulls at his collar and tries again. 'My head. My eyes.'

'I did,' Tim says. He leans over and puts a hand on Jack's belly. Feels the muscles under his palm harden up. But Jack doesn't move, doesn't flinch. He can't help himself. 'I did do it, right enough. Do you want me to do it again?'

He keeps his eyes fixed on Jack's face. The redness, the puffiness, the slicked-back wisps of gingerish thinning hair. Closer now, so he can feel the man's gravy-scented breath on his cheek. He is so ordinary that for a moment Tim is nearly overcome. Jack has closed his eyes but he must feel Tim staring at him, because now he opens them, frowns, and moves off. The hand holding the cigarette is shaking, and he throws it away.

'Let's agree then. I collect the board weekly. Most lodgers like to leave a marked envelope in the fruit bowl on Monday evenings. Netty will sort you a rent book. Ask her, if she forgets. She gets tired. Our lodgers don't tend to require credit, neither are arrears permitted.'

Tim laughs out loud, steps back and thumbs his wallet out of his back pocket. Hands Jack three crisp new blue fivers and enjoys Jack examining them, surprised. That was him just about done now; but they mustn't know that. They weren't idiots; even Jack was suspicious. They mustn't think it was anything to do with the money. Jack folds the notes in half and slips them into his shirt pocket. Tim tries not to seem as if he wants to snatch them back again. It's an investment. You've got to speculate. That's how the world works. No one gets something for nothing.

'Tell me when I've used that up and you can have some more,' he says. And, 'Where's this trifle I was promised?'

The girl comes out then; Netty, perhaps, has sent her out to fetch them, but she's pushing a doll's pram and it makes a rattling noise along the crazy paving at the back of the house that irritates Tim — he glances at her sharply and sees that instead of a doll in the pram, she's taken one of the rabbits from the kitchen table and tucked it in there, under a blanket.

'You don't want to do that,' he goes to her and

59

lifts out the rabbit. 'It's a warm day. We want to get this little man's suit off and get him tucked up inside your refrigerator so you can have him for your tea tomorrow.'

The girl stares at him, her dark eyes inscrutable. She says nothing as Tim takes a length of string out of his pocket, ties the rabbit's back legs to the head of the outside tap and uses his penknife to make a start on loosening the skin between them. He's done it hundreds of times before; he's familiar with the greasy smell of the rabbit fur and knows exactly the right pressure to apply as he works his fingers between the muscle and skin. The fine webs of fat that marble over the thighs and flank adhere to his questing fingers. The rabbit isn't as fresh as he's pretending, the last in the lot nicked from Gregson, the skin soft, the fat slick. It's not a hard job, all he needs to do now is pull, not too hard, towards the rabbit's head and he's half done. But a shudder passes through him and he's embarrassed. Damn rabbits. Cost him a job and now he was near to fainting at the sight of them. What was wrong with him? Squeamish? With his professional experience? He was a joke, and a bloody bad one. Jack is staring but asks for no explanation. This piece of showing off feels boyish and silly — another little trick that no one asked to see.

'Come along, Annette,' Jack says, 'leave Mr Richardson to his work and see if your mother needs us.' They go back into the house and the late-afternoon sun warms the back of Tim's neck as he continues to skin the rabbit. He has to go into the kitchen and joint the little carcass with his eyes closed, the sting of bile at the back of his throat. When he's done, he rinses the stringy body in the sink, breathing through his mouth to avoid the thick ferrous smell of it. He finds a pot, places the pieces into it then stows the pot in the fridge. When he returns to the dining room he is wiping his hands on a towel, sheepish and shamefaced.

'All set, Tim?' Netty says. There are circles of sweat under her arms. She is standing at the table and serving the trifle into little glass bowls.

'All done, Mrs Clifford.'

'You're very thoughtful. Here, will you have some extra cream?'

'Sit down, will you, Netty?' Jack says. 'You've done enough. Let us serve ourselves.'

Netty looks ready for her bed, but sits at the table and pretends to eat the trifle. She's noticed nothing, and of the two of them he'd had her down as the sceptic. Jack must have spent some time working on her — convincing her to let him into the house. But their belief, he could see, was fragile. Ah well. He would tough this one out. Find that smile that his mother promised would open doors for him.

He picks up his spoon and eats. She's used powder to make the custard instead of cooking it herself from scratch, which he'd prefer, but it is still very good. Even though he expects the trifle to unsettle his stomach even further, he asks for a second helping, which pleases her.

He can tell.

4

On a weekday Netty aims to have the lodgers fed and watered and the dining room emptied by eight o'clock at the very latest. She has to hustle to keep to time if the boys all want something cooked and most mornings they do, but so long as she gets the hob fired up before seven and juggles tea and toast and bacon and handing out the morning papers without too many mishaps it works out all right. With Tim, there's a full house, so sticking to a routine is important. How long she'll be able to keep all these plates spinning, she doesn't know. It's gone half seven.

She brings in the teapots on a tray and regards with pleasure all five of her young men reading newspapers in their shirtsleeves and opening their post. It's only been a couple of days but they seem to have accepted Tim all right, who is sitting at the head, leaning back in his chair and gesticulating with his cup.

'Trouser legs are getting narrower and narrower,' he's saying. 'They're cutting them that fine now that the line of the calf, if you've got a good strong one, becomes part of the line of the suit. If you've got a proper cutter, that is. None of these fifty-shilling off-the-peg jobs, but a real bespoke.'

She pauses in the doorway. The tray is heavy today and the morning sunshine is shining right through the bay window behind Tim so Netty can't see the expression on his face at all, just the shape of his curly hair, the tip of his nose, his open mouth. Like a stamp.

'Tea's up, gentlemen. While it's hot, if you don't mind.'

'Thank you, Mrs Clifford.'

That's Pete Jackson, who's been with them for nearly three years now. He's a porter at the Grange Hotel and though he keeps saying he's going to move onto something better one of these days, he seems pretty well settled where he is and Netty's glad of it. He's a good boy: no trouble for them, and always leaves them a bit extra at Christmas.

Danny Matthews stands up, insists on taking the tray from her.

'Today you'll have to let me be mother,' he says, and does the rounds. She's grateful. It was all she could do to get dressed this morning.

Jack's always saying that one of these days the Cliffords will come into their own and shan't have to let the house out the way they do. That they can move downstairs and Netty can have her own sewing room, and a music room too, with a piano, if she wants one. Privately, Netty has come to realise this is just a pipe dream of Jack's and any road, what the hell would she do with a piano? She never bursts his bubble. Only smiles and convinces him that she'd miss the boys, all of them, because she's so used to having a houseful to look after.

Danny finishes pouring, and sets the tray down on its mat, the way she likes it. He works taking tickets at Victoria Hall. He's in the box office and sometimes out front and in the record shop at weekends, to give him a bit extra. He's only been here six months but has fit into their routines like he was born to them. Alan Gravesend, a junior accountant, chews toast behind his paper and says nothing. He's one that takes a while to come to life in the a.m., but no one minds that, they're all used to him — and if a bulb goes in the night or you want the bins putting out last thing, he's the one to ask; the light shows under his door until the early hours every morning. He says he's up studying for his exams and Netty's content to believe him.

'Will you sit and have a cup with us? Tim here is just putting us straight on a few things.'

Nicky Robinson is the youngest. He's buttering toast and listening to Tim, who is talking about Edinburgh now — the layout and history of the city and what he found to get up to there.

'Is that right?' Netty says. She sits. 'Just for a minute then.'

'My very first job,' Tim says, 'was at a tartan mill. I can't say it was the most stimulating position for an ambitious young man and the noise of the looms used to give me terrible headaches. I didn't last there long, as a matter of fact. But you could say it whetted my appetite for the career I have in mind now. If nothing else, it gave me a working knowledge of the background to the business that will no doubt come in useful to me. I'm hoping, quietly confident, if you catch my drift, that it's just the kind of detail that will put me head and shoulders above applicants without similar experience.'

'They make many tartan suits on Savile Row, then? For the Caledonian patriot with a shapely calf?' Nicky asks.

Danny splutters, and Alan and Pete, who are that bit older, turn back to their newspapers, merely smiling.

'You chop up pigs. That's how you're earning your living, isn't it?'

Tim smiles calmly. 'I'm nowhere near 'chopping up the pigs', as you put it. Nowhere near. Takes a damn sight more training to master the techniques of butchery than it does to — off the top of my head — flog tickets across a counter and work a counting machine.'

Pete folds his paper, and takes a long, slow sip from his teacup.

'It takes years to be competent — only competent — and longer than that to get really good at it. Same length of time as you'd expect to spend on a medical degree, some say,' Tim says.

'So you're telling us it's as much of a science as it is an art, then?' Nicky is still teasing him and Netty wants to intervene, but can't find the words.

'You laugh all you want, Nicholas. The fact remains that there's only two men who can transform a corpse into something you'd want to eat. One is the butcher. Do you know who the other is?'

'Spit it out, man,' Danny says, 'I'm growing cobwebs over here.'

65

'Your priest.' Tim lays down his cutlery with a flourish. Alan and Pete laugh and Danny busies himself opening an envelope.

'You've a great big cocky gob on you, for a man whose highest achievement is an understanding of the sacredness of best sausages,' Nicky says.

He's got a point. Tim is laying it on a bit thick. But he's unruffled and only laughs.

'You're not having some tea, Mrs Clifford?' He holds her gaze, as if between them they have a secret that the others aren't in on, and she looks away quickly before the others notice. The house won't be worth living in if the boys think she's playing favourites.

'Not this morning,' she says. 'I'll be in the kitchen if you need me.' She stands.

'Could I trouble you for a pot of coffee, if you have it?' he asks.

This is par for the course. She roots frantically through the cupboards for the packet of coffee she knows she has in there somewhere. Whenever a new one arrives, there's a bit of jostling and banter while they sort out the pecking order between themselves.

They come from all walks of life; city boys, boys down from the farms and the lakes. The grammar school lot and the lads from the moderns. They've all got to rub along together. She stifles her urge to go back in there and defend Tim, to gather him up and away from the others who don't understand how important he is, and bring him into the warmth of the little kitchen to sit at the table with Annette. She

66

watches the kettle, waiting for it to boil while the fantasy unfurls itself into the room along with the jet of steam from its spout. Annette hums under her breath, slowly stirring golden syrup into her porridge.

★　★　★

At five to eight Netty bustles into the dining room and takes away the teapots and the cruet set. The cruet going away is her regular signal for the boys to clear off and get out from under her feet and usually they're all very good about heeding it. Tim is still nursing his coffee, so she leaves the pot by his elbow. The others call through to her as they leave, wishing her a good morning. She tells them it's rabbit casserole tonight and she won't wait for them if they're later than six. By ten past eight the dining room is empty.

Empty that is, except for Tim, who is lounging in his chair and looking out of the window like a man who's just woken up on the first day of a very long holiday. Netty eyes him curiously. She's learned, over the years, to trust her instincts when it comes to these young men. She's very rarely wrong. But Tim is impervious to her scrutiny: an unknown quantity.

'Did you sleep all right?'

'Oh yes. Very comfortable. It's a lovely room.'

She knows it isn't. There's nothing to be done about the damp, they've all to suffer it, to varying degrees, but the room is dark, and poky, and she hasn't had the time to get the curtains

67

washed and dried and up again. He is being very gracious. She'll do them for him at the weekend, if her energy lasts.

'You're not liverish? I've got a bottle of Fennings'. Indian Brandee too, if you want it?'

'I've never been better.' He leans back in his chair. Doesn't look as if he's planning on shifting himself any time soon.

'And you're getting on all right with the other boys? No problems getting to the bathroom or anything like that?'

'I'm happy to wait my turn, Mrs Clifford. There's a routine, I'm sure, and a whole set of domestic politics around the matter of soap and badger brushes that I've got to get used to.'

Netty empties the coffee pot into his cup. The pot is heavy in her hands, fuller than she expected.

'So long as you're settling.'

He smiles at her gratefully. The coffee is thick and soupish; Netty notes the grains trickling down the inside of the cup and is embarrassed, but he is drinking it and doesn't seem to mind. She'll have to boil the kettle again at this rate. And buy more, if he can get through it this fast.

'You'll probably find it much quieter here, after Morecambe,' she begins, almost apologetically, though she's never felt the need before — not with any of the others. 'People will say the place has changed, that it's less like itself since the railway came. The older generation. I don't know about that. But you should know this place isn't for paddling and donkeys and slot machines. It's for people who like a bit of quiet.

We're probably a different sort of town from what you're used to.' She pauses, wondering why she's trying to put him off, as if part of her doesn't want him here at all. 'Some days we get a load of cheap trippers in on the steamers from Morecambe. Lads your age with their pay packets. Shop girls. But they soon go.'

Tim finishes his coffee and motions for her to refill his cup again.

'I've lived all sorts of places, Mrs Clifford. Back home the council put us in one of those concrete high-rises. They said it would be just like the old street, except it would go up and down rather than across. The windows didn't open properly and it got mouldy because there was nowhere to hang out your washing. It was different all right.' How many places can he have lived? He's nineteen at the absolute most, Netty thinks. Is he spinning her a tale? 'I like a bit of fresh air. Some space to breathe.' He stretches, laces his fingers behind his head. 'I'm sure Grange-over-Sands will suit me perfectly.'

'That's good.' Netty takes the tray into the kitchen, decants the clarty plates into her sink of hot water, washes Annette's porridge bowl then goes back in with a cloth. He's still sitting there. She glances at the clock.

'You not going to work?'

It's been so long since they've had a new lodger (they stay, she prides herself, because they feel so welcome, because she runs such a happy house) that she's quite forgotten how to induct them into the invisible rules and routines that they all keep, the ones that keep the house

69

running smoothly, that stop them all getting under each other's feet too much. He can't be blamed for not knowing about the cruet. She wipes around him and looks at the clock on the wall.

'You wouldn't want to be late, would you? Gregson wouldn't like that.'

As soon as she opens her mouth she wishes she could bite the words back, could clutch them out of the air and throw them away before they reach him. Jack would shake her if he could hear her talk now. The boy's hardly had a chance to unpack and here she is flapping about like a fishwife, harassing him about his work and his bowels and probably putting off any good intentions he had regarding her.

Tim coughs. 'Since you mention it, I thought we might talk about that.'

He can't have been bagged, not already. It wasn't possible. But if he wasn't able to cover his board and then Jack asked him to leave, well, what would happen to her? Nothing was set in stone, she knew that. Jack had told her the boy had been vague, hadn't wanted to commit to anything. But still, the signs were hopeful, or a damn sight more hopeful than they would be if he lost his job and had to go back home to his mother. Or perhaps she could keep it to herself and not say anything to Jack at all. It would be a hard thing to hide and what the other boys would make of it if they ever caught on wouldn't bear thinking about.

'There's been no trouble for you, has there?'

Tim pushes out a chair.

'Why don't you take the weight off your feet? I don't like to think of you running around after me with a tea towel all morning. I'll get this table cleared when I've finished with my coffee. It's the very least I can do.'

Netty tucks her cloth into the front pocket of her apron and sits down. The table is speckled with dropped toast crumbs and grains of sugar and she sweeps them into a pile with the side of her hand. Imagine being told to sit down in your own house! Like being called in to the headmaster for the strap.

In the coming weeks Netty will look back and try to pinpoint the moment when she first started to believe in Timothy Richardson, butcher's apprentice from the city of Edinburgh. Not just when she started to hope (seeing Jack with that silly knitting pattern, his eyes screwed up into slits), nor when, in her desperation, she became willing to give any foolish thing a try (much earlier — that first time with Candy, probably, loosening the sash on her housedress and thinking that as it cost her nothing but the woman's bus fare she may as well play along with it) but the exact moment when she let herself fall and really began to believe. She will keep returning here, to the sharpness of the grains against her hand and the steady ache deep down inside her pelvis, like her monthlies, but worse.

'Don't look so worried, Mrs Clifford.'

She watches her hands move across the table, sweeping and tidying the crumbs, then scattering them so she can tidy them again.

'I'll do you the honour of being direct. Mr Clifford told me about your trouble.'

The grit of spilled sugar prickles between her fingers. She finds herself unable to meet his eye. The muscles in her jaw tighten.

'He was very discreet. You mustn't feel embarrassed. I don't want to pry into your business.'

'That's quite all right.'

He waits.

She expected that he would want a medical history from her sooner or later. So she tries to find the start of the thread so she can show it to him and get him to understand. But it's no good. The first symptoms had been puzzling and inconvenient; no more than that. A few times a month she'd had to scrub her bloodied knickers in a sink of cold water like a fifteen-year-old girl caught short. She put that and the blood that sometimes appeared in her bed after she'd been with Jack down to her system getting ready for the change. It had gone on for three years.

The past is ruined now. When she looks back at the photograph of Annette on her first day at school, she can't enjoy it. The picture (upstairs in an envelope in one of the divan drawers) shows Annette standing on the front steps of the house, framed against the front door smack bang between those blasted trees. She was what — five? Her face still chubby, like a toddler. Baby teeth. And wearing, pleased as anything, her school uniform. The first hand-knitted cardigan (Netty had been proud of that — the effort it had taken!) and new white socks, fresh out of the packet. She'd been laughing as the shutter clicked so the picture

72

came out blurred and was spoiled. She kept it anyway. She must have been dying without knowing it even then.

She didn't worry, not really, when she went to her GP. She thought she'd get away quick with a tonic and a prescription for her hormones but instead they sent her off to Manchester to see a specialist. A white coat with a funny accent and a slick hairdo. He felt around a bit, like a midwife, and said she'd to have an operation, fast as they could get her in for it. The short notice and inconvenience was her own fault for not going to her GP earlier. She shouldn't have let coyness get in the way of her safeguarding her own health, especially with a little one at home to think about. But at least she did already have a little one. It could be worse. The smug bastard; they were toffs and frigid bitches, the lot of them. She hated them all, none more than the hatchet-faced nurse they'd sent into the ward on the morning of her operation to shave her as if she was having a baby.

'All right, Mother?' she'd said, as she pulled the sheets back.

They wheeled her off to theatre. The black rubber mask they placed over her face smelled bad. The rasp of the stiff white sheets against her bare limbs almost hurt. Deep, dry breaths, counting backwards from ten. Then she was out.

Out.

Out, then opening her eyes four hours later (they said) feeling like she'd only blinked, just once, and no real time had passed at all.

She didn't think about anything then, only

73

dumbly regarded the flowers on her nightstand. The nurses clopped up and down the wards in their stiff little leather shoes all night, like horses pulling landaus back and forth along the prom.

'Where's Jack?'

'Now then, Mother.'

They gave her a jab and put her back to sleep.

The sticky-mouthed haze she emerged into lasted for days. They said it was normal, just a reaction to the anaesthetic, and when she asked to see the parts they'd taken away from her, they ignored her. She wanted to meet the surgeon but he was too busy to deal directly with patients.

One of the Hatchet Faces came back.

'We'll have none of that carry-on, please,' and this is how Netty learned she'd been crying in the night. She said Netty wasn't to be a nuisance but should lie still and concentrate on getting herself better. So Netty was good. She lay still and felt blood seeping into the thick pad tucked between her legs. Every couple of hours a Hatchet Face would come and pull the curtains around her bed. Sometimes they wouldn't even talk to her before tugging the sheets back to peel the soaked hot pad away from her, inspect it, and replace it with a fresh one. Jack could only come once or twice in the evening when she was too tired to say much anyway.

The operation hadn't been the end of it. Not by a long chalk. They said the surgeon had found something nasty. An infection? Never mind about that. The only thing she had to worry about was the little bit of follow-up that was needed.

She'd lost count of the hospital visits since then; the train journeys to Manchester, the long afternoons sitting in The Holt with untouched knitting in her lap. The place stank of disinfectant and cheap soap. There was a fancy word for the follow-up but she'd either written it down wrong, or it wasn't in the dictionary in the first place. Doctors were always making up words. And they only had a little Collins *Gem*, for Scrabble games.

It really hurt. Jack said she'd get used to it, but she didn't. They'd told her she'd be under sedation when they did it, but all she felt was seasick. 'The source', which was radium (Collins says 'pure white alkaline earth metal', but she never saw it), got stuffed inside little metal tubes. And the little metal tubes got stuffed inside her, like hot spikes, followed by a pack of wadding and gauze to stop them moving about. She wanted to complain about her feet being cold, because of the stirrups, but her mouth felt like it was full of cotton wool and she couldn't get the words to form properly. She had to stay in bed for days afterwards, hooked up to a catheter with her ankles strapped together to stop her moving about and getting the radium out of place.

'Oh Jack, I feel like a right Christmas turkey. Stuffed to the gills and roasting.'

She was trying to cheer him up and be positive, like the doctors had said, but Jack only squeezed her hand and squinted at his crossword because he was ashamed of her. She was ashamed of herself.

The consultant came and sat by her bed and

described the sickness to her as if it were an invader to be battled with; a Martian wreaking havoc in the territory of her own flesh.

'You've not to let yourself be beaten. Think of your little one. Keep positive, yes?'

She nodded. Remembered her manners and said thank you nicely.

But she's not soft. She knows what beaten means and anyway how's she supposed to fight when the cells of her enemy are so similar to her own that whatever poisoned them, poisoned her too? How could it be something separate to her when it whirled around her most secret places, burrowing into her flesh and unfurling through her body to so thoroughly entangle itself with her organs, her glands and her blood, that no further surgery was possible? She and it had become one flesh and nothing short of a miracle, the kind of miracle Timothy Richardson and people like him claimed they could dispense — like coloured handkerchiefs from top hats — was just about the only thing worth hoping for. She was swiping at shadows. Hurting no one but herself.

★　★　★

Netty does not know how long she's been staring out of the window considering her situation. It happens to her sometimes. She'll find herself somewhere in the house, a duster in her hands, with no idea how she got there.

'We've had this house a long time,' she says. 'The plan was always to rent it out. Let the

76

rooms. We hoped the house would work for us, give us enough money to live on. I thought we might get away for a few weeks every summer. There's lots of places I wanted to see. Europe, mainly. I've never been on a plane.' She swipes at the spilled sugar again. 'But we didn't know we'd end up working for the house. Being tied to it. I don't think Jack minds as much. Or maybe he didn't expect any different. Over twenty years, we've been doing this now. A long time to be frying sausages and filling teapots.' She frowns. This isn't what he wants to know, is it?

'Just start by telling me how you feel,' Tim says. 'Are you in pain?'

There are tears on her cheeks and she wipes her face quickly.

'I'm all right today,' Netty says. 'There is pain, but it comes and goes.'

The truth is that some days her limbs are like lead, and at night she pours with sweat to the point where Jack once had to ask her if she'd wet the bed.

'I seem to have turned a bit of a corner.' She touches her hair, still lank and dry, but long enough to have a wave put into it, to be able to feel like she can take care of herself again. She kept meaning to ask Fiona to come round with the bleach and a box of Twink. She should make a bit of an effort for Jack and Annette.

'I look less of a sight than I did, any road. I have something for the pain, but it puts me to sleep and there's no point in spending your life in bed, is there? So I just try and get along. For as long as I can do.'

'I'd probably do the same thing,' Tim says, not like a doctor at all. Netty is heartened by this, and finds her courage.

'Jack told me about the way you helped him. His eyes. How did — '

'I understand,' he cuts her off — almost, if she's not mistaken, a little embarrassed. 'Can I ask you something?' He doesn't wait for an answer. 'Would you mind standing up for me? Nothing else. I won't touch you. I just need to see you standing.'

Netty hesitates, then wipes her hands on her apron and pushes her chair back. She'd had enough examinations. Doctors poking at every inch, eyebrows to breakfast, as if they were midwives. No point getting squeamish about another one. Tim stands and circles her, the coffee cup in his left hand. He points low at her abdomen, his finger at her pubic bone.

'Here,' he says, and she blinks quickly, and nods.

She never said that to him. Jack wouldn't have either. He really wouldn't have. Some things are not for talking about. Shouldn't be for public consumption. The hairs on her arms are lifting; she can see the gooseflesh but she's not cold. Tim traces a line in the air up the centre of her body and round, to the small of her back.

'Here, too.'

'Yes.'

He circles her again and moves his hand, all without touching her, until he's pointing at the lump she's never even mentioned to her doctor because she's too bloody terrified, in her left armpit.

'Here.'

Netty is astonished. He could have broken in somewhere and looked up her medical records. But nobody knows about that swollen place in her armpit, not even Jack. He gazes at her, examining every single inch of her frame. It feels like an x-ray: something and nothing, all at once.

Is this the treatment? Does he do it like Candy does, without touching? He touched Jack though, didn't he? Grabbed him, more like? Maybe he's got different methods for different people. More gentle with women, perhaps. What would she know about it? It might as well be quadratic equations or voodoo, as far as she's concerned. Best not to ask.

She takes a deep breath and tries to open herself up to whatever he is doing. Buck up; make a proper effort. But nothing changes and even with her eyes closed she can sense Tim moving away. He sits, tries to take a sip from his cup, sees that it is empty and pours again from the seemingly inexhaustible coffee pot.

'You can sit yourself down, Mrs Clifford,' he says, amiably. 'I just wanted to see, that's all.'

She won't sit. She rubs her bare arms, then runs a finger under each eye, to neaten up her mascara. She won't lose her dignity. Not in front of a nineteen-year-old lodger. She may have come to a low pass but she's not at the bottom of it yet.

'Are you able to make any recommendations?'

He taps his finger against his lip.

'You recall that I mentioned my position at Gregson's?'

79

'Yes?'

'I said that it wasn't entirely suitable. That I was looking for something better. You remember?'

'Men's outfitting, wasn't it? The clothes. Like you did back home. The mill.'

'That's right!' He praises her like she's a young girl getting her sums right, and Netty is surprised to find herself blushing with pleasure at his approval.

'I was wondering how it would affect our arrangement — my staying here, that is — if I were to hand my notice in to Mr Gregson. I'm thinking I'll be needed here, and it isn't fair to carry on apprenticing if I'm not planning to stay long term. I'm not sure it feels decent.'

'I see,' Netty says, slowly. I'll be needed here. This is it, isn't it? He's saying he will help her — that he'll be in the house, doing to her whatever it was he did to Jack? It's his round-about way of promising her something, isn't it? She could reach out and grab his hands over the table, but only wrings at the cloth in her apron pocket.

'I only ask because I know some landladies are extremely cautious about the employment prospects of their lodgers. And rightly so, of course.'

'You'd have to speak to Mr Clifford about that side of things,' Netty says. 'If you're asking about finances.'

Tim gasps, and claps his hand over his mouth.

'Oh no. Oh no, Mrs Clifford, I didn't mean that at all. Not at all,' he laughs. 'Were you thinking I was asking for some financial . . . leeway?'

'I'm not — '

'This is not a quid pro quo arrangement.'

He looks almost offended. She doesn't know what he's saying. Quid? She's not to worry about paying him? She wipes her forehead with the back of her hand.

'Please do rest assured, those envelopes will be appearing in the fruit bowl, right as rain. You've no worries there. Gregson's butcher boy or Head Cutter at Huntsman's, I intend to pay my own way.'

Netty's back hurts and she wants to get into her armchair, or even better into her bed, but Annette is clattering in the kitchen and the washing-up water is cooling in the sink. The polite, easy way Tim has with her makes her uncomfortable. Is he making fun of her?

'Like I say, that's something you'd have to speak to Mr Clifford about.' Stiff and embarrassed. The moment of him seeing into her — if that's what it was — has passed, and they're left talking about practicalities. 'You'll find him very approachable. Very fair.'

'Message received and understood.' Tim mock salutes her.

How he can joke around like this when he's just looked through her skin and into the most secret places of her body is beyond her. But he smiles and she relaxes. There's no point in inviting him to the house and asking him to help her if she's going to get all hoity-toity and defensive when he asks a simple question.

'I'll bring you some more toast. Shall I? If you're not in a rush to be off?'

'I wouldn't say no,' Tim says. 'Perhaps a sausage or two as well? On the side? And if it isn't too much trouble, might you do me a chop for tonight, instead of the last of that rabbit? Could that be arranged?'

5

Annette loiters in the garden just staring at the house, as if she is trying to measure with her eyes how crooked it really is. She's there so long that her pan boils dry and her over-boiled egg explodes. She used to blow up empty crisp packets and pop them — all the kids at her school did — and that's what the noise of the egg exploding in the dry pan sounds like. It stinks. She ditches the pan in the skip — not worth scrubbing it, there are more pans here than you could shake a stick at and she's not going to be here long enough to get through all of them — then takes another one out, runs the water, and tries again. The water boils. She eats.

She could, if she wanted, eat from a different plate or dish every night and just chuck them out afterwards. Empty out the kitchen gradually. And no washing-up. And now it's fully dark and she sits in the kitchen for a long time, even after she's finished eating. She's staring at the eggcup and saucer, at the soap dish on the windowsill, at the black scuffmarks on the door frame. The work. The endless work. Too much to hope that someone would buy the house as is. She knows that. Annette taps a finger against her lips — like she's telling herself to shut up — and goes to the little window. One of the panes has broken at some point and she's taped a bit of cardboard over it that's already wet and sagging, and that's one more thing to add to the list, though perhaps she should be more realistic. Getting the place up for sale is the main thing. A little pane of glass in need of replacing isn't going to stop someone who really wants to buy it, is it?

No.

The garden's a mess too. It was always kept neat, the edges of the lawn cut straight, and her dad's precious brassica patch resplendent in twin beds at the back. The privet marked the exact spot where home ended and everywhere else began. What does she remember? That she wasn't allowed to mess about with the begonias. That she had to keep out of the way, not annoy the lodgers. She had to entertain herself. She remembers hushed conversations, half overheard and not understood. Doors closed in her face. Boring afternoons in the garden. That lawn. The state of it now! Her dad took such care of it. She remembers the springtimes — always around Easter — when he'd have to go and dig out the sycamore seedlings that sprang up in the lawn, front and back. They'd shoot up inches overnight, even in the gutters and the moss growing on the shed roof — and he'd curse them. The cursing seemed to cause them to multiply rather than shrivel: it was a job that burdened him until the end. She remembered that, right enough. She'd even said something about it to the tree surgeon this afternoon: the persistence of seedlings, the constant rooting out.

'If we could just get the trees down, it would make sorting out the garden much easier.'

Eve smiled. 'Another bit of bad news for you, love,' she said. If she fells the trees, she explained, Annette will have to keep up with the job herself, or pay someone else to do it, because even when the trees aren't there to drop their keys, hard winters of the future — maybe the next ten or fifteen of them — will crack the buried samaras of seasons past and shock them out of their dormancy. The seedlings will spring up out of the ground every April for years and years, like ghosts, like resurrections, like revenge.

Annette shook her head.

'I won't be here for that,' she said. 'It won't be my problem.'

No.

We test our voices again but we've lost them. We hold our hands up to our faces and no matter how loudly we shout we can't feel the warmth of our own breath against our palms.

Annette doesn't throw the plate and cup away, but rinses and dries them and puts them back in the cupboard. There's broken eggshell in the washing-up water and when she tries to fish it out it floats away between her fingers. We paddle our hands through the water without feeling it and there's nothing we can do to help. Her sleeves are sopping wet when she stops, pulls out the plug and watches the grey water swirl the broken fragments down the plughole. We want to remind her about the drains. She needs to take more care. But she just stands there, with the water running along her wrists, sliding down her palms and dripping from her fingers to patter on the ripped linoleum.

Now she thinks about it, her father wasn't always so houseproud. He'd maintained the place as well as he could, but there was a season — towards the very end — when he'd wandered around the place with fresh eyes, suddenly seeing cracks and cobwebs and scuffed paintwork and discoloured ceilings, and set about fixing it all with something like fury. It had become obsessive. Something had changed. Something had made what had been invisible to him previously too obvious to be tolerated. What was it? The faded ribbon curtain flutters in the doorway, as if disturbed by a breath. There's a new bottle of something on the draining board — she must have picked it up from one of the shops in town. Wine, it is. She opens it up.

This bloody house, she thinks. It was about time. About fucking time, after the crap jobs and the crap flats and the crap landlords, moving every six months, having to pack up her stuff and dismantle and rebuild cheap, flat-pack furniture so often that it fell apart, getting too old for living like a student and doing it anyway, having no choice but to do it, and after avoiding the place for years, after avoiding even picturing the house in her head, and after being forced back to it by circumstance, it was about fucking time she had a bit of luck, a bit of money under the floorboards, or a quick sale, or a priceless painting in the attic (she snorts), or something. She is entitled to it. She is. She drinks.

★　★　★

Now we remember that the neighbours, too, used to tell us to get shut of the place while we still could. They'd advise us to buy a semi-detached in Morecambe or Ulverston and invest the rest of the cash for our retirements. It wasn't only the general dilapidation or the trouble the trees were causing; both were less pronounced then than they are now, of course. It was because of Netty, quietly wasting away behind the net curtains. They whispered and worried Jack wouldn't be able to manage the house when she was gone. Better to get rid while the place was still a going concern, they said.

And yes, maybe we should have taken the trees out earlier. Made it a matter of urgency. We hated them for the shade they cast in our front garden: nothing would grow but anaemic grass and springy privet. And we hated them for their leaves, which they'd shed in a rush, spitefully early and before (Netty, for one, was convinced) any other tree on the street. In better times we raked them out of the grass and made piles of them under the hedges. When autumn arrived, bringing clouds that touched the ground, the whole house would smell like brackish water, mould and the woods. The leaves would yellow and rot and turn to slime on the path.

We hated them but we never, ever suggested we should have them taken out. It might have been the money but more likely it just didn't occur to us. You worked round things and played the best hand you could with the cards you'd been dealt. That was our way. Whatever the neighbours said and however badly we needed the money, we clung on, as if the house wasn't a gift to us from Jack's dead parents, but their flesh and blood itself.

★ ★ ★

Annette is rummaging in the kitchen cupboards, a mug half filled with wine in one hand. Taking out a tarnished coffee pot and a sugar bowl with a brown and orange flower pattern along the rim — the kind you'd get in a vintage tea shop now — and endless Tupperware and not one box with a lid that fits it. She finds a torch tucked away in the odds and ends drawer. It won't work, she thinks, and tests it, and she's right so she leaves it in the drawer. The back door always sticks — more often in wet weather. She kicks it a couple of times to get it to open. Muttering. The patio glitters with frost. The sheets have gone stiff on the line. She leaves footprints in the crunching grass as she stamps over the lawn and to the end of the garden. The light from the kitchen door doesn't go far — she's heading into the dark with the light her strange little telephone makes guiding her footsteps. Towards the shed.

She won't wait. That's what she's saying. Won't stand around and do nothing while the place falls around her ears. Won't let the dust and damp eat into her inheritance. It's freezing. There used to be a padlock, a giant gold-coloured thing her father would spray with lubricant now and again. The light from her telephone sweeps over the door and yes, the lock is still there. Speckled with rust and sparkling with frost. The key?

She strides back to the house, shouldering her way past the cardboard sheets, to the kitchen and the odds and ends drawer. There are all kinds of keys in there, lying loose and muddled in with all the other things. Some of them have lain undisturbed for so long that they have left rusted imprints of themselves on the drawer bottom — reddish shadows to mark where they have been. She sorts through them and takes anything padlock-sized. There are four, all unlabelled. She has to prise one of them up with her fingernail. It hurts.

She stands for a while. She's trying to remember if there used to be a key-box or a labelled board. She's sure her mother would never have left them scrambled up in a drawer like this. Her father would have wanted to have a system for keeping the spare keys to the lodgers' rooms in order. They were never professionals, though. Not real business people. Opening the house to lodgers was as much about kindness as it was about generating the income needed to maintain the fabric of the building. They seemed to consider themselves more as hosts than landlords, waiting desperately for their slice of the gods-in-disguise pie. She puts her hand against her throat, thinking, too angrily, about us. We want to touch her but the wind picks up and we're blown around the garden like handkerchiefs, flitting through the hedges, wheeling up high and snagging in the branches of the old rotten cherry tree.

No. Wait. Don't.

She rubs her face. Pulls her hair back and knots it up high with a rubber band she's been keeping around her wrist. It seems to help.

'Don't start,' she says.

Her voice. Her voice is so different to ours. So loud and steady in the dark. We whisper but even we can't tell which noises we're making, and which come from the dry branches and the dead leaves that rustle around us where we sit.

In the garden she struggles to hold the telephone steady, train its light on the padlock and wriggle the tiny key into the lock all at once. She drops the telephone. We watch it go — it bounces and tumbles over the grass, the light swinging crazily, to illuminate the bare stems at the bottom of the hedge. Is there no one who could help her?

Annette retrieves it, swears and grunts at the padlock *fucking stupid thing* (words we never taught her) but when she loses her temper and tugs at it the metal clasp it is looped through comes right out of the wood. The screws fall away into the darkness. She pushes at the splintered door frame with her fingers. This is no miraculous feat of strength. The wood is so rotten that a child could have done it. The shed holds nothing now but some folding garden furniture that should have been treated annually with teak oil, but wasn't, and is now powdery with mould. Plant pots in their dozens, stacked neatly inside each other, lean in a corner. The bulk of her father's tools went long ago. Candy's nephews asked to borrow them, or promised to take care of them; have the lawnmower serviced and so on, and they never came back. Annette's got no use for them. She will hire someone to do the garden once the trees are out.

The remaining tools are mounted on the wall, hanging from lopsided nails. A pair of pliers, a hammer, a chisel and saw, a spool of electrical tape, a spirit level, some other thing with a winding handle Annette never saw used and does not know the name of. She leans in and takes down the saw. It is only when she is halfway back to the house, the kitchen doorway a bright rectangle of light and warmth drawing her — us — through the frozen garden as if we are fish on the end of a line, that we realise she has left the shed door open and the wind, if it picks up, will bang it to and fro all night.

6

We didn't know. We didn't see. We were away upstairs or sleeping or distracted or in the garden or away somewhere else but now we have it all back we understand things differently. We see Annette trudge around the house with her saw, poking in cupboards, drinking more of the wine, and punching at buttons on her miniature telephone. We don't know who she wants to speak to, but no one answers. We see Timothy Richardson too, padding around in the middle of the night, plucking one of Jack's shirts from the maiden in the kitchen and now we can follow as he takes it into the living room to try it on.

It is old and worn and the buttons have been lost and replaced with new ones that don't quite match but he likes the soft feel of the fabric under his fingers, likes the way the collar fits. The sleeves are a bit too short; the yoke a touch too narrow, but the feel of it good, all the same. He can tell it was once a good shirt, the seams hand-felled, and the cotton thread-count high. And with approval he buttons it right up to the top and then, sure that everyone in the house is away or asleep (it is very late — he did pad around the house at all hours, we knew that) he sits in the chair next to the gas fire, the Rexine one with the best view of the television, the one that Jack claims for himself.

He doesn't turn on the television. Doesn't

mess around with Jack's items on the coffee table: his smoky glass ashtray, his water glass, his Fleming paperback and his crossword and his pencil. Doesn't lift the *Radio Times* or fetch a cushion or reach for the playing cards or the dominoes. He just sits, his hands on the arms of the chair, staring at the curtains and the dark curved glass of the television screen, thinking.

It would be very nice to have a place like this. A house to be the man of. He pats his breast pocket the way Jack does when he checks for his spectacles (we know old habits die hard, or not at all — we always knew this). He finds Jack's tobacco tin on the coffee table, helps himself to a hand-rolled cigarette (Jack is economising) and smokes it with his head leaning back against the antimacassar, just the way Jack likes to sometimes at night when the lodgers are out and the house is quiet and he can get a bit of peace and time to himself for once.

Tim breathes deeply and carefully enjoys the sensation he imagines Jack enjoys every day — the comfortable knowledge that every brick of the place belongs to him, and the wife, and the girl, and a rotating set of lodgers to keep the folding money coming in, and every old paperback and worn-out rug and net curtain and bent teaspoon in the whole structure belongs to him too, is predictably his, familiar against his hands and each item knowing its place on the shelves and in the drawers and cupboards and spare beds.

What a thing. What a bloody thing!

We watch, silent as mice, as Tim smokes, and

as he smokes he tries to put himself in a place like this. A wee house in Morningside or Stockbridge. A garden. A woman with an apron in the kitchen, a car to run her into town for her messages, people round at the weekends for meals and card games and drinks parties. Teacups with gold rims. A little grabber for getting sugar lumps out of the bowl and maybe a garden plot of his own, where he could go out and fiddle with his own brassicas at the weekends, the way Jack does. The man must get some pleasure out of it, or else he wouldn't do it, would he?

And will there be drives out into the country on Sundays and roast dinners in nice pubs? Will there be the cinema now and again, and a babysitter he'd pay in crisp pound notes to come in and mind the angelic, cherub-cheeked child that would be occupying the nursery upstairs? Will he walk down Princes Street with this woman — in a fur coat? — on his arm and feel the envious gaze of other men? Will he hold his own in conversations and tell jokes and get his accent right and carry a handkerchief and an expensive cigarette lighter and be admirable without being vulgar, notable without being famous, respected without being feared? Will he be able to do that? Pull off the most unlikely transformation of all?

He's ready for another cigarette. There's a creak above his head and he freezes, wondering what he'll say if he's caught like this, wearing the clothes of the master of the house. The shirt smells of Jack — clean and musty all at once

— of gardens and cooking and cheap soap flakes. A door closes, the toilet flushes and the cistern refills noisily. He's helpless, he knows. The second he got himself installed in a house of his own, the clocks would be going wrong, the neighbours looking at him funny, a steady stream of the lovelorn and afflicted making their way to his door. He can't even lay his hands on someone in bed without wondering what is going to happen to them.

And why do you no' stop it, then?

The trouble he'd made for his ma. The people that would turn up.

Just settle down, will you? Get a wee job. Live quietly. Be ordinary.

She made it sound like the trouble was something he wanted. But it wasn't him. It was other people. They sniffed him out, some charm he gave off, like sweat, and they wanted him — and what was he supposed to do? He could suffer it, or turn it to his advantage.

It's just the way I am, he'd said, and smiled, and smiled and smiled until the smiling didn't work on her any longer and he'd had to leave and promised himself pastures new where nobody knew what he was and he would keep himself to himself and mind his own business and work up to having a gig like the one Jack had, here, in this house. Then he'd call his mother and invite her back. Show her his house, all of his things, his car and his wife and his sons (three, why not?) and a garden in the back and a roof that never leaked and walls that never grew mould — not like the modern high-rise they'd been put in, the one with no room for the lot of them, never mind someone like him. Someone too big for his own boots. And he'd show her all this, a regular estate agent of his own life, and she would — what would she do? — she'd say *Wheeee, would you look at that?* and that would be enough. That was what he had planned to do and this place was a good enough stepping stone even if already he was prepared to admit his ambitions were beyond him.

There's a cry from upstairs that startles him.

'Jack?' he whispers. Not sure if he's hoping for a reply, or not.

He holds his breath. Starts to unbutton the shirt. But the cry comes again and now he's listening out for it, paying attention, he understands that it is only the girl. Moving in her sleep and shouting in her dreams. Nothing more. He puts out the cigarette, takes off the shirt and replaces it on the maiden. They'll never know. He will never let them know. Never allow them to suspect that he wants them as much as they want him. He closes the door and goes upstairs to bed though he does not sleep. He never sleeps. We don't sleep any more, either.

7

The tree surgeon is long gone but we are still curious about this woman. The first guest over our threshold in years. And because we can, we follow her away down the road, the van's engine noises picking up as she reaches the edge of town, joins the slip road for the motorway and heads south. She hums absently until she reaches her exit. She stops to fill up her van with petrol and now she's picked up Tom from football practice and time is no longer against her, she drives the long way back to the house, sharing a bag of chips, two battered sausages and a can of warm cola with a dusty-tasting top.

They talk for a long time about the match. Tom has plenty to say about various substitutions and decisions from the referee and he speaks in a manner that nearly prompts Eve into opening a discussion on the matter of good sportsmanship. At the last moment she changes her mind and distracts her son by coaxing him into a game. They spend the rest of the journey giving marks out of ten to the various displays of coloured lights in the windows they pass. None, they agree, is a patch on their own.

Eve has a lot on her mind. Not Annette. Not the trees, or the house; the woman's strangeness flickers uncomfortably at the edge of her mind from time to time but her own worries are closer to home. There's a school trip planned — the boys in the football team invited to a school in France, to play against their team in a 'friendly' and then to take a tour of the countryside and visit some museums. Practise their French. He's going to be taking exams soon enough. Before they know it. But Tom hasn't even got a passport and they're not mad keen on him staying with strangers. He's their only one. Not a baby any more, but still. Maddy has hidden the letter about the trip under the microwave, and Tom keeps bringing it out again and laying it on the kitchen counter. Yesterday he went to the post office on his bike and brought back a passport application form, shocking them both. He says he'll put towards the cost with his own money, if that's what the problem is. Get a paper round or something.

It has been causing arguments. Eve keeps him chatting, hoping the subject will not come up. Tom points out the coloured lights strung from the trees along the high street, the nativity display in the corner-shop window all lit up with electric candles. He's holding his hands — not so little any more — in front of the air vents and rubbing the heat into them. His fingernails are filthy. Eve might forbid him from going on the trip. She could. She and Maddy could do that, if they wanted to. And they do.

They arrive home. She parks her van in the drive, unloads a stack of logs and sawn-up branches from the back into the garage with Tom and finally goes into the house. Inside, Maddy has got the telly on too loud as per usual and *Come Dine with Me* is blasting out through the whole of downstairs. The meal being prepared is something fancy and unappetising to do with raw white fish and limes and homemade flatbread. Eve hopes that Maddy isn't doing raw fish for their tea, goes into the kitchen to inspect the pots on the cooker and tells her she's promised Tom he can stay up a bit later tonight and watch *Parkland*. The letter about the trip is on the dining table again. She folds it up and shoves it under the microwave. Maddy watches. Says nothing. They are united on this. Agreed that to watch their son grow up and away from them is a special kind of horror; the temptation to put a stop to it almost unendurable.

Outside, Tom lingers on the drive. He takes his football boots out of a plastic bag and knocks them against the wheel of the van to dislodge lumps of mud and grass from the studs. After a minute or two of this he puts the boots back inside the bag, looks up and down the street as if waiting for something to happen, then goes inside the house, banging the door closed.

8

We don't stay with Maddy and Eve and Tom, in their house. Our worries are closer to home too. We return to our own place, swept across the gently undulating land and the wide flats of the bay like slips of paper in a gale. And we're here. And here she is. Our little girl, alone again in the garden. Tiny now, with mud on her knees and a grass stain on the back of her pinafore. She is busily collecting the biggest leaves from the rambly hedge out front. Gathering them, damp and greasy, by the handful, empty snail shells crunching under her shoes. She knows she's to clear off and entertain herself outside. She's not to be noisy and she's not to go into the street and annoy anyone because Dad is busy helping Mum in the bathroom. Mum's having a bath in the middle of the day and needs help with the pouring jug to get the soap out of her hair. There's nothing to worry about.

She has a good collection of green leaves. They are the shape of eyes and she holds two over her own eyes to see if they fit. They do. She stumbles over the grass, seeing nothing. What does she look like? What she should do is get a little stick and poke holes in the leaves so she can hold them over her eyes and still see through them. She could look at herself in the hall mirror. But she's to stay out of the way in the garden and anyway she's supposed to be getting the tea

100

party ready because what will the guests think if they arrive in their best clothes and there's nothing ready for them? It would be completely mortifying. She picks a few more leaves. There are rules about this game. It's all right to pull leaves off the hedge but not to pick flowers or to mess about with the brassicas or to eat any berries or to make a mess. She stops, takes her green handfuls towards the house and lays them out in a circle on the front step. She admires it. She likes sitting between the trees like this. Likes hearing the whispering they make when the wind blows through their branches. Then she gets daisy petals (daisies aren't flowers, they don't count, so it's okay to pick them) and puts them on top, and then little bits of crumbly mud or twigs. There's a song to sing about getting the party ready, a private song she makes new words up for every single time, but mainly the song is like the one she hears being sung when the big kids play Boatman in the street.

Boatman, Boatman, can I pass?
You can't pass!
Boatman, Boatman, can I pass?
If you're wearing yellow, you can pass!

But instead of saying *wearing yellow* she says *invited to the tea party*, which is better, and anyway she's not allowed to play Boatman because sometimes the bigger boys can get carried away with wanting to stop you getting over the river and it can get a bit rough. Here's Mister Jackson with his suitcase.

101

'I nearly stood on you, there,' he says.

He's not annoyed. Instead of going away he puts his suitcase down flat on the step and sits on it and holds out his hand for a plate.

'What's for dinner today, then?'

'Scones and jam and crab paste sandwiches. You don't have to have the sandwich if you don't want. I have three different sorts of pink cakes with icing on the top.'

Mister Jackson takes an invisible cup of tea from his palm and raises it to his lips. He does it like the Queen, with his pinkie in the air. That's the proper way to do it.

'Wait,' Annette says, 'just a splash more milk, I think. It's good for your bones.' She pours and the two of them sit and drink tea for a while. He says it's very good, and that her cakes are nearly as good as her mother's are, but perhaps she'd want to consider putting a drop of rose water into the icing next time.

'Are you going on holiday?'

'I'm going to live somewhere else, Annette.'

'I know.'

The misters do come and go and she's not to get attached to them because they won't stay forever. Mum is good at picking the lodgers and runs the house very carefully, with lots of rules so that everyone gets on and nothing is broken. Maybe now and again one of the misters will stop giving Dad money or steal something or come back too late at night and then he has to go and live somewhere else. But the misters *have* been behaving themselves. Annette has been behaving herself very carefully, too, and not making a nuisance because she doesn't want to have to go and live somewhere else either.

'Are you getting married?'

He chuckles. 'Not yet. Your mother's a touch poorly.'

'She's not so good but she's fine if she has a morning and afternoon sleep,' Annette says. Which is interrupting. But it's true. She has lie-ins and naps and early nights and she says all these things help a good deal and that's why she has to do them every day. After a while she'll stop doing them because she'll have got the benefit of them. Then things will go back to normal, which means having chocolate Nesquik sometimes, and Ludo in the afternoon, and trips to the shop with the tartan shopping trolley which Annette is allowed to pull along so long as she's sensible and doesn't batter it up and down the kerb like she is driving a flaming bumper car.

'When you get married, can I be a bridesmaid?'

Mister Jackson puts his teacup down on the step and lets Annette take the leaf back, for washing up. It's bad manners to push yourself forward but those who don't ask don't get.

'Once I meet her, I'll suggest it to her. I'm sure whoever she is, she won't mind.'

Annette nods.

'My tooth fell out and I put it under my pillow and in the morning there was a penny and after a while my old tooth grew back in my mouth where the gap was.'

Mister Jackson laughs at this even though it wasn't a joke. There's a noise from inside. Mum shouting out, as if she's slipped in the bath. That would be no good. Annette cranes her neck, looks up at the attic windows. The sun has made them black and glittery. She can't see in.

'I'm sure it's nothing,' Mister Jackson says, 'the doctor will come soon enough and make it right. But us lodgers are out on our ears for the time being. All except Saint Richardson, that is.'

He says the last bit more quietly, but she hears it.

'You mustn't worry. Try not to think about it. People get ill all the time. And then they get better. And what's this?'

He puts his fingers behind her ear. Scrats about in her hair. She holds her breath.

'There's a lot of junk behind here. You need to have a good clear-out. What's that? A tallboy? A rocking horse? A coal scuttle? Now I am sure I left a tanner behind here. Have you gone and lost it? Perhaps got it mixed up with a bag of jumble? Left out for the rag-and-bone man?'

Annette laughs until finally Mister Jackson shows her his hand. There's a shiny sixpence resting on his palm.

'Very careless of you. Some people prefer to use a piggy bank,' he says.

Mum isn't that ill. She is still having cups of tea in her armchair and giving Dad lists of things that need doing in the house. She still likes the Dansette playing in the afternoon now and again. But the lodgers have been packing up their things and leaving, lugging boxes of books and records down the stairs and into waiting motor cars, bundling up dirty sheets and towels and leaving them on the ends of their stripped beds for Dad to deal with. They all want to give her presents. Mister Robinson and Mister Matthews made magic coins come out from behind her ear too. Mister Gravesend gave her a whole bag of aniseed balls for herself. The landings are too quiet now and there's no one to talk to. And Annette has to be really quiet because she's not nearly as good as a saint which is like being an angel or as good as gold and she hasn't even got a suitcase for her things.

'Be good,' Mister Jackson says. 'Thank you for the tea.'

He should stay. One extra mister won't be too much trouble, especially if he makes his own breakfast and lets Mum have long rests in the afternoons and who is she going to play with now? He's off, picking up his case and going away down the path. She holds the coin in her fist and runs to wave from the gate. We watch her waving, waving and waving until he's gone round the corner and her arm is sore. We watch her and we wait with her and we crowd her by the gate and this time we do not leave her alone. We don't. We don't leave her alone. But it doesn't matter now. It can't help.

9

It's nighttime now. In the sitting room the two remaining men of the house are drinking steadily and listening to the late news. More on the mail-train raid. Jack is still interested, and won't let Tim talk until the bulletin is over. They're silent until the pips.

'I knew they'd get away,' Tim says.

Jack grunts. They sit with a bottle between them on the coffee table. It isn't something he'd usually do with a lodger but it's just the two of them left now and things feel different. And he's something to broach. Jack's no good at small talk. Has never been comfortable in company. Can honestly say that Netty is the only person in the world he actually likes speaking to. He needs a drink if he's going to say what he needs to. And now he's had too much.

'It's been three weeks,' he says. He rolls the cigarette card into a tube, flicks his Zippo and watches it glow blue and yellow before tossing it into the ashtray.

'I warned you it might take a while.'

'You've not even started. Not even tried.'

The boy stands up as if he's going to leave. Something flares in Jack. He stands too, and crosses the room to the doorway. The burnt card stinks.

'Let's have it out,' he says, swaying. 'Tell me what you're playing at, Richardson.'

The boy's expression is unreadable. He moves closer, silent across the carpet in his stockinged feet. Jack tries to remember what you're supposed to say when you want to start a fight. Something to do with coats, and offering out. It's nonsense. He'll just talk to the boy. Find out what the state of play is.

'She's waiting for you. She's done everything you've asked.'

'I've no' asked her for anything.'

The boy's accent slips when he's been drinking. A bit of the real him showing through. Jack isn't sure he likes it.

'Is it a matter of money?'

'Come here.'

The boy takes Jack's head in his hands. Now he is pressing his palms hard against his ears, is shaking his head violently. Jack's jaw clicks. His skull is like an eggshell with a dumb wet yolk rocking about inside. His ears pop. He is about to vomit or cry out when Richardson lets go of him and stands back, smiling slightly, out of breath, a sheen of sweat on his top lip.

'I'll start when I can,' he says.

Jack trembles like a little girl. Denning is on the radio now. And after him, something about a plane crash. Reeling off the names of the dead and missing. The noise of it is incredible. He's got to move. Got to turn it down, before it wakes Netty. The boy is whispering — they are close, he can smell the coffee and whisky on his breath — but even so he hears him so clearly it is as if he's shouting. Jack sways on his feet and whimpers.

'Shh. Shh.'

'You come up to me, Mr Clifford. Come up to me whenever you like. I can do things for you, can't I?'

The boy's hair crackles as he runs a hand through it. There's more tiny sounds: the carpet fibres rubbing together as he steps forward, passes him, leaves the room. Every step he takes up the stairs, across the landing. His door opening and closing. The buzz as the boy opens his fly to undress for bed. He hears it all. All of it.

Jack turns off the radio. His balls ache. He stares out of the window at the garden. The leaves on the sycamore trees are whispering and he hears them, even through the closed window. After a while he sits, reaches for the whisky.

★ ★ ★

We move around the room but he doesn't see us, and look, the world doubles in that strange way it has lately, and here's Annette, banging the door open with her elbow because she's carrying the wine bottle in one hand and her mug in the other, coming in, crunching leaves all over the bloody carpet, seeing nothing but the objects in front of her. The cleaning that needs to be done is endless but she just sits, the saw in her hand, dust puffing out from the rotting settee. The television set is gone (where? We don't know) and the broken radio put into the skip but the coffee table is still there, dented and scratched. She puts her feet up, just because she can. What

108

a thing — a woman of her age relishing this disobedience. But there it is. She clicks her heels on the table and finds no pleasure in it.

She drinks, sitting alone in the dark like this, and feels the cool space and emptiness of the house unfurl around her. She should have visited Candy. Made more of an effort. It wouldn't have cost her anything. Candy always said she'd send money for the ticket, if that was the problem. She'd been the nearest thing to family. It is hard for Annette to picture her own mother now — she's got to start by remembering the things she held in her hands and extrapolating outwards from there, filling the whole thing in tentatively, like a paint-by-numbers missing its key.

Her hands. Red, with cracks over the knuckles. Gold wedding ring, and an engagement ring with a speck of diamond so small you had to hold it up to the light to see it. *I scratched mine and your dad's initials onto someone's privy window once, just to prove it was the real thing,* she'd said once.

Her voice.

Hard to remember what it sounded like now. What else?

She always had tea towels or dusters tucked into the pockets of her apron in case a spill or smudge crossed her path while she was on the way to somewhere else. That's what she smelled like too. Annette remembers it now — the smell of her mother, inseparable from the smell of the tea towels. Pledge and sweat, face powder and fags and bacon fat. It was nice. Those apron

109

pockets. Stuffed with pencils — always. She was never without one. Behind her ear, too. And her hair was blonde and crackled like leaves because the bleach made it so rough. She kept the pencils for the food orders, and the coal bill, and the rent books — who owed what, who was using the phone, how many baths people had. Wasn't one bit of the house that wasn't her business, that wasn't reckoned for and recorded in a little notebook somewhere.

What else?

Frying pans and cruet sets and magazines and crossword books. Knitting, too. The knitting. She had this way about her, that last summer, of parking herself in a chair with her knitting and, without wanting to put anyone to any trouble, without wanting anyone to go out of their way, not at all, inveigling the whole house to wait on her hand and foot. Food being brought in. The dining room being turned into command central headquarters — her spending whole days in there.

You couldn't go and ask your father to bring me a box of ciggies, could you, love? Click click. *Don't bother Mister Richardson while he's on the machine, love — get out and have some fresh air while it's fine.*

There it is. She has it now.

His name. Richardson.

And he was allowed in command central headquarters. Allowed anywhere he felt like going. Wasn't prevented from messing about in the shed, sitting in the back garden, even sitting with her mother and using her sewing machine

110

while she knitted. That's all she did. And he was allowed, because he was paying, while Annette herself was banished to the garden. She remembers the whispering, tidal sound of her mother counting under her breath, and hissing if someone came in because she didn't want any noise in the room — no talking or music, no television, no games — in case it made her lose count and knit when she should have purled, or some other irrevocable disaster of immense importance. Knitting — as if there was nothing more important she could be doing, if she knew her time was short. And she did know, didn't she?

Annette thinks about time. About what she'd do with it if she knew she only had a little left. The scores she'd settle. The secrets she'd want to tell, and the ones she'd want to take with her. Easier for her than for some, perhaps — but she's not responsible for anyone else. Not got children or dogs or even a goldfish to worry about. She can please herself and not worry about hurting anyone and that's the way she likes it. That's the responsible way to do it.

She lifts the nearly emptied bottle, tips the dregs into her mug, mops up the spilled drops from the coffee table with her thumb and licks it clean. Sod the dust and murk and her filthy shoes. No one ever died of a bit of dirt. She's getting stupid now, and looks at the saw in her lap as if she doesn't know what it's doing there. Finishes what's in the mug. Laughs. Sets the saw on the coffee table next to the empty bottle. Could do with another drink. But that bottle

111

went too quickly — people get into trouble that way. She gets up and boils the kettle. The steam billows around the kitchen and dampens the corners but it can't warm our faces. We watch her wrap her thin hands around her teacup and when the tea is done she goes back to the sitting room and sits some more and always her hands return to the saw.

They sent her away too. That's the thing. He got to stay. So when it came to coming home, visiting her father, replying to Candy's letters, even telephoning once in a while, she didn't. She didn't owe them it. Didn't owe her father anything. Treated less than a lodger she was, so why should she act any different to one? She runs her fingernails along the teeth of the saw. She's going to take matters into her own hands, that's what she's going to do.

No. Don't.

She cocks her head as if listening to something. Holds her breath.

Annette. Don't.

She pulls the edges of her cardigan over her chest and shivers and what's the use of all these words being returned to us if nobody listens to anything we have to say?

We didn't know. How could we have known what he thought of us? What he wanted from us. We didn't even understand all that we wanted from him. It has taken so much time for these things to become clear. How to tell her? We follow her as she stamps around, closing curtains, checking windows. It isn't only that the place has draughts — all old houses do. It's

112

worse than that. The movement of the cold air seems more pronounced in the night: as if the house itself is breathing; sucking the outside in. Some mornings, we can taste sea salt in the condensation on the inside of the windows. When Annette first arrived she pulled the damp carpets in the guest rooms up and discovered the floorboards were covered in sand.

She picks up the bottle from the coffee table, hoping for a drip, a dribble, just a little something to stop her mind from turning and help her to sleep. It's heavier than she expected, though, and when she pours she's able to fill her mug to the brim. She's only mildly surprised. She has luck like this sometimes. Things lasting a little longer than they should. But astonishment sets us fluttering into the corners of the room. Why didn't we notice the influence our guest had on our little girl; the way the best and worst of him rubbed off on her?

Her stomach rolls but she drinks anyway, still on her feet, still wandering around the down-stairs rooms. And now she's in the hall, the entire height of the house open and empty above her, the stairwell its own column of damp air and heavy cobwebs. She considers the saw. Doesn't remember picking it up, but here it is in her hand again. It is light and springy, the blade spotted with rust. The teeth are wide apart and — she runs her finger along them curiously — perhaps too blunt to do much damage to anything at all. Perhaps. It's late now. She should sleep.

10

Even with the lodgers gone Netty does not slow down. She does two or three things at once and performs all her tasks with a new and wearied sense of urgency. She's managed to get one of the sleeves of Annette's school cardigans started, but that's nothing to write home about seeing as there's another two cardigans to finish before the end of the fortnight when school begins again and she's having to force herself not to think about the fact that she's started much too late. She regards her progress by smoothing out the nearly finished sleeve on the arm of the chair, then holding the edges of the ribbed cuff together to check her seams are straight. Her tension has always left something to be desired. The cuff is narrow but it will probably grow in the wash — her knitting always does. She picks up the needles and begins again. She'd hoped to do a cable along the front, each side, but (she looks, now, at the wall clock, running at least a quarter fast, she's sure) perhaps she'd have to scale down her plans. Better plain cardigans than no cardigans at all. If she gets on with it she'll be able to start the second sleeve before Candy turns up. The royal blue wool slips over her fingers and she drops her needle for a moment in order to turn the page of the mag, before retrieving it.

She's been reading about this cracking new

diet where you only eat certain foods on certain days of the week. Nothing but fruit on a Monday, bread and potatoes on a Tuesday, all vegetables apart from tomatoes on Wednesdays, pork and chicken on Thursdays, cheese and red meats on a Friday and normal service resuming over the weekend. No eggs or milk in the week at all. According to the article, this diet cleans the system and allows the body to cure itself of any problems or imbalances. No milk in your tea all week. She'll ask Tim for his opinion. She can't say she much liked the look of it, but if he says it might help, well, it's worth a try.

'Mrs Clifford! Will you open the door for me?'

'The door's open, love,' she calls, but still she lays down her magazine and her knitting and heaves herself out of her chair. She goes slowly, checks her lipstick in the hall mirror. Her hair has got thin at the temples and she touches it, then traces the ashy shadows under her eyes. There's a slim drawer in the top of the hall tallboy for pens and notebooks and odd bits of things and she slides it open and pulls out her compact.

'Just give me a minute.'

He's struggling with the doorknob, unable to turn it because he's got something, some huge parcel, by the looks of it, resting against his shoulder and he is trying to steady it with one hand and turn the knob — which is, like everything else in this bloody house, loose and in need of some attention — with the other. Tim is a dark shape behind the rippled glass in the vestibule door but Netty knows the tilt of his head, the way he stands.

'Just wait. I'm nearly there.' She snaps open the compact and blots at herself though it'd take a can of paint and a trowel to make a difference these days. She sighs, slams the drawer closed, leans forward and opens the door. Tim nearly falls into her arms.

'Ta da!' he says.

He's only gone and bought an entire bloody bolt of some fabric from the haberdashery. It's wrapped in brown paper but she'd recognise that stamp blindfolded.

'Did you get a lift?' she dreads the cost. Where he gets his money from now, she doesn't know. She doesn't like to ask. The envelopes must still be turning up in the fruit bowl: Jack would have mentioned it otherwise.

'I walked,' he says. 'Carried it over my shoulder, like Dick Whittington. It weighs a ton.'

'I bet you were a right sight for the neighbours. Get in, will you. Candy'll be here soon.'

'She will, will she? You're having a treatment today?' Tim makes a face, as if he's amused, and wants Netty to know that he's trying not to show it.

'It's not fair just to drop her. She'll wonder if she's done something wrong. I'm not trying to rush you along. I know it comes in its own time. I don't pretend to understand. But if you think Candy might be holding things up a bit . . . ?'

'You do as you like, Mrs Clifford, it makes no difference to me.'

'Sure?' Netty says, but he just winks and pulls

116

the bolt into the house, bumping it over the doormat, as bold as you like. She helps him prop it against the wall. Once he has it settled, he tears open the paper. He's nimble. Fleet-footed, darting around unwrapping it. Netty is so slow now herself that she likes to watch him, likes to see how easy moving is. He whistles, pleased. It's a bolt of fine, white cotton, bloody good quality — she can tell that just by looking and a quick rub between finger and thumb confirms it.

What the hell does he want all that cloth for?

'Shirts,' he says.

The first few times he answered her questions before she'd had the chance to ask them, Netty had eyed him suspiciously. It wasn't nice. Wasn't nice to think that someone could get inside your head, where they'd no place to be. It felt like a trespass. But as they'd got to know each other a little better, she'd accepted it not only as one of his peculiar ways (and he had plenty of them) but also as a token of how nicely aligned their characters were. Almost like he was one of the family.

'Why do you want to make yourself a shirt, Tim? Jack'll have a spare one if you've got an appointment you need to smarten up for.'

The boy might have a job interview. Never mind that the only white shirts Jack owned were threadbare and were that old they had Utility labels in them.

'You can't get the type of shirt I'm going to make in the shops, Mrs Clifford. These are going to be a cut above. Bespoke, which means cut from a pattern personally designed by me, in

117

response to detailed measurements taken from the client, by me, and adjusted for fit and drape at sixteen different points, by me. Better than a second skin, because what I'm going to do will not just replicate the shape of the man, but improve it. And this isn't a shirt for me. I'll be starting with the man of the house,' he says, and Netty laughs, her hands against her stomach.

'A fancy shirt,' she says, struggling to catch her breath. 'A fancy bespoke shirt is just exactly what Jack's been hanging out for. How did you know? He can wear it while he's digging out the potatoes and mending the roof tiles, can't he?'

It's not the laughing that takes her breath away, so she has to lean against the newel post and put her hands on her chest for a minute, it's the pain what the laughing brings on. Still, most days it doesn't stop her.

'Mrs Clifford, I'd advise you to sit down before you fall down,' Tim says, in that fake doctor's voice he has that always sets her off. 'Every man, no matter what he does for a living, should always have at least one crisp white shirt ready to be pressed into service at a moment's notice. It's your armour for modern life. He'll feel more ready to face the world just knowing it's hanging in his wardrobe, never mind whether he wears it or not.' He bounds to the foot of the stairs.

'Mr Clifford? Might you be available to assist me for a moment? I'd be most grateful.'

He does talk funny. When Jack makes an appearance, rolling up his (blue, ragged) shirtsleeves and panting from his run down two

118

flights of stairs, Netty can tell just by looking that he thinks Tim is calling him down because he's decided it's finally time to start her treatment.

'There's no need to bloody bellow,' Jack says crossly. 'What's the problem?' He puts his hands against the side of his face, his fingers pressed against his ears.

'No one's bloody bellowing. Leave your ears alone, Jack.' He's crabby today. Been crabby for a while, now she thinks of it. It's his sleep. Every little sound wakes him: the strike of a match, a smothered cough, even the rustle of Annette turning over in her bed at night rouses him. Then he lies awake muttering, claiming that the creaks and sighs the house itself makes are stopping him from nodding off again. He's not had a full night in days and days.

'It's nothing urgent,' she says. Jack's face closes up and he won't look at the boy, has to be cajoled and persuaded to let Tim measure him up for a shirt. Netty can read him like a book. Haven't you got anything better to do? Isn't there someone here who you're supposed to be fixing? She lays her hand on his arm.

'The grouting in the bathrooms can wait one more afternoon,' she says, and because she wants him to, Jack agrees to go into the dining room (so she can watch from her chair) and stand with his arms outstretched while Tim darts around him with his tape measure, reeling off the numbers. Annette has appeared out of nowhere, drawn to Tim like the rest of them. She insists on helping, picks up a pencil and jots down the figures. Jack looks like a scarecrow, standing there with his arms out like that. Even Annette is smirking behind her notebook.

'You've a fine figure, Mr Clifford,' Tim says, as he measures. 'Your left shoulder is slightly lower than your right, but that's because you're right-handed. We're all a wee bit lopsided like that. But let me tell you,' he goes on, the tape measure dangling around his neck, 'you will never have a shirt that fits you as well as this one will. Not ever.'

'Right enough,' Jack mutters.

Tim measures to the sixteenth of an inch, opens his book and goes through the anatomy of the pattern, making sure he's got the right measures for each of the pieces. He makes Annette read the numbers in the notebook back to him, and checks them all again. You can't blame him. What that material must have cost!

'We're aiming for perfection here. That's the job of the cutter. Perfection. Have you ever wondered how it is possible for fabric — a material that by its nature is flat, featureless, without shape or contour — to be coaxed into not only dressing the body, but enhancing it? The real cutters can make a jacket that will make a man look four inches taller, disguise his hunchback and make you forget he lost an arm in the war.'

Netty laughs. 'Are you practising your patter as well, Tim?' The mouth on him!

'It's all about the detail, as a woman as eagle-eyed as yourself has no doubt already noticed. You've got to think about the type of man I'm going to be working with one of these

120

days. He wants what he wants, and he wants it exactly. He's not going to fit himself into a standard pattern — some blocky scratch-job made for anyone. A man like that wants to be treated in a certain way.'

'Well. Those that want don't always get,' Netty says, sourly.

'They do though, Mrs Clifford. It wouldn't even enter their heads to think that they wouldn't.' He drapes the tape measure around his neck (it reminds her of the way the hospital doctors like to wear their stethoscopes), leans against the door frame and puts a hand on his hip. 'There's a man who sacked his cutter because he'd specifically asked for his braces buttons to be attached to the outside of his trousers on the front waistband — because he liked the look of it — and on the inside of his trousers on the back waistband, so when he was driving without his jacket on the buttons wouldn't make marks on the leather seat of his Rolls. The tailor thought someone had made a mistake on the pattern and made the trousers up in the usual way. Heads rolled at that fitting, I can tell you that for nothing.'

Jack puts his hands in his pockets. Netty tries to catch his eye, but he's gazing curiously at Tim. Jack wouldn't know what to ask for even if he did have the money to waste on braces and leather seats and fancy buttons. He'd have no idea. His shoulders slump.

'Are you done with me now, Richardson?'

'That will do nicely, Mr Clifford. You're my very first customer.'

'Customer?' Jack says. He frowns. Takes his hands out of his pockets. Maybe those envelopes aren't finding their way into the fruit bowl after all. It would be beyond the pale for the boy to get behind on his board, give up his job and start charging Jack for shirts what he never even asked for! They might have made an exception for him but there's got to be limits.

'Client, I think. That sounds more dignified, doesn't it? But either way, there will be no charge,' Tim says, very grand. 'Mr Clifford, you are doing me a favour. This is practice. I've a book to consult,' he rolls the tape measure up and tucks it away into his pocket like a real professional, 'and Mrs Clifford has kindly agreed to donate the use of her trusty old Singer to the cause.'

'She has, has she?'

Oh, he is taking the biscuit now.

'She certainly has. Because she is an empress amongst landladies.'

Netty rolls her eyes. Tim just winks and she finds herself trotting off to the under-stair cupboard to retrieve the machine and sewing box, where they've been languishing since hemming curtains for the back room, and that must have been over a year ago now. The cheeky get, she thinks, not annoyed at all, but grinning with pleasure.

These moments feel like gifts — the whole family together, all smiling, and no one worrying about Netty, no one being all po-faced because they're thinking (she can tell, she's not bloody stupid) even in the middle of a nice time, like the day at the lido, how long before Netty isn't able to do things like this, how long before she's stuck in bed all day, or worse, not even knowing her own family? Jack is flicking through the figures in Tim's notebook as Tim rattles on about the way he's going to make the pattern and Annette is playing some sort of game, jumping about the squares on the carpet between them both. No one is thinking about Netty being sick except Netty herself, and she's going to stop any minute now — and just enjoy this moment for what it is.

'You behave yourself with my Singer, Timothy Richardson,' she says, for Annette's benefit. She's not forgotten promising to give the girl this machine for herself on her sixteenth birthday. She wonders if that's something she should tell Jack about. 'I have plans for that Singer,' she says, winking at Annette. 'It's a good model. Don't snarl it up. Treat it gently. Do you know how to thread it?'

Tim gives her his mock innocent look and Netty sighs and motions for Jack to plug it in, to slide it across the table to her where she sits. She glances back at the wall clock. Candy is never less than punctual.

'Pay attention, the pair of you,' Netty begins. 'You always start here.' She slots a spool of cotton onto the metal rod on top of the machine. 'Are you watching? I'm only going to show you this once. You'll have to remind each other in future: you can't moider me about it.'

★ ★ ★

123

By the time Candy raps at the door the boy has fully taken over the dining room and is practising hemming on an old stained tablecloth. Netty can't face the stairs so she has to take her final treatment in the kitchen. If Candy considers the venue beneath her, she never mentions it. Her tightened lips give her away clearly enough.

'It will do,' she says, and brushes off the kitchen counter with her palm before placing her handbag on it. As if Netty keeps a dirty house. The two of them sit at the small folding table tucked in against the wall. Netty pours the tea Jack made for them and motions towards a plate of biscuits.

'Only a drop for me, as you've made it already,' Candy says, delighting, as always, in asking for nothing, and taking little. Once tea has been drunk, the begonias in the garden admired through the back window and Annette's health and diet enquired after, Candy leans back into her chair, clasps her hands on her lap and tilts her head to one side. She stares and Netty awaits this week's prognosis.

'You look done in,' she says, 'the worst I've seen you for a long time.'

Netty laughs lightly. 'And there was I, thinking that we were friends.'

Candy shakes her head. 'What's he doing in there?' She jerks her head towards the dining room. 'The noise! I thought you were getting rid of the lodgers? Didn't you speak to Jack about it? You need rest. A very long rest. Even the quack says so. Can you not convince him to get rid of them?'

124

Netty, who has spent the day resting — first in her chair, then in her bed, then in a deckchair in the garden, and then in her armchair in the dining room — already knows she isn't going to tell Candy about the specialness of Tim. About what he'd managed to do for Jack's eyes. About what he was going to do for her. The decision had been made the day he arrived: she and Jack were going to keep him to themselves. And anyway, the boy is no work. He makes her laugh. He even brings Jack out of himself. He's a breath of fresh air through the whole house. So what if he hasn't started yet? It's her job to have faith in him. To think positively. Even Candy, if she knew the full picture, would tell Netty there was no point getting the treatments if she didn't think they were going to work. No. The boy is gathering himself, and will start in his own time. That is all there is to it.

'It's the Singer,' Netty says, 'that's all. He's making Jack a shirt. To say thank you for being allowed to stay on, I expect.'

'You're not waiting on him?'

'He eats with us. It's no extra work.'

Candy shakes her head. 'Is it the money? Write off and apply for national assistance. You're entitled to it. Christ, you look terrible.'

Netty yawns. She's desperate for a ciggy. Has been for a couple of hours, but didn't want to interrupt her knitting with it.

'So you've said. I had a bad night. I couldn't sleep.'

'Your light's going out,' Candy says, ominously.

She always talks like this: mysterious utterances about light and energy, about flow and presence and vibrations. She refuses to call what she does healing.

'The Lord heals,' she'd said sharply, correcting Netty when she'd first gone to her and asked for her help. 'I invite his spirit to work within you. I'd be happy to visit you at home. There's no charge. A donation of food or good-quality clothing, clean and pressed, to the children's home, if you felt moved to offer something other than prayer.'

Candy made her first visit two days later. Netty had bought real coffee and filled a vase with fresh flowers. Sent Jack and Annette away on a coach trip, told them not to come back until after four, and to bring a fish supper with them. Candy was practical, even stand-offish. She didn't even do so much as light a candle, just instructed Netty to take off her shoes and undo any zips, clasps and buttons on her clothes and underwear.

'You don't need to fully undress,' Candy said, 'just loosen everything.'

Netty untied the strings on her apron, undid the button and zip on her dress and slipped off her shoes. She unclasped her bra and unfastened her stockings. She sat in her armchair with her eyes open as Candy had swept the air around her with a series of jerky hand movements. Netty tried to suppress a thought, but it came anyway, and along with it, a giggle. *She looks like she's swatting flies.* The treatment lasted ten minutes, if that — though Netty only realised it was finished when Candy turned away and started to put on her coat.

'Don't expect to feel different right away.' She tied a firm bow in the belt of her coat. 'You'll sleep well tonight, I bet. Send Annette round with a note when you'd like me to come again.'

Netty, still sitting in her chair with her dress slipping down over her shoulders, struggled not to raise her eyebrows. Was that it? Candy seemed to be waiting for something, her handbag on her arm, her coat buttoned to the collar and her hand resting on the doorknob.

'Sometimes people like to give me a little bit towards my bus fare,' she said. 'No payment is expected or desired, but to offer travel expenses is polite.'

Netty leapt up to scrabble about in her handbag for loose change, her stockings flapping about her ankles and her dress gaping open at the back. She was better prepared the next time, and had ready a little coloured envelope with a few coppers in it. The third time, Candy accepted a small glass of water. The fifth, she had a cup of tea and enquired after Jack — his health, of course, and what line of work he was in. After a few months, Candy had warmed up further and started to take an interest in the other side of Netty's treatment — her regular trips down to the hospital, the various pills and potions. Sometimes they'd even have a bit of a laugh together. Maybe a cup of tea and a bit of a laugh is all the difference she could expect a treatment like this to make, Netty thinks.

'My bloody light is not going out,' Netty says.

'I'm knackered, that's all.'

Candy pushes her teacup away from her and puts her head to one side. She's a good-looking woman — early forties, same as her and Jack, but wearing it better because she has no husband to wait on, no children to give her grey hairs and sleepless nights. She is never caught without lipstick and eyeliner, and is the type who has a handbag to match every pair of shoes. Glamorous, in a stiff, shabby sort of way.

'What's the quack said? Are they going to send you back to Manchester?'

Netty will not look at Candy now and takes a slow sip of cooled tea. She's impatient to get on with it, get it over with, for all the good it does her, and get back to her knitting. It is difficult to swallow.

'No. They've said there's nothing more.'

Candy blinks a few times and dabs at the inside corner of her eye with her ring finger. 'It made you sore anyway, didn't it? And you'll be glad they won't be cutting you open again.'

'There's that, of course.'

'Still, they're not even going to give the radium another chance?'

'No point in it, that's what they said.'

'What are they going to give you?' Candy frowns. 'They must have something.'

'Morphine for the pain, a vitamin tonic to keep my strength up. The district nurse if I need — when I need help with the toilet.'

Candy clasps her hands together and Netty wonders, uncharitably, if the woman is thinking of offering a prayer. Sing a hymn or two and get the priest round for the last rites, while she's at it. Why not? Anger blooms in her bones and gathers in her blood. Its heat tingles in her throat and between her legs. She clenches her fists and says nothing.

'You could write to your consultant. Ask for a second opinion.'

'That's what Jack says. He wants to write a letter.'

There's a silence. Netty is counting her breaths, willing away the negative thoughts that have allowed her disease to take such a hold of her. She has shrunk the space she allows her thoughts to occupy. The house. Jack. Annette. Nothing else. Most people probably have a bad cell inside them, waiting for an excuse to start multiplying. There's a personality type that makes the body more susceptible. It's not helpful to throw tantrums, to lie in your bed and give up, to weep and feel sorry for yourself and spend afternoons planning your own send-off. She'd spent a whole morning sorting out old dresses and cardigans to be given away to the neighbours, but people who succumb to the temptations of negativity and self-pity leave the door wide open for the disease, so she'd pulled herself together and shoved it all back into her wardrobe. The key is to accept the terrifying fact that there must always be hope. Netty exhales sharply and sets about the task of hoping.

'Let's not make a fuss. You're still giving me treatments, aren't you? We might put it on the run yet, eh?' The quick shame of hot tears on her cheeks makes her close her eyes.

'Shall I call Jack?' Candy asks.

Netty shakes her head.

'Annette then?'

Shakes it again, more forcefully.

'Does Annette know?'

Netty opens her eyes and wipes her face.

'The less she knows about all this, the better. There's always a chance.'

Please, God, let Tim start soon. Why won't he start? Why has he got time for shirts and not for her?

'She'll know something's up. What did you tell her about the lodgers going?'

'I needed a rest.'

'And everything else?'

'She's eight years old. Head in a book all day. Dolls and teddy bears the rest of the time. Dressing up in old net curtains. She doesn't need to be worried. It still might turn out all right.'

Candy raises one plucked eyebrow.

'The last lady I worked with, in your position, she decided to say nothing too. It was a drawn-out thing, and she opted to go to hospital as early as she could. Never came out. Her son — a bit younger than your Annette; four, he was — knew something was going on. His father's sister moved in with them, and he knew his mother hated her, that she'd never have wanted her in the house under normal circumstances. Little things, too. His aunt started checking his homework and she was the one who paid the coal man.'

Netty tries to ignore Candy but her voice, low and slow, as if she takes pleasure in the physicality of talking itself, no matter what is being said, drones on.

'You'd think he'd have put two and two together himself, but he didn't. It's different for a little one. He asked his father, his aunty, but neither of them would say anything. It came out in the end that he thought his mother had been sent to prison. Before she was sick she used to do a bit of cleaning and take in ironing. He thought she might have been accused of taking a piece of jewellery and sent away. Where he got that from, I don't know, but that's what he came up with. So he stopped asking questions, and just as his father was hoping he'd begun to come to terms with it in his own way, he asked when she'd be coming back. He'd been waiting patiently. Thought someone might get sent away for five years, perhaps, for stealing a really nice piece of jewellery. Diamonds, or what have you. And five years apart was terrible, course it was, especially as he knew there'd been a mistake and his mother would never have nicked anything. After she'd done her bird, she'd be back. As the months went by this little story he was telling himself became more and more complicated. But he believed it as if it were true and didn't really have a full appreciation of what had happened until years after the fact. He was haunted by it. That she'd been gone, all that time, and he hadn't properly known.' Candy taps her temple. 'He won't ever be right, you know.'

Netty tries to give herself a minute to digest this but she can't. Her anger licks over her like a fever and by God she knows about those. This time, she's unable to master herself, lays her hands flat on the table, leans forward and gives Candy what-for.

'Does every lady you work with, every lady in my position, end up kicking the bucket?' It's mean and cruel and it isn't fair. She knows it, but she also knows she'll get away with it. She can do what she likes now. 'Maybe you'd better find another job because what you're doing obviously isn't working!'

Netty wants to sound fierce. To make Candy blush, but Candy has tears in her eyes and is looking back at Netty with infinite patience and pity and as well as that, a new kind of respect; as if Netty has acquired a depth of wisdom and knowledge usually reserved for canonised saints and — she might as well say it, what harm can it do now? — the dying.

'I've thought the same thing often enough myself,' Candy replies, wearily, 'but you can't sit and do nothing, can you?'

Netty clamps her hands over her mouth and begins to sob. Her chest heaves. Those cardigans, not knitted yet! After a minute or two Candy pushes a screwed-up paper tissue into her hand.

'Enough now,' she says firmly. 'You're not doing yourself any good.'

Netty tries to smile and finds herself unable to. This sets off a fresh bout of weeping, which Candy ignores.

'Your lodger's not half making a racket in there with that machine,' Candy observes. 'What did you say he was making?'

Netty dabs at herself. 'A shirt.'

'I'd charge him extra for use of the communal

areas. He's robbing you of your own dining room. You're too soft.'

She folds up the tissue and tucks it away. 'Don't be daft. He makes me laugh.'

★ ★ ★

Sometimes, Netty wants to tell Candy all about Tim. About kindness arriving at the door: an angel with dark hair and the best-fitting suit this side of Manchester. About the afternoon she spent standing in the kitchen watching him teach Annette the twist in the back garden. He'd held her hands and they'd danced barefoot in the grass until the soles of their feet were black. The way he helped Annette to stand on the Ewbank and pushed her up and down the upstairs hall, the shrieking and banging echoing round the house until even Jack stopped his work and smiled up at the ceiling. Timothy Richardson was almost too good to be true. He was like something out of a film.

One night a couple of weeks back, Jack and Tim had stayed up to listen to the last news on the radio. She'd lain in bed for several sleepless hours waiting for him, first with her knitting, then with a novel. Eventually Jack came stumbling up the stairs, banged their bedroom door closed much too hard, grasped her by the shoulder and shook her gently — as if to wake her. She let the novel slide off the bed and hit the floor, to find a home with a pile of Jack's James Bonds.

'I'm up. I'm up. You're fit to wake the dead! What is it, love?'

'Come up here,' he pulled her arm until she was sitting next to him on the edge of the bed. Her feet brushed the rug, the mattress creaked under them and Jack, his head bowed, swayed slightly and kneaded at her hand.

'Sorry. Sorry for waking you up. You need your rest, I know.'

'I wasn't asleep. I thought I was tired, but I can't seem to drop off.' He was still rubbing her hand between his, as if he thought she was cold, and she squeezed back, as hard as she could, and laughed a little bit. 'Did you open the Christmas whisky? Oh Jack, you reek of it.'

'Shut up. You're so loud.' He put his fingers in his ears and laughed. He was absolutely steaming. 'You just be quiet, woman.'

The pair of them had the giggles then, for no good reason at all. What was there to laugh at, when you sat down and thought about it properly? They put their hands over their mouths and rocked until the sound of the lavatory flushing and the thought of Tim overhearing cooled them down and helped them get control over themselves.

'You're up too late,' Netty whispered, 'you'll regret it in the morning.'

Jack was still smirking.

'What's tickling you?'

'Just the radio,' he said. 'Tim was right: they didn't catch them. The farmhouse was empty. Clean as a whistle. They got away.'

She knew immediately what he was speaking about: he'd been obsessed with that Cheddington lot since the news had broken.

134

'Just for the time being.'

'They've been poking about inside the house where they were. No signs.'

'Everything will catch up with them in the end. I guarantee it.'

Jack wiped his hands over his eyes. He never could hold his booze, especially whisky. What was he playing at? She'd have a word with Tim in the morning.

'You've had too much to drink, love. That's all it is. Come to bed.'

'They've been inside the house where they were hiding,' Jack repeated, 'and while they were there they'd passed the time by playing Monopoly. You know that game our Annette has, with the houses?'

'Yes?' Netty was not following his drift, not at all. She was wondering if she had the energy to go down and make him a cup of tea. Milky, with three sugars and a digestive. That's what he needed.

'They'd been holed up and playing that. With the money that they nicked. With real money. Ten-bob notes, pounds, fivers.' Jack laughed again, and wiped his eyes. 'Real money.'

Netty was struck then, with something like guilt. It wasn't just the whisky.

'Come here.' She tried to slip her hand out of his so she could put it around his shoulders, but Jack kept hold of it, and loosened his flies. Netty put her head on his shoulder and listened to the hitch in his breathing as he held her hand and wrapped it around his penis. His fingers tightened over hers.

135

'Jack . . . '

He shushed her.

'Don't say anything, love. Will you?'

She would, and she couldn't blame him for asking. He'd been patient with the limitations her illness had placed on them both, but he was still a human being. She'd still got to be a wife to him, as much as she could. A proper wife. After she'd brought him off, Netty kissed his cheek and went to rinse her hands. When she got back, he'd fallen back on the bed and gone fast asleep like that, without a word. She had to tug the blankets out from underneath him just so she could tuck herself in. She lay awake listening to him snore, feeling hot and bothered, then old and useless and not like a wife at all.

After that night Jack's requests in the bedroom (and not only the bedroom, she thought, staring into her teacup, smiling and willing herself not to blush as she considered the kitchen, the empty downstairs bedroom, even the bloody garden shed!) had become more frequent. It was like that first time was him testing the waters. Checking if it were all right by her for a married couple — together twenty years — to do this furtive, teenage thing.

But there is something odd about him. A change that runs a bit deeper than what he likes in bed, or how far he can see without his specs on. He's angry too. Steaming angry, and keeping it locked down tight like a pressure cooker on full blast. She wants to shake him and say, 'Well, life's not fair and whoever told you it was going to be?' but mainly she wants her shortsighted, shy, awkward husband back. The skinny boy with a patched jumper and thick glasses. Tongue-tied Jack, a lanky orphan, left lonely in a big house that was dropping to bits around his ears. He didn't know what to do with it.

'We'll patch it up together, Jack,' she'd said. 'You and me.' And he'd stared at her through his bottle-bottom lenses, his eyes huge and grateful and owlish, as if he couldn't quite believe his luck.

That's what he was like when she met him. That's what she wants now. But some days she doesn't even know him. Like today. Messing about with the shirt. Pretending it was for her benefit and to keep Tim sweet when she could see the idea of owning something fancy just for himself had started to appeal to him. Why wasn't he leaning on Tim more, and telling him to get things started? Was she daft to think that Candy might be able to shed some light on this? Might be able to provide a listening ear, or even a suggestion or two? It would be confidential. Only like talking to a doctor or a nurse. And medical people heard details of people's married lives all the time.

'Have you ever had intercourse with a soldier?' they'd asked her. 'Have you had or ever attempted to have an abortion?' It was to find out how she'd caught it, she knew that, but it was still shocking to be asked. Medical people were unshockable.

But Candy wasn't really a nurse and she probably wouldn't understand. Never married and with no kids of her own, she wouldn't know what an unexpected pleasure ordinary family life could be. She'd take it the wrong way. Think Jack was some kind of pervert. A sex case. Or worse, Candy would ask why they just didn't get rid of Tim altogether, if he was stirring things up, and then Netty would let something slip about the healing Tim was going to do.

He was waiting for the right time to start. The house itself was holding its breath; the tension had galvanised them all and she was sure he was gathering himself to begin any day now. Candy would take it as a slight. It would be like telling Fiona she'd decided to go to the salon on the main street for her wash and set instead of having her come to the house with her vanity case full of rollers and curling papers. No. It would be a snub. That's what was bothering Jack, too. The tension of waiting for Tim to start his work. The poor man was seeking comfort from her the only way he knew how. That's all it was.

★　★　★

Netty dots at her cheeks with the folded tissue, takes a deep breath, and smiles.

'We just like his company, that's all. Annette loves him. He helps Jack around the house. He'll earn his keep.'

'You're keeping something to yourself, Netty,' Candy says, and shakes her head. 'It's your own business. I won't ask again.'

'There's nothing. Come on now, shall we get started on the treatment?'

She pulls her chair forward. She's already undone her buttons and for the next fifteen minutes Candy's shoes creak on the linoleum as she moves around making her funny little hand movements. The sawing of the Singer sobs through the walls.

11

We lie on the floorboards in the front hallway, leaves in our hair and forgotten-about post slipping through our fingers. *This is a good place to live*, we want to say. It isn't just a place for guests and tourists, for the passing through. She could make a home here. We want to say yes, it is true that the town has always been a place for the sick and for travellers but now the sanatoriums have gone, Grange generally begins to empty out in the early autumn. When the wind comes the tourists know it is time to leave and the people who work at the hotels and cafes start to bring in their outdoor tables and chairs. The tennis courts on the promenade close at the end of September and a fortnight later the ice-cream shop on the sea front packs up and prepares for its winter closing. By October the town's welcome to visitors is wearing out and the residents are preparing for the reduced income, thinned prospects and blissful silence of the off season.

When winter comes, everything changes. Didn't she see? The water in the bay loses its bright metallic sheen; the tidal pools and tributaries at the estuary no longer act as mirrors to the rough sky but become muddy brown lakes, hopping with sand shrimp and siphoned by crowds of godwit, stopping off on their annual migration south. Even before the summer is over there is a certain coolness to the place. The wind does other things too. The bay is dangerous and unpredictable: it always has been. It changes daily and without notice: that's part of the microclimate of the area and the reason for the siren charm and danger of the edgelands. The gullies and channels shift, the sands run like mercury: no one can trace the same path across them twice. But these daily fluctuations are part of a larger turn — in our time there was a beach here but now the salt marsh is encroaching on the foreshore and we gaze, without recognition, on a landscape transformed.

The Kent, which flows alongside the promenade, is on the move. The wind has taken it further and further away from the town. It will continue to retreat inch by imperceptible inch, taking whole decades to make its slow migration south and away from the town. The beach got choked up with silt, then disappeared entirely under a harsh scruff of spartina grass. Those of us returning after years away will lean over the old railings to measure the view against our memories, squint at maps, and consider ourselves lost. We'll wonder where the water went, where the ice-cream kiosks disappeared to and where the amusements have gone.

There's nothing to be done about it. It is the nature of all deep-water channels to be cyclical; to go where the wind takes them. Those who stay say the salt marsh covered the sands so slowly that the locals in sight of it every day didn't notice the shift at first. Now farmers graze lambs there. Because the creatures eat samphire and seaweed they're something of a speciality; the restaurants charge a lot for them. Salt marsh lamb: raised on the tidal range of the town, their short lives lived on the very spot where the pleasure boats used to plough up and down with their horns tooting and their passengers waving to queues on the shore. It's all gone now and even if people did still want to come, the mill towns don't keep the wake weeks any longer; the Glasgow fair that used to see the city empty and decant itself down here, discharging from the train stations and filling up boarding houses and hotels in Blackpool, Morecambe and Grange, is only a memory, reminisced about in half-empty pubs in need of modernisation and refurbishment. The odd confused tourist still arrives at the train station and immediately heads for the coast in search of the sands, loaded up with picnic baskets and windbreaks. Bored cafe owners stare out of drizzle-speckled windows and smirk. What the visitor finds is a beach transformed into grey, mud-streaked grass, the odd sheep skull, and silence. On bright days the sea is a shining thread on the horizon pressed between the salt marsh and the low-slung swollen clouds. Miles out.

But one day the wind will turn again and when it does the Kent will remember itself and advance on the marsh to drown the cordgrass. After the spring tides new channels will emerge overnight and turn the sea-washed turf into a treacherous maze of unmapped islands, slippery knolls and sucking mudflats. Those that mourned the disappearing beach will, if they last long enough, live to grieve the eroding salt marsh. Farmers will move their grazing lambs inland, the sea will return the sand to the town and the curlews and oystercatchers will come home. Walkers trying to take their bearings from the old coordinates between Holme Island and Great Crag will become disorientated: the tide will boil through the channel, proceeding at the pace of a galloping horse and the outcrops will seem to move, to change appearance, to shift their relation to the mainland entirely.

★ ★ ★

Annette does not feel like sleeping tonight. She leaves the saw by the door, goes up to the attic rooms and runs a bath. Her body is pale and thin in the water. There are scars on her knees and tattoos on her arms we have not seen before. The skin under her eyes is transparent; the blue of her blood shows through. We can see everything. Her chipped toenails and the old purple nail polish almost worn away on the tips of her fingernails. The callouses on her feet. The hair under her arms and between her legs and the way she tilts in the water, as if she'd prefer to be lying on her side rather than on her back. Her eyes move under her eyeliner-smudged lids.

We wait. Her hair floats around her face. We hold our breaths. We sit. Steam comes off the water. The tap drips and plinks. We run our fingers along the walls and the shiny soap-flecked surfaces of the tiles. She is dozing now, her chin against her chest in the cooling water. She's half thinking about money — not quite worrying (she's always had a special talent for

143

slot machines and a knack for the scratch cards) but wondering how to get out of this fix. She could, if she wanted to, stuff her things in her bag and get out tonight. Catch a train somewhere. Pretend the keys had never arrived. Leave the house for someone else to deal with.

No.

We know she can't hear us but we hammer on the tiles with our fists, calling and calling and still she doesn't open her eyes. But then. Something happens. There's a horrible noise. Her eyes snap wide open and she reacts like a newborn baby set down too quickly: her hands fly out of the water and up, as if to catch onto someone or fend off an attacker. The old mannerism makes us smile. But she's awake now. And we are still here. We are still here.

Shh. Shh. It's nothing.

She sees what's happened. One of the tiles on the wall over the bath has fallen off and smashed on the taps. That's all. That's all it is. Did we do this? We look at our soft hands, capable of nothing, and marvel.

She gets out of the bath, shivering. Her hair is dripping, plastered in wet strips between her shoulder blades but before she can reach for the towel she notices the bare place in the plaster is riven by another crack which steps away downwards behind the rest of the attached tiles. Annette moves closer. Her cloudy reflection swirls across the shiny surface of the remaining tiles. The water from her hair runs between her breasts and along her legs.

Here. Here. We're here.

The effort we make tears at our throats and three more tiles detach themselves, fall against the taps and rim of the bath and shatter into the water. More of the crack is exposed, widening as it heads down towards the corner of the room. Annette moves quickly. Her dress is hanging on a hook on the back of the bathroom door. She puts it back on. Her hair soaks it. Down the stairs in bare feet, grabbing the saw from the tallboy in the hall. The house is actually falling apart. She could have been killed. If the tiles had fallen more this way, or that . . .

No. No.

She puts on her coat, heaves back the bolt and goes into the front garden. We can be sure that no one is looking at her. The well-to-do neighbours started training their eyes away from the rapidly overgrowing garden in the sixties. The house must be all but invisible to them now.

Get them down, she thinks. And she knows this is an idiotic idea but she's half mad and still drunk; her head feels like a crowd of starlings has been let loose in it. She kneels at the foot of one of the trees. We kneel too. Nothing to do but stay with her.

The roots here have thickened, pushing up the flags across the path and splitting the ground open in painful fissures. Annette rubs her little saw against the pitted and swollen skin of the tree until it bites. There's hardly any sound at all, just the patter of broken flakes of dry bark dropping into the bowl her dress makes as it falls between her knees. We want to cry out. We want to ask her to stop. To leave all this the way it is,

145

the way it has grown, the way it should be. But she continues to scrape at the bark and the smell is wickedly green and for a long time we feel quite drunk on it.

12

We sit in the cold garden with Annette, waiting even as the blades of grass stiffen with night frost and harden between our fingers. And from where we sit, we can look through the windows of the house to some other day. We see Jack aim an empty cigarette packet at the wastepaper basket. He throws and misses. Netty wants to go on one of the bay walks. She has read about the new sand pilot in the *Gazette* and she won't stop going on about it but he can't have it. People drown out there. They get stuck in mud that doesn't look like mud to begin with and the tide comes in and they drown. Or they slip and fall in the wet sand and they can't get up and they drown. Or they get lost and confused by the pier lights and they wander out too far and they drown.

'You're not to do it,' he says.

Netty laughs. 'Lost? There's nothing to get lost in.'

Jack pushes imaginary glasses up his nose, snatches the folded newspaper off her lap and shakes it open. 'The water is the same colour as the sky, same colour as the sand, same colour as the mud. Mist comes in, vapours. Sends people loopy.'

'You're talking tripe. The air is good for you. It's medicinal. And there are lights,' Netty says, 'along the promenade, and this sand pilot is a proper, official guide who works for the Queen,' (Annette, a junior royalist, pricks up her ears) 'and any road, it will be during the day.'

Jack ignores her. Carries on reading the newspaper.

'We always used to go on walks. And it's embarrassing, living here and never doing what people travel miles to come and do. It's not at night.'

'It says here,' (Jack's eyes have found with a still-alarming, still-joyful clarity the very article that she'd been reading) 'that the walks are a momentous event. That the sight of the sunset is something to be treasured.'

'Well, there you go,' Netty says. 'Momentous. Aren't I allowed a momentous event? Just one?'

Jack glances over the paper. She's shooting daggers with her eyes. I'm sick and you're not, and you can go and do what you like and I have to have help to get up out of chairs and I don't gripe about it. But this small thing. I want. I want it. I want. Sickness has made her selfish. Maybe she's a bit grateful too. He can put his foot down, which means she can sulk and keep believing that she would have been able to drag herself across the sands if only he'd let her. She can hardly get up the stairs these days.

'Sunset,' he quotes the article again. 'You're not going out wading through two feet of mud at night.'

'I'm feeling much better. Don't you feel better too? Less on your mind? Now that Tim has finally started? The waiting was the worst of it. Things will improve now, you'll see.'

Jack wants to snort but he stops himself. Yesterday morning Tim vanished after breakfast. He'd half promised Jack some help with the grouting in the smallest bathroom which was getting towards a crisis point and had been put off long enough. With no lodgers any more the general cosmetic upkeep was less important but still, letting the house go to rack and ruin along with everything else was hardly going to help matters and as the boy wasn't paying rent any more it was about time he made himself useful for something. He turned up late in the afternoon, red-faced and kaylied, carrying his jacket over his shoulder. Jack wondered if he'd been in a fight; there was a scratch on the side of his neck and another on the back of his wrist, but he decided not to ask.

'All right,' the boy had said, no less able to enter a room and read exactly what was happening in it drunk than he was sober. 'All right. I will make myself useful. Is the lady of the house around? Tell her to go upstairs and lie down on her bed. Face down.' He actually winked. 'She needn't undress.'

Jack had never been in a fight in his life. Had only been drunk on a handful of occasions. Had, on account of his eyes, never played a sport other than chess and the occasional humiliating bout of table tennis with a cousin at Christmas. Had spent the war ignominiously tending potatoes, row on row, and getting filthy, white-feathery-style looks from land girls he wouldn't have looked twice at anyway. But even knowing all that about himself, he still wanted to take a running jump and kick Timothy Richardson up his smug drunken arse. Instead, he went into the kitchen, washed his hands under the cold tap and quietly told Netty not to overexcite herself, not to get carried away, but that he had some news. The boy was ready to start.

There was no way he'd have her alone in the bedroom with him though. Jack sent Annette out to check on the brassicas (the aphids were cracking on something wicked this month, it was the warm snap they were having — summer's last hurrah) and insisted on leaning in the doorway, half aware that he was trying to make himself as big as possible and feeling ridiculous about it. Netty lay fully clothed and face down on the bed, her house shoes tucked neatly together in front of the gas fire. Her face was turned sideways, her eyes closed. Tim sprawled in her chair, his shirt tails untucked, his feet resting on a pile of dog-eared paperbacks. He reeked of ale.

'Let's not stand on ceremony,' he said, in his put-on English voice. He got up, bent down, grabbed Netty around the hips and shook her. The bed creaked, up and down, up and down, but Netty remained silent and Jack remembered the thrill — the cold water down the spine, hairs standing on end, violent, sexy thrill — he'd got when it had been his turn to feel Tim's hands on him. The smell of the boy's palms. Wondered if Netty felt it too. When Tim gave her a hand to help her demurely up from the bed, Jack saw her breathless and blushing, turning her face away to smooth flat the candlewick, and he knew that she had.

'I'll meet you halfway,' Jack says. 'No walk across the bay. Not a chance. But we will take the train in to Morecambe and go for a walk along the sea front. Hire a couple of deckchairs. Annette can have a paddle, and we'll go to a cafe for tea and fish and chips and ice cream. We can see a picture if you feel up to it. Or we can come back on the early train. The forecast says tomorrow will be decent. Let's go while we can.'

Jack could cut his own tongue out. While we can. He means 'while the weather holds' rather than 'while you can still manage' but there's no way to correct himself now, not without drawing more attention to something that he'd be better to just let slide. Netty thins her lips and gropes down the side of the chair for her knitting — the woman can't leave it alone lately — but Jack knows this means she's agreed. He hides behind the newspaper again, feeling like a bastard; relieved and wretched all at once.

★ ★ ★

Because she's not been allowed to do the walk, Netty gets her own way about everything else. Everything. The fanciest cafe she can find for fish and chips — white tablecloths and all — followed by an ice-cream float in the lobby of a stuck-up hotel. Jack orders black tea with bread and butter, flicks open his wallet to look at the diminishing notes and grits his teeth. It doesn't matter. No one will starve to death in this

151

England, and he'll sort the rest of it out when he comes to it. On the beach he buys ice lollies, and a fishing net for the girl as well as a set of Russian dolls from a stall on the sea front, and a packet of paper flags for her sandcastles that she only opens and lets blow into the water. Gone.

They perch on a blanket spread across mounds of egg-shaped pebbles, all shades of white and grey. Annette goes paddling. Jack warns her not to go out too deep, not to even think about going in after the flags, which float a mile or so out on the unbiddable bay. Netty is smoking; her dress pulled up and tucked in around her knees so her legs can get a bit of colour. She'll ask him to get up and get her some tea in a minute. Her eyes are trained on the foggy horizon; no clear line between where the sea ends and the sky begins. He fancies he can see their own place, perched up on the limestone slopes on the other side, over the Kent channel, but when he turns back to point it out to her she's still staring, staring so hard her eyes are screwed up into slits, her forehead furrowed with lines. She's not trying to find their house; she's looking for something in the shifting tides and channels of the muddy bay itself.

'Annette will be all right,' he says. 'I'm keeping a close eye on her. She's too pleased with that dress to go in any deeper than her ankles.'

'I know, I know.' She's irritable.

'It's a nice day, isn't it? Won't be many of these left. Shall I get you some tea?'

'I really wanted to go out on that walk, Jack.'

'I know you did, love.'

152

'Could we take a boat out instead? There'll be a place to hire a little boat, won't there?'

There are boats on the bay. Nobbies for shrimping, bay boats for the pleasure cruises. Prawners. The odd show-off with a yacht. Steamers to ferry them back across to Grange or Arnside if that's where they want to go. Netty doesn't want to buy a ticket and be a passenger on a little chugger making a circular trip back to the end of the pier. She's got an urge to set off entirely. She's still sitting next to him, and he wants very badly to wrap his hands around her calves and hang onto her like that. Instead, he says, 'It's a bit expensive. You know, with the lodgers going and all. I thought we'd be wanting to economise.'

Netty sighs and flings herself down on the blanket. Jack has to get up then because Annette starts calling for him. Not frightened, but on the brink of it. She's sinking into the mud, laughing and shouting and convinced that the cockles are biting at her toes. He makes his way to her with some difficulty over the shifting stones, plucks her out, dangles her in the sea so she can rinse her feet and helps her pick her way back over the pebbles.

'There's no cockles here,' he tells her, his face against her cheek, her hair in his mouth. 'You'd hear them. They sing under there. Make a pattering noise like the rain falling. That's how you watch out for them.'

(He was right about that. He couldn't have known, of course, that in years to come it would be one of her favourite things to do — out on the sands in the early morning, muddied up to

153

the ankles, listening to the strange click and rattle of the shells under her feet.)

When they get back Netty is lying on her side with her hands laced at the nape of her neck and her elbows over her ears as if she is trying to blot out the entire world. All that work to convince herself that she is feeling better has just about wiped her out. He has the urge, for the fifth or sixth time that day, to put his hands around Richardson's bloody throat.

* * *

By teatime the Cliffords are walking slowly back along the crowded sea front towards the train station with the low sun on the side of their faces. All in all, not a bad day. Annette is sucking on a stick of rock and Jack, despite seeing Netty's constant longing glances at the blurred murk of the bay, is feeling almost straight with the world. They've decided not to bother with a picture, there's nothing on that appeals. No point in wasting the money for them to sit in the dark for a couple of hours being bored when they've a perfectly good television set at home. He's no idea what the nine o'clock film is, but it's bound to be at least half as good as anything showing at the Royalty. And at the right price. Jack carries on musing, almost entirely unaware of the crowds and noise around him, until Netty grabs at his hand.

'Can we go in?' she says.

She's pointing at a wooden booth on the main drag tucked in between a pub and a toyshop. It

154

looks like a big garden shed decorated with a black and silver sign proclaiming that Gypsy Rose, whoever she is, is in residence. Palm and tarot card readings are available. The font is an italic script, mysterious and homemade at the same time. *I will reveal affairs of the heart, financial worries, family problems, health and travel*, it says. *You will be amazed and satisfied.*

Jack thinks this is ridiculous and morbid and very possibly the biggest waste of money he's had to supervise today but because Netty is grabbing at his arm and smiling at him and he can see how tired she is, how her pain is coming back, he says nothing. Jack resolves not to think about the gas bill or the account at May's and instead stretches out his arm towards the booth, the shack, and smiles.

'After you, ladies,' he says, realising too late how, when he is trying to be confident, he sounds as if he's doing an impression of Tim.

The booth is sweaty, damp and smells like creosote, cats and unwashed hair. It's bad enough in September but Jack can only imagine what it is like in this dark box during the midsummer heat. Rose, whose real name is probably Barbie or Hilda or Peggy, is sitting behind a card table hunched over a crossword book with a teacup and saucer on the table beside her. Plump, middle-aged, kind-faced and eager to fleece them.

'Come right in, sit down,' she says.

The three of them crowd in and take their places on the narrow bench in front of her. The walls of the booth are covered in tacked up patterned scarves and phrenology posters. There

155

are framed photographs too, of the woman with famous people who've come to have their palms read. She's even got one of her with Ken Dodd. She's staring at his outstretched palm, ignoring the camera, and he's looking right into it, brandishing his tickling stick as if Rose doesn't exist. Jack tries hard not to scowl. They're not the type of people to get their pictures taken and put up anywhere. Not famous for anything, not important. There'll be no 'Jack and Netty were here' carved onto trees, scrawled on park benches. Nothing, after they've gone, to prove that they've existed in the world at all. Not unless you count Annette, who is wide-eyed and excited about the palm reading, egged on by her mother, and egging her on in turn. They're as bad as each other.

'Who's first?' Rose says. Netty leans forward and holds out her hand but Rose or whatever her name is keeps her lips buttoned until Jack has opened his wallet and passed the money over to her. Six bob! Once she's got the coins in her paw she tucks the crossword book away and pushes the sleeves of the shapeless coloured sack she's wearing up her forearms. Her bracelets jangle.

'Now what do I see here?' she says.

Netty is strained and hopeful. Annette shrinks against her — frightened, perhaps, now it's actually happening. Rose cradles her, running her painted fingernails across the palm.

'The left hand is for the past. This is very good. A happy life, filled with love and family. An early marriage, with many good years behind you.'

Netty nods.

'You've not travelled much,' she glances at Netty's right hand, 'and travel isn't in your future either.'

Netty draws breath and Jack sees Rose frown slightly. Netty's giving the whole game away. She's never had a poker face. Nothing the woman says will be reliable now.

'No travel in the future is all right. It isn't a bad sign. Some of us are just homebodies, my dear. That's you, isn't it? Happiest at home in your nest. Keep yourself to yourself.'

Netty nods again. She needn't look so eager. Jack wants to kick her under the table but keeps it to himself. Rose goes back to Netty's left hand.

'All the same, I see there are lots of coming and goings over your threshold. Many, many visitors.'

'Oh yes,' Netty says. 'We've always taken in lodgers. From when we were first married. Had to stop recently because . . . '

'Sickness in the family.' Rose peers closer. 'You're sick.'

Jack realises he is holding his breath. Mustn't get carried away. Netty's declined something terrible in recent weeks. Anyone looking at her would know that there was something not right. You needn't be magical to be able to tell that.

'Here,' Rose runs her finger along the centre of Netty's palm. Her fingers curl. 'The life-line. Young girls want to know when they're going to get married, how many children. But everyone our age, in the end, wants to know how much time they have left.' She pauses. She's trying to be portentous, but the sounds filtering in from the front, children laughing, music pouring out of the pub window next door, bells jangling as donkeys trudge up and down on the beach, float into the booth and destroy any atmosphere she's managed to work up.

'What did you see?'

Rose grins and leans back in her chair.

'You're going to get worse before you get better. The path ahead isn't going to be easy. Perhaps more painful than you think. But I don't see you leaving that house of yours for a long time.'

Jack lets the air rush out of him in a great sob of relief, despite himself, and Rose starts to pay him attention.

'Do you want me to do you?' she asks. He shakes his head. 'The little one, then?'

Annette, to his surprise, already has her hands out, palm up on the table, fingers spread. Jack is about to say no, of course not, out of the question. She's too young to understand it's just a silly game, that there's nothing to it, that no one really believes in these things, but Netty reaches into her bag for her purse and puts more money on the table.

'Go on, Jack,' Netty says, 'let her.'

Rose begins with Annette's right hand. But she says nothing for a long time, only looks into the child's face searchingly, as if she doesn't like what she sees there.

'You've a good many years ahead of you, young lady,' she says. 'No children, but lots of travel. And always a home to come back to.'

Rose cradles Annette's hands, gently closes her

158

fingers against her palms and squeezes gently before releasing them. Annette is looking at her expectantly. Rose shakes her head.

'You be careful what you apply yourself to. How you use your gifts.'

Jack doesn't like this. Has no inkling what the woman means, and he can see Annette hasn't either, but he doesn't want her to get any funny ideas. He's about to stop the whole debacle when the woman lets go of Annette's hands and clears her throat.

'That's more than enough for a small one,' she says, then reaches under her chair for her crossword book. The Cliffords are dismissed.

'See!' Netty says, red-faced and excited. She looks like a painted doll. The brightness of the sunshine is starting to hurt Jack's head and he puts his hand over his eyes. 'See, Jack, it's going to work!'

Jack looks meaningfully at Annette. Slips her a penny and tells her to run on and see if she can find a bubble-gum machine before they get to the station. He means to speak to her about the palm-reader and make sure the girl knows it is just a game, but a second after the thought has formed, it disappears because Netty is still before him, breathless and happy, and she needs dealing with first.

'You can't say that,' he whispers. 'You can't say everything's going to be fine just because some old — '

'Jack . . . '

'Some old lady tells you that it is. How would she know?'

159

'If you don't believe in it, it won't work. That's what Candy says.'

Jack doesn't need to have faith. He doesn't need to think positively, or hope for the best, or throw the bad energies out of his body or any of the other rubbish Candy is filling his wife's head with. He can safely rely on the facts because the fact is that he can see Annette, a good deal ahead of him now and trotting away further. He can see her down to the detail in the lace on the top of her socks, the twisted red piping along the sleeves of her dress. And the things he can hear — the girls on the beach half a mile away speculating about which one of them will get in the family way first. The man in the ice-cream van rinsing his scoop in a jug of warm water and whistling 'Greensleeves' under his breath. Some man in the back room of the pub they've just passed asking for his drinks to be put on a tab. There's a reason he's not dared tell Netty what the boy has done for his ears, and why he's done his best to keep the terrible improvement to himself. It felt like having an affair: sneaking about downstairs while Netty was in bed, having himself improved when she was up there fading. It felt like stealing. Maybe she'd see it that way too. Why was there all this for him, and nothing for her?

'I'm not saying he can't do it,' Jack says. He doesn't know what he's saying. The boy has started, at last. What more does he want? 'We don't know anything about him.'

'Why's that? You want to know something about him, you ask him. He's doing his best to be friendly to you. You're awkward around him. You need to try harder with him. Draw him out a bit. You don't chat to him properly. That's why you don't know anything about him.'

Jack takes a breath.

'I wrote to the consultant,' he says.

Netty's eyes widen.

'I want to see if they'll have you in again. Have another look. That's all.'

She shakes her head. The horror of the hospital and what they did to her has been slow to leave her. He knows this. He tries to touch her, but she bats his hand away.

'What's wrong with you?' Netty says. 'You were the one who invited him back. You were the one who got all our hopes up, asking him to come and stay with us, treating him like royalty. Start when you like, there's no pressure. Make yourself at home, feel free to use the garden!' She imitates Jack and her face becomes a picture of impotent obsequiousness. He recognises himself immediately, and is disgusted.

'Do you blame me? Seeing something that might work better than anything you've tried so far? Wanting to try it? Do you blame me for that? Even if I was wrong?'

Jack has begun to suspect Tim might be a leech. Sucking them for the free meals, the house, the adoration he's been getting from Netty. Sucking them dry, and pumping them full of some magic that has cast a spell on them all and made them forget their brains. Forget everything. If he had half a backbone about him he'd of slung him out on his ear by now. But just

161

as he sets his mind to do it, to throw the boy out to wherever he came from, Tim will do something that makes it impossible. Will flash a smile, or get to work on that ridiculous, beautiful shirt. Will tell Annette a joke that will have her falling about laughing, will compliment Jack's work on the house and the garden in a way that coaxes him into feeling, just for a moment, like a man standing on the ramparts of his own castle, owning everything he sees for miles and miles around him. Or, worst of all, he'll take Netty upstairs and start touching her in a way that fools her into thinking her body can carry her over the sands without failing her.

'It's no wonder he waited so long, with your attitude stinking everything up!' Netty says. 'If it's too late to make a difference, I'll know whose fault it is!'

She turns quickly and walks away from him. She catches up with Annette, holds her by the hand and crosses the road to walk along the promenade, the skirts of her too-big summer dress swishing around her knees. She can't keep up the pace for long though. Once she's over the road she stops and presses herself against the railings, pretends, for Annette's sake, she's looking out over the water instead of catching her breath. Annette climbs up and stands on the bottom rung, leaning out as far as she can to see — what? There's nothing out there — and Netty points, to some aspect of the view, a boat, or someone in a funny bathing costume, perhaps. There are telescopes mounted on the railings at intervals right the way along the length of the prom, and Netty is feeding a penny into one and leaning over to look. She turns the telescope on its revolving stand until it's pointing out to the west and the open sea. Annette waits patiently, not even getting a look-in. He'll cross the road himself. He'll go over there and intervene. Before he can get to her Netty leaves the telescope and starts walking away down the prom, weaving rapidly through the crowds without seeming to see them at all, as if in a dream. Annette follows and Jack picks up the pace.

(Later, safely at home with Netty snoring lightly in bed beside him, he will remember his heart beating furiously in his throat, the stickiness of sweat gathering in his armpits and the idea forming — bubbling up from the depths somewhere — that Netty was running away from him. His wife was getting dragged out by the high tides and she wasn't struggling but was determined to throw herself into the water head first. He will long for her and, troubled by an erection, lie awake until morning.)

There are jagged rows of deckchairs in his way; all filled with shop girls and secretaries in short skirts stretching their legs out under the last of the watery sun. He approaches an ice-cream van with a snaky queue a mile long that he has to dodge and finally break through, muttering a dozen 'excuse me's before he can catch them up. He drops his good hat, watches it roll away into the gutter, has to stop and wait for a car to pass before he can bend to retrieve it, dust it off, and measure the damage.

When he finds her — and they've really only

been parted for five minutes, if that — she's with Annette in front of the Midland Station, feeding more pennies into the gum machine. Annette has her hands cupped under the machine, catching the coloured balls, shiny as beads, as they drop down and roll out of the hatch. The machine must be broken, because Annette already has enough to fill her cupped fists and her pockets are bulging with sweets. Lucky her.

This walking off is something Netty has always done when she's been annoyed with him. He remembers fondly the time she left him in a cafe with two bowls of oxtail soup on their honeymoon, just because he'd made some comment about her not needing to ring her aunt every morning. He'd grimly set to and eaten them both, and by the time they'd reunited she'd forgotten entirely what the fuss was about. Now Netty is weighed down, her straw bag stuffed with their purchases and he says nothing, just leans in and gently takes it from her.

'Steady on,' he says, 'one or two is enough, Annette.'

'It's only gum. Let her have what she likes. This is supposed to be a happy day, isn't it? Something to remember? Someone might as well have a nice time.'

'All right,' Jack says. 'All right then, Netty. Have it your way.'

Netty eyes him, such a look of naked hope on her face that it hurts him to look at her. She's done her hair nice for today, put on a string of pearls and some lipstick. It's like painting the front door when the house is on fire, he thinks, then mentally shakes himself. What a dog he is. What a dog, to be tormenting her like this.

'I won't say any more about it. If this is what you want, well, maybe you're right and I'm wrong. What would I know?'

'Really?' She purses her lips. 'You're not going to make a fuss? You're going to make Tim welcome, and let him do whatever he thinks will help? For as long as it takes?'

'If that's what you want.' He is utterly defeated, and Netty is suddenly smiling, vibrant and rosy.

'Thank you,' she says. 'I'm only asking for the same chance as he gave you. With your eyes. Why should you get it and not me? Isn't that what you said in the first place?'

Jack says nothing. It's far too late to tell her about his ears now. She has enough to think about, he reckons, and deeper down: *she'd hate me for it*. He follows them both into the shade of the station. They've missed their train and have to wait for an hour on the platform, so Netty gets to see her momentous sunset after all, against the noise of Annette's cow-like chewing. We wait with them and watch: the sky is grey and orange, streaked with purple, and the sunset is really not that different from the ones we see out of the attic windows at home.

13

Annette saws for hours, even as her fingernails tear and her teeth chatter. We hover as close to her hands as we can and we wait for her to speak and we murmur blessings she does not hear while the tree bark splinters and drops onto the path. Blisters form on her palms and her eyes are running with the cold. She's drunk and quiet except for the grunting noise she makes as she digs the saw into the trunk of the tree.

Be all right. Be all right.

Even her dad, she thinks. Even he treated her like she was too stupid to know what was going on. She remembers him standing in the kitchen with his hands over his ears, the radio playing in the next room, the volume on its lowest setting, buried in the pink armchair under a pile of cushions. He'd pretend he could hear every word — recite the football results one after the other, even though no human could hear that, or bear it if he could — in some attempt to what, entertain her? Was he trying to pull his own version of the old coin trick? No. He was a hypochondriac. Constantly checking his hearing. Worried about his eyes. Always said he wasn't fit for office work, not with his poor sight, which is why they were stuck with the lodgers. Wasn't his fault, her mother had said. Everyone had limitations.

But after, when they'd gone to live in

Ulverston — what's the first thing he did? Get a job in an office. Pushing paper about. Filing and ordering and dealing with forms and ledgers. All the stuff he said he couldn't do. He was promoted too. And there was more money, so the problem that their old house had become (that's what they called it, dug in as snug as ticks inside the centrally heated new-build bungalow — all brown bricks and glass, with white plastic windows and matching fascias. They called it *the old house*, as if it had lost its real name along with its occupants) wasn't so urgent any more.

Promoted. His boss said he was the right-hand man. Eyes and ears of the company. Able to discern the lie of the land like nobody else. He'd been made a deputy manager and started wearing his new suit to work. Candy had made prawn cocktail and they'd invited people round and drunk snowballs together so she could brag to her friends about him. But all Annette could think of, forced into her best skirt and blouse and forbidden to have a snowball, teenage and sullen at this point, was the way he'd used to struggle with the newspaper when he was tired, and sometimes needed her mother to read it to him because apparently, his eyes were too bad to manage. So much for that.

Annette's thoughts are a swirl; a lifetime of moments running through her every hour. The words come back now that she's searching for them. Mr Richardson, who used to sit with her and teach her how to do magic tricks with matchboxes and sixpences and pieces of knotted string. Showed her how to move her hands and what to say to distract people while she slipped the coin into a pocket or unknotted the string with a flick of her thumb. It felt important, learning these things — Mr Richardson wouldn't leave her alone until she'd perfected it, even though she'd always pick it up quickly. Too quickly. He said it would come in handy when she was older. That she'd to watch out for herself, and be careful who she let know about her talent. And then he'd change the subject, laugh at her father's obsession with performing his homemade hearing tests and light another cigarette. He smoked like a chimney, though they all did then, even in the house. He used to chuck little pellets of bread onto the lawn and try to coax the starlings out of the trees and down onto the grass. Wouldn't let her join in, because she was only eight and couldn't keep herself quiet long enough.

She stops sawing for a moment, and looks upwards into the branches of the trees. The starlings used to roost in there. Is that what birds do at night? Not sleep in their nests, but roost in the branches, never fully asleep because they'd fall off and hurt themselves? She holds her breath. She can keep herself quiet now, can't she? She never says anything now. Closed book. That's what her workmates — because she doesn't have friends, only people who exist in the same places as she has to — say about her. Doesn't like answering questions. Doesn't want to get tangled up with other people. Nowhere feels like home. Might as well get used to it. Make an advantage of it. Travel light.

The branches are silent. Bare. Wherever the starlings go at night they're not here. What was it with Richardson and birds? Rabbits too, she thinks. Or no. That's not right. One got into the garden once, and her dad, who was still in his dressing gown, wanted Mr Richardson to go out and chase it off because he was worried about it devouring the brassicas, and Richardson wouldn't — wouldn't say why, though Annette sees now that he was scared. Scared of a scabby rabbit, bumping its way around the raised beds, blind and half mad with myxie and Richardson refused point blank to go out and shoo it away. A regular Doctor Doolittle, he was. And her dad had just taken it — as if Richardson were the landlord and he himself were the guest.

She lifts the saw — it's slippery but she thinks the moisture is sweat — wipes her hands on her dress and starts again. She saws and saws and we want to say that we did not mean any harm. We want her to speak to us. We want to hear her voice so much.

Come in. Come into the house. It will be all right.

★ ★ ★

Hours pass. She cries out and the saw falls into her lap. Her hands are slick with blood.

She can't get rid of the trees.

She can't.

She leans back onto her heels, staring. Her palms look like they've been burned. Like she's pressed them to the stovetop and left them there.

169

We hold onto her shoulders and comb her hair with our fingers and smooth our thumbs over her eyebrows to take her headache away but she doesn't turn to look at our faces. She must be so cold.

Come back inside.

She tries to stand and fails to manage it even though we are standing beside her. But it's too much for her, now, to get back into the house. We can tell by the way she moves that her joints have seized and her face is numb but despite the freezing temperature and the lost sleep, the hours of frantic sawing that she can feel in her aching arms and shoulders, Annette has nothing to show for her pains except a paperback-sized wound on the side of the tree, white and sticky. All she's done is rubbed away some of the bark.

Her hands.

Her hands are burning; throbbing and wet and hot — rubbed red raw. Her phone is in her pocket and she brings it out and starts to look through the numbers even though swiping at the screen hurts her fingertips. There must be someone who can help. Whose numbers does she have stored in there? A couple of temp agencies. A Chinese takeaway in a city she hasn't lived in for three years. The solicitor and the tree surgeon. She lets the phone drop. There is nobody who she can call to help her short of an ambulance, and she's not that far gone. In need of a friend, not a paramedic. The only thing she can do is kneel for a moment and attempt to gather herself. She shuffles backwards, off the wet grass and onto the front step, letting the saw clatter onto the path.

She'll wait till the sun comes up and thaws her out a bit. It's still dark. Small hours. Not long before morning, perhaps, but in Grange, in December, the morning is slow to come. Annette herself is not what she used to be. How old now? We try to count the years but time slips away, the tide dragging wet sand out from under our heels until we fall and slip into the grass.

14

We are the night watch. And we do keep watching. Of course we do. What else is there? There's Jack, fleeing to the pub because the newly heightened sounds of Netty's relentless coughing make him want to put his hands over her mouth. The tables in the taproom are small and round and the tops of them are covered in old pennies and halfpennies that have been fastened on somehow in regular concentric circles. It is Jack's habit to run his fingers over the coins while he is drinking or reading the newspaper as if they are a book in Braille and he can read the years on each of their faces just by feeling them. Someone (he smiles), some little get has taken out a penknife and tried to prise the pennies up. There are gouges in the milled edges and deep scratches in the table where the edges of the coins don't touch. It's some poor sod who's that hard up for cash. That desperate for a drink, perhaps. But he knows what that is like. Why else is he here, rather than at home, where he should be? The drink dulls the sounds he can hear. Blurs his vision a little. Returns him to himself, or who he used to be before Richardson got hold of him. The smile drops from his face and he stands, leaves his paper and goes to fetch himself another pint.

The girl serving is cut in half by the edge of the bar which means he can't see her legs, only the fussy, halter-neck blouse she's wearing. He can tell she's wearing heels by the sound of them chapping against the tiles, the way the flesh on her bare upper arms swings and jiggles. Her headlights are clear as day against the flimsy material. He realises he's staring at her and turns his eyes to the pumps, ashamed.

'Another bitter,' he says.

'Pint or half, love?'

She must think he's had too much already, to be offering him a half. That's it. He's made a fool out of himself in some way. He tears his eyes away from the soggy beer mats dotted along the edge of the bar, his own fingers against the rail making little anxious auras of condensation on the cool polished brass, and dares himself to look her in the eye.

'He'll have a pint. On my tab, Alice.'

The voice comes from behind him. Is fuddled with drink, but familiar all the same. Jack turns and there's — what's his name? — one of the boys they turned out at the start of the month, and flushes with shame. He unpeels his hand from the rail and tries to wave the drink away, but it's already in front of him, dark and foaming, and without knowing himself, he picks it up, sips, and pinches the foam from his top lip with his index finger and thumb.

'There was no need for that. But thank you. You'll have to let me get one for you. Are you staying on?'

He tries to remember the boy's name, but can't. Jack must be more gattered than he realises, because he is clapped on the back and

173

guided to another table, in another part of the taproom, his newspaper abandoned, and as he sits with the creak of warm leather under his arse and the polished wood of the back of the chair against his shoulder blades, he realises he has no recollection of walking away from the bar. He regards the glass in his hand gladly and with mild surprise and takes another long gulp. Was it James? Jamie? Something like that?

'How is Mrs Clifford keeping?' the boy asks. Jack studies him carefully before answering. He has a young face, pudgy around the corners, as his mother would have said. Shaving rash on his throat and a forehead full of plooks, poor bastard. Peter. Yes. Peter Jackson. That's the one. A porter or something at the hotel.

'As well as you might expect,' he says, which is the neatest and most polite way he has discovered of refusing to answer that type of question. His head clears for a moment — he suspects just for a moment — and he remembers his manners.

'I'm right sorry we had to ask you to go. You and the rest of the boys. I hope you understand. Did you find another place? Somewhere decent?'

Peter shrugs. He has a packet of baccy and busies himself making little cigarettes for himself and Jack.

'I'm staying in the hotel for a bit. They've a dorm behind the kitchens. It's not much and the noise in the morning is fucking shocking, but you do what you have to. Something will come up.'

Jack accepts the cigarette, tilts his head

forward for it to be lit and inhales deeply. 'I hope there's no hard feelings. The short notice, and that. Mrs Clifford couldn't keep up any more. It wasn't right to charge you, when she couldn't cook for you.'

'We'd have been willing to work round that. I can cook. I can even iron. National Service is good for something. All that marching about and putting up telephone poles made a proper girl out of me.'

Jack takes another pull from his pint. The glass in his hand is wet and he lowers it to the table slowly, afraid it might spill. He is clapped on the back again. Peter is standing above him. (Jack realises he has missed a moment here, feels his eyelids drooping. Did he fall asleep? The nights are long at home now; Netty wakes often and needs to be settled, like a baby.)

'Darts. Come on.'

Jack shakes his head and the taproom tips and spins but he is already on his feet and Peter is taking a little wooden darts case out of his jacket pocket, tapping on the bar to get darts for Jack, and fiddling with a nubbin of chalk at the blackboard.

'I've never played before. It'd not be much of a game for you.'

'You've never played?' Peter laughs. The colour in his cheeks is high, his forehead is shining. 'I don't believe you!'

'My eyes,' Jack begins.

'Of course.' Peter taps himself on the head. 'I never thought. They kept you out of the war, didn't they?'

'I spent it on a farm. It was war work.'

'They stuck you in with the C.O.s and the queers, did they?' Peter makes a chalk mark on the floor, motions Jack to stand at it. 'My father went to France. Never came back. Lots didn't, of course.'

Jack nods. 'A generation fatherless,' he says, which he is sure is a quote from somewhere or other — some radio programme, perhaps, or a newspaper. It feels strange in his mouth, and for a minute he thinks Peter is going to argue with him, to complain, to shame him, somehow. He's not the boy's landlord any longer: there's no upper hand to be had. But Peter puts a dart in his hand and mimes the motion of throwing it at the board.

'Aim for the middle,' he says, 'it'll be all right. I'll stand behind the proper line,' (it's marked on the floor with gaffer tape) 'but I've drawn another one. Seven foot for me, five for you. On account of your eyes. We'll see how we get on.'

'You go first,' Jack says, 'show me how it's done.'

Peter tips his head, stands behind the throw-line and aims. The dart bounces off the spider and drops to the floor. Laughter rumbles around the taproom. Someone calls out: 'Fanny!' and Peter points into a shadowy corner, mock threatening. 'Just warming up, gentlemen. I'm letting the beginner have a chance.' He throws the next two darts in quick succession; they hit the board and stick.

'That's 21, Pete,' Alice says. She's leaning over the bar. Probably taken a shine to him already.

'Your turn,' Peter says. 'Don't make a show of me in front of the lady, will you?'

Jack steps forward to the chalk mark on the floor and feels the eyes of every man in the pub on him. His shirt is damp under the armpits and the woollen tank he's wearing is starting to itch. No way of getting out of it now. The dart is snug in his hand, the brass barrel weighted perfectly, feeling like an expensive pen or a bullet. He leans forward and throws. There's a surprised, ragged cheer.

'Beginner's luck!' someone calls.

'That's 50 right there,' Alice says.

Peter frowns. 'Throw again, Jack, you get all three.'

Jack lifts the dart and throws again. He can't pretend he isn't trying. Closing one eye, drawing his arm back, feeling the dart fly easily from between his fingers, sail through the air, and land, more or less exactly where he intended it to.

'25. Oh he's doing well, isn't he? Make him stand back a bit. Even it up.'

Alice is drinking ginger beer from a little glass bottle. Jack glances at her, then takes two steps backwards and lines the toes of his shoes against the black throw-line.

'Here?'

'There you go. He doesn't want showing up, does he?' She raises the bottle to her lips as he makes his last throw, but lowers it again, without sipping.

'You never did!' she says, and laughs. 'Pete will have you for that one. Another 50, that is.'

Jack wants to ask if that's any good, if he's done well, but he can tell by the look on Peter's face that it is, and he has.

'Bad eyes my arse. I think this round is on you, isn't it, Mr Clifford?' He slips his case back into his pocket and goes back to the table.

'Ah, is the baby throwing his teddy out of the pram?' someone shouts. Jack puts his head down and goes to the bar. When he returns with the drinks, Peter is staring at him.

'Call it a fluke,' Jack says, 'I could barely see the board. Seems like a pointless sort of game to me anyway. There's no money down, is there?'

'I suppose that's the curious thing about eyesight,' Peter says slowly, flipping the beer mat over and over in his hands. 'No one else can know what you see. Even the optician has to ask you to read the letters out to him and take your word for it. Medical boards work in the same way, don't they? Stand in front of a chart, read a few letters out. Or don't read them out, if that seems more sensible. Bob's your uncle, Fanny's your aunt and you've got your class D.' He lifts his glass and drinks steadily. 'You've not got your specs on. Three years, and I've hardly seen you without them. Mrs Clifford once told me you slept with them next to your pillow in case there was a fire in the night.'

'I don't like to wear them out of the house, you know that.'

Jack tries to light a cigarette but the matches won't strike, his hands are damp, and he's about to give up when Peter flicks his lighter and lights it for him. Jack can hear the gas hissing through

178

the lighter; he believes he can even distinguish the different pitches the gas makes as it rushes through the various holes and gaps in the top of it. The men three tables over are talking about his surprising win, and the men two tables behind that are discussing Alice and the things they'd like to do to her. An elderly father and his middle-aged son are sitting at the other end, next to the door, and they're talking quietly about their employer, who by all accounts is a right piece of work. Underfoot, someone is changing a barrel. Jack puts his hands over his ears and closes his eyes. Peter will just assume he's drunk, that's all, but when he opens his eyes a long minute later, the boy is still staring at him, part curious, part accusing.

'Come on, son. We've both had a drink. No point saying things we'll regret in the morning. You know me and Mrs Clifford always thought of you as family.'

Peter snorts. 'Until push comes to shove. Then we're just back to being lodgers. Paying guests. Out on a week's notice.' He catches Jack's eye, gives him a half-smile. 'All except for Mary Poppins, that is.'

Jack is baffled.

'That's just what we call him.'

'Who?' He knows. Course he does.

'Walks-on-Water Richardson. He's a cousin, I take it. Your nephew, something like that?'

Jack says nothing, and Peter seems to mistake his silence for anger. 'Look. I didn't mean anything by it. I was born in '42. What do I know? Would have got out of it myself, if I'd

179

been in your shoes. My old man too. No one wanted to go; not after the first time. Even I know that. It's human nature, isn't it?' Jack's face burns but still he keeps silent, not trusting himself to be civil. 'We'll have a whisky, shall we? I've not slept right for a fortnight. But I'm getting a room up the hill. Next week. Meals and shirts included, and it will be nearer to work than your place was. So I've nothing to complain about. It's the drink. Ignore me. It's all right.'

'He's not family,' Jack says, slowly. He finds his tab has gone out — these hand-rolled things always do, unless you smoke them like you're waiting for the hangman to come — and he lays it carefully down on the edge of the ashtray. If Peter doesn't notice, he'll pick it up again and tuck it into his pocket for the walk home. No point wasting it.

'What do you mean, not family?'

'He's nothing to do with us.'

'Not family to Mrs Clifford?'

'We've known him a few weeks. He's the same as the rest of you.'

Peter considers this for a moment then shakes his head slowly.

'He's not though, is he? I wouldn't bother if it was the lot of us. We're not blind, we can see Mrs Clifford's needing a — ' he pauses, looks away from Jack at the black and white framed photographs above the bar as if something of great interest has just appeared there ' — a rest. But when it isn't the lot of us, it's all except for one, and that one in particular. The mollycot. We're going to wonder, aren't we?'

180

Jack tries to nod, finds his head unsteady and concentrates his attention on the muscles in his jaw, the nape of his neck. Mollycot? It was a strange, old-fashioned-sounding word. But he thinks he knows what it means.

'It's difficult to explain.'

If Netty were here, she'd smooth this over. Never had to explain anything she didn't feel like going into. Would bustle in with more drinks, and nuts, and packets of cigarettes, and ask for a game of dominoes, and all the awkwardness would be forgotten. She's good at distracting them like that, heading off an argument at the pass. But she isn't here, and Jack is still searching for something to say when Peter speaks again.

'I wouldn't have said anything against you. Not if he was family. But . . . '

Peter stares at the pictures again. Jack follows his gaze. Young men in uniform. Football or rugby, he doesn't know which, arranged in rows and staring straight-faced at the camera. Peter sips, sniffs, and continues.

'I can see why you'd have some use for him. He said you needed a qualified hand, what with him being in the medical profession.'

This finds its way through to Jack slowly. He is half shocked, half amused.

'In what? He's not a bleeding doctor, you know.'

'An Edinburgh drop-out, more like. He said he'd been near to qualifying then he'd had to leave. Money, or something.' Peter pulls a face. 'Is he helping you nurse her?'

'That's what he told you?' Jack doesn't want to

see the funny side but he has to take up the extinguished tab end and grope for matches to hide his smile. He should buy Peter another drink. He checks their beer levels, the lacy smear of foam dragged up inside their glasses. He'll wait five minutes. No point rushing to empty his pockets.

'He did. He says they learned their stuff on a — excuse my French — a cadaver. They had him in a cold drawer at nights and weekends, and during the day wheeled him out to chop him up and look inside his guts. Named him, he said.'

'Did he tell you what he was called?'

Peter looks at him sideways, trying to tell if Jack is joking, or not. Jack strikes a match and inhales, tasting the harsh, burned part of the cigarette first. The effect of it immediately combines with the drink and the roots of the hairs on his head prickle.

'He was full of all sorts of shite. There was a pub they went to. The tourists would come in and take pictures of them drinking in their white coats. He said they'd all sit there together learning their textbooks between drinks, testing each other on the names of the bones.' Peter looks at Jack earnestly, not knowing if it is his story or Tim's that is being disbelieved. 'I'm telling you the truth. He could reel the whole lot off. Easy as anything. I've heard him do it.'

Jack can't control himself, and laughs openly. He is seeing little butcher-boy Richardson, or whatever he was before he left home, on the edge of a crowd of rich toff white-coats, peering over their shoulders to get a glimpse of their textbooks: big green-bound tomes with nuddy pictures in them. Jack doesn't know if what he's thinking ever actually happened, but it feels right enough, and it gives him pleasure, so he embellishes the scene, painting in Timothy Richardson as a skinny seventeen-year-old in a shabby shirt and trousers being slung out of a university lecture as an interloper, an information thief and a fake.

Jack meets Peter's eye. He forces himself to stop laughing but Peter raises his eyebrows anyway.

'What's tickled you?'

'It's nothing,' he says, 'let me get you another drink. Winner's prerogative.'

It's a cheeky thing to say, but the awkwardness has passed and Peter lets him get away with it. Jack stands, careful not to stagger or weave, but once he's up and on his feet the taproom seems to clear around him and he's able to make his way to the bar without impediment. Alice remembers his order and has two pints on the bar before he's had time to form the words he needs to ask for them. He asks her to throw in a bag of Seabrook's as well and she smiles but even in his state he can see there's nothing in it. She's tired, her eyeliner is smudged and her eye is on the clock over his head when she takes his money.

'We'll have bad heads in the morning,' Peter says.

Jack agrees. 'Mouths like the bottom of a budgie's cage.'

Peter is laughing, but Jack's thinking about

Netty alone in her bed, the mess, the washing to do before the nurse arrives in the morning. She can't turn up to find him crashed out on the settee stinking of ale and wearing last night's shirt.

'And how's your Annette?'

Jack shakes his head. It's not that he doesn't care about her; she's his flesh and blood, of course he does. It's more like there's only room for a certain number of things in his head at any one time. And Netty is taking up all the room. There should be family for Annette to go to: an aunt or a grandmother somewhere near. But there's nobody. Just some elderly relatives of Netty's in Scarborough, who are no good. Whenever he tries to consider the girl, to think about what might be done about her, his head skitters back to Netty, black-eyed and gaunt, and apt to wander away from him if not held onto tightly. She's like a slip of newspaper on the edge of a pier — likely to blow out to sea altogether were it not for Tim holding her firmly down and keeping her with them.

'We're all just doing our best. Pulling together.'

Jack's words are meaningless and Peter doesn't question him further, doesn't stop him when he pushes his half-empty glass away from him and stands. The heat of the place has become too much, and Jack wants to get out and walk down through the town to the esplanade. It will be empty this time of night, the lights out, and nothing to see out on the bay but shadows and the eerie, greenish glimmers of foxfire.

'That's me. I'm off.'

We watch him as he goes slowly, walking unsteadily and thinking about Richardson's cadaver. We get up from the taproom and go with him. He hums under his breath. The university would keep them in cold storage at night, he supposes, the carcasses stacked like sides of beef in narrow refrigerated drawers. Tags on their toes. Rows of them, unlocked every morning like bank safety deposit boxes. He can see it clear as day: Tim leaning over someone's shoulder, crowding the one with the knife in his urgency to see the body opened. He's keen to see the skin peeled back and everything inside uncovered. Heart, lungs, spleen. It's how doctors have always learned their trade: practising on those who can't complain; the shed corpses of criminals, prostitutes, vagrants. It's not like that now, though. Jack is letting his imagination run away with him. They don't dig people up in the dead of night any more. You can donate yourself and volunteer your parts to be of service to the next generation.

We stop where he stops — on the promenade. He can tell the tide is in before he's near enough to see it, just by the smell. It's thick and green, salty and mossy all at once. The water slaps softly against the promenade wall and the dark shapes of the fells loom against the sky. It is oppressive. Like being watched. The clouds are moving, so the stars come and go. He stands there for a while, his hands getting cold on the railing, his head swimming. It's not right to stay out so long. Netty might wake up, is almost

185

certain to wake up, and need him for something. The doctor came in the evening, gave her a jab that he said should last her until morning. But it isn't guaranteed. He should get back, and even as he thinks it, feels himself rooted to the spot. We know Jack does not want to go home.

Eventually a young couple wander up, arm in arm, her boots clattering on the flagstones. They're giggling and whispering to each other. Jack hears everything they're saying and it makes his face redden in the dark, and does not shock him, and he misses Netty. The girl is wearing a white coat and a short skirt — her thighs are pale in the dark. They're waiting for him to clear off so they can sit on one of the benches and the boy can put his hands inside that coat of hers. They catch him watching.

'Fuck off, you old perv!' the man calls.

The girl laughs, the tinkling louder than he can stand.

'Keep your eyes to yourself, Dad!'

He is embarrassed, turns away from them and walks quickly, heavily, towards the house.

15

The grass must be icy-wet at this time of night, but we lie in it and feel nothing, waiting, thinking of nothing. Annette whimpers a little but there's nothing we can do, we can't even stop up our ears, so we wait and we try to sleep but we've lost sleep too and nothing changes until our idea comes.

And yes.

There it is. There is one thing we can do. One tiny thing. And so we do it.

We leave Annette and we move away from the house. We do not want to. We do not like to do this but it needs to be done. We move over the town, following the unlit roads, and we sweep along the curve of the coast and find — we don't know how — a little house with a gravel drive and a white van parked out front and all the windows dark apart from the tiny one at the side, because someone's left the bathroom light on again.

Eve opens her eyes in her dark bedroom. There's something soft patting at the side of her face. What is it? We twitch at the curtains impatiently. She suffers one of those terrible moments — having no idea where she is, who she is or what is supposed to happen next. It passes quickly, drowned in a quick tide of irritation. Maddy has forgotten to put out the cat and it's scraping with its paws at the pillow, stamping and yowling right next to her face and wanting to be let out. The automatic timer on the central heating has already clicked on and if she's going to have to sort the cat she might as well get up properly. For the love of . . . While she's still convincing herself to get out of bed and start the day she's on her feet and unhooking her dressing gown from the back of the bedroom door. And now she's fully awake.

And not alone. There's Maddy, who sighs and turns over in her sleep and Eve's mind snags, briefly, on the way the washed-out tee-shirt she wears to bed always rides up under her armpits but before she can allow herself to consider seriously the possibility of getting back in beside her, looping her arms around Maddy's waist and bringing her close to feel the way the small of her back fits perfectly against her abdomen, she is tying the cord of her dressing gown, hissing at the cat around her ankles to shut up for Pete's sake, and heading down the stairs, where it is noticeably cooler. She draws the gown around her more tightly and shivers.

Now the front door is open and the cat is nimbly streaking away across the lightly frosted gravel as if it were a bed of hot coals. No doubt to shit in next door's garden. The sky is navy blue and slowly lightening, the frost not as bad as she'd feared. Something is nagging at her, something other than the cat, and even though she is feeling the chill of the early morning in her hands and feet and a rawness at the back of her throat as she sucks in a good few lungfuls of the cold air (just to wake herself up properly) she loiters for a moment or two more, searching herself. What's wrong? She's not sick. Not hung-over.

From a few streets away comes the rattle and clatter of glass and cans as they tumble from their bins into the recycling truck. Eve checks, and notes that while Maddy forgot to put out the cat, she remembered to put out the bins. At least there's that. She thinks of the warmth of her again. Too late to go back upstairs? She decides against it: Maddy is murder if she's woken early. Eve brings in the milk.

Coffee. Kettle. She turns on the radio to a fragment of news; a local piece about a group being set up to raise funds for the refurbishment of some old outdoor swimming pool, fenced up and left to dilapidate for a couple of decades now. They've got a blog, a Facebook page. They're trying to raise awareness, whatever that means. She turns it off, still fretting, churning at her thoughts. Did she dream last night?

It's been years since she had a nightmare. Not since the boy was tiny, and so fragile that pictures of him being lost, damaged or broken filled all her sleeping hours. He's a big lad now, nothing to worry about with him; it isn't that. And Maddy is all right too. Healthy and driven, grumpy and outspoken. A pain in the arse, to be honest. But they are all right. They keep each other on their toes, still. She loves her, and remembering the fact of it makes her smile and she's still smiling as she takes her coffee into the sitting room, opens her laptop and starts scrolling through her emails.

189

What is it? If it's not a worry about family nagging away at the back of her head, then it will be work. An appointment she's forgotten. Some permit she should have applied for and hasn't yet. Something and nothing. She's her own boss. She's good with the details, usually. It won't be anything that can't be sorted out. She has several new emails. It's the right time of year for enquiries from new domestic customers — high winds or frost causing boughs to shatter or alarming fissures to appear at the site of old pruning cuts.

The emails are either tentative, from prospective clients who have already worried themselves half sick about the cost and the disruption, who are asking for worst-case scenarios before she's even been onto the site, or they are terse and demanding and they insist on emergency out-of-hours visits, with liberal use of attached photographs. She examines one of these pictures. The beech at the gable end of the house in question has tipped forward, knocking off slates and fascias and smashing through an upstairs window. The hidden systems of the roots are exposed in all their complexity, pulled free of the soil yet clinging to it still. She dispatches this message and the others quickly, making appointments, offering reassurance, forwarding several to Alec, who she knows will be out today making initial inspection visits. She is satisfied that nothing is amiss and now she's in the flow of it, she is about to open her word-processing program and use the template to prepare a few new invoices — may as well be useful as she's awake anyway — when she stops.

It's the house. Not this house: the woman's from yesterday. What was her name? The panicky one with the gnawed-at fingernails, living in a building that was dissolving around her. Clifford. Something slots into place alongside the name and it feels almost like relief. It is the thought of the woman on her own in that house that woke her early this morning, not the cat. There it is. She heaves out a sigh, closes the laptop and gets up from the couch.

She promised her an estimate. Yes. She'll discount her. Offer a climber cash-in-hand to come in one weekend. Eve will have to write to the council herself to double check the specimens aren't protected, no doubt about that. She'll have to insist on it. But an estimate won't do any harm. She wants to go and check on her.

Maddy has a desk in the kitchen and Eve gets up and goes to it, coffee mug drooping from her fist. She pulls open drawers and searches for the nice writing paper and the matching envelopes she knows Maddy has stashed in there. For some reason she thinks she'll like that, this Clifford woman, a hand-written note, better than an official estimate on the company headed paper. And anyway, if you're going to do the job under the table, you might as well keep official paperwork out of it. She stirs through the desk drawers, finding crisp packets and crumpled receipts and a half-finished piece of knitting. Tubes of hand-cream and old broken pens. Finally, the writing set. A present from someone, no doubt — the cream watermarked envelopes and sheets of paper aren't quite Maddy's style. The packet is unopened. Eve shrugs off its plastic wrapper, leaves it on the desk and takes a pen from a jar next to the keyboard. She sits at the kitchen table.

Her handwriting is poor and the pen feels uncomfortable in her hand but she scratches out the words laboriously, with patience. A hand-written estimate. A third of what she should be charging, and that's presuming the job isn't more complex than she guesses. She'll drop it through the woman's letterbox first thing.

16

It is unusual for a man to spend much time in the kitchen. When Jack decides, without any fanfare, enough is enough and he is going to take care of the dinner himself, the sight of him standing at the cutting board becomes an actual event. The rest of the diminished household drift in to watch, to assist, or to interfere.

'You've to cut here,' Tim says, brushing Jack aside. We see him turn the chicken over so that it lies breast-down on the chopping board. He runs his finger along the underside, tracing an imaginary line along the backbone. 'Take the knife and put it into the carcass. Inside. I've drawn the giblets already. You just need to take out the spine.'

Jack is fumbling, trying queasily to joint the bird without touching it. He keeps wiping his sticky hands on his trousers and getting fluff over the carcass. There's a blue soup bowl on the draining board where Tim, after removing them, has placed the bird's head and feet, the lungs and guts and heart. The organs are bluish dark and glossy, puddled in their own fluid. There's no dog in this house, but it doesn't matter. Later, Tim will make stock for a thin soup that the nurse will spoon into Netty's mouth, more of it ending up on the bed than inside her.

'Let me,' Tim says, and starts to unbutton his cuffs. But Jack won't take any more help and waves him away. He is insisting on cooking for them all this evening. No more fish suppers or cold cuts. He's got to learn to do it sometime, and it may as well be now. He fumbles with the knife again and the chicken slides across the board.

Tim, who picked the bird up from some old duffer down the side of the market, can't be sure how fresh it is. Either Jack or the bird is starting to stink; the kitchen is heavy with the smell of blood and sweat and warming fat — the smell he never got used to, even after all those months up to his elbows in guts and heads and tails and feet at Gregson's. He sits in one of the kitchen chairs and lights a cigarette. He doesn't particularly want one, but he thinks it will clear the air. The missus doesn't hold with smoking in the kitchen — she worries about ash in the food — but she's up the stairs more often than not these days, and now there's a cut-glass ashtray on the table when there never was one before and Tim leans his head against the wall and blows smoke at the lampshade as if to spite her.

Jack leans over the bird, his elbows sticking out at right angles, and Tim wonders when the pair of them last had a fuck. Must be months now, months and months. How long does a man go on like that? Not that he's interested in doing the job himself, though he's fairly sure he could cadge Jack into it, if he needed to. He's just curious. Maybe one of these days he'll ask. He suppresses a snigger. Jack grunts and mutters.

'Mrs Clifford would have done this twice a week for you; it's not hard,' Tim says. 'Ease up.

You're not trying to cut through the ribs. Just remember: the bones are stronger than most domestic knives. You've no need to hack through them so don't bother yourself by trying. They're held together by muscles and ligament. Slip your knife in between the joints and take the bird apart the same way as God Almighty put her together. It's no more than a fancy jigsaw puzzle.'

Jack hoicks his trousers up at the back, reinserts his knife into the cavity and proceeds to saw at the bird. The jaggy knife he's using grates along the rib cage. Pink water and slime pool on the cutting board and drip down the front of the kitchen cupboard.

'For Christ's sake!' Jack knocks the bird with the back of his hand and it tumbles into the sink.

'It's already dead, Jack.' Tim looks out of the window. The leaves are starting to drop. Where he comes from they have a phrase they use to indicate when hunger has passed into being ravenous. *My stomach feels like my throat's been cut.* That's just about how Tim is feeling now.

'Turn the oven on and peel some potatoes,' he says and Jack, still staring murderously at the chicken, tells him to fuck off out of his kitchen. Tim laughs, and does as he's told.

The girl is out in the hallway, messing about with the streamers in the kitchen doorway. She's no bother, most of the time. Tim touches her hair as he passes her, and she follows him up the stairs like a dog, her feet thumping up each tread. Yesterday he taught her the mindreading trick — some silly piece of business using a notebook and pencil and a deck of playing cards. He'd had his suspicions before then, and sure enough, she took to it like a right wee natural. Didn't matter what card he picked, she was able to scribble it down after a few guesses. She'll make money out of that one day, he reckons, and feels sorry for her.

'What do you want, hen?'

She's trying to tell him something, tugging at his unbuttoned cuff, but she's whispering, as they've all to do now when they're upstairs.

The missus is in her bed up in the attic and all is quiet up there. Tim's not supposed to know about the steel bedpan tucked bashfully under the valance she more often than not can't get to any more, or the mopping Jack has been doing. There's a nurse been this morning, fair enough, but the woman has been told (even Candy, in the face of Netty's fading, has relented and urged her to listen to her quack) to get herself into hospital and she won't because she'd rather be here — nearer, she says, to Jack and Annette, and in her own house with her own soap and towels and bed sheets, and she won't be forced out of the place, not now, not ever (the last thing to go in these cases is the spark; the sheer bloody-mindedness of a person determined to carry on being a person long after it's stopped being good for them) but really, Tim knows, Netty wants to be nearer to him. He's the magnet for her and for Jack and Annette too: the solid ball of pure sunshine they all orbit around. He smiles.

'What is it, Annette?'

She points at the open door of his room, and he nods her inside.

We know now that Annette has been, against instructions, haunting the emptied lodgers' rooms and marvelling at the treasures the disappeared men have left behind for her. She has retrieved and placed under her bed a collection of talismans. First, a screwed-up monogrammed handkerchief, then three odd playing cards from different decks, an empty tobacco packet, a single leather glove, a pointed key-ring that was also a tin-opener, and last and best of all, an empty brown pill bottle with nothing inside but the smell of oranges and a plug of cotton wool. In Tim's room she has found the limp-necked, cloudy-eyed rag of a starling lying on the floor in front of the window. There's a loose jet of shit across the bedspread and a dusty, bloody smear on the inside of the window pane.

Tim sits on the edge of his bed, carefully avoiding the mess of white and grey droppings, and starts to unlace his shoes.

'They come down the chimney sometimes, hen. It's a shame for them, but we can't do anything about it.'

The girl crosses the room and stoops to pick up the bird. Tim's about to tell her to leave it be — he'll get a piece of newspaper and use the fire-shovel to dispose of it later, but she's got it in her hands now, cradling its body between her palms with its head hanging over her thumb.

'They stand on the roof ridge and the chimney pot,' Tim says. 'Listen.' He puts a finger to his lips and they wait, listening to the cooing and trilling of birds on the roof echo down the chimney. 'The fire must put them off. But when we don't have it lit . . . '

Annette is walking slowly towards him, the bird held as delicately as if it were made of paper. Her face is flushed, her dark fringe sticking to her forehead. Maybe she was up here when the bird came down. He worries about her seeing it wheeling around the four walls in a panic, throwing itself against the window, shattering its skull and breaking its neck against the glass. He wonders if she cried, and why she didn't call for help or open the window.

'It won't have felt anything. It won't have suffered. These things are very quick.'

She hands him the bird, gently passing it into his hands, steps back and stares at him.

'Make it better,' she says. 'Fix it.'

Tim knows that it is dead — snuffed out like an old candle — and shudders. It is disgusting to him. The limpness of it, the way the body, useless as food, has now become litter. It's nothing. Fix it! What have they been saying to her? The bird is still warm, its yellow beak cracked slightly open, like a cockleshell. Does the girl know anything about death? Has she ever had a kitten go under a car or a pet mouse crushed underfoot? Jack's parents weren't on the scene; that's how he had this big house and no money to do it up, but perhaps Netty's mother and father? That's what small animals and grandparents are for. He shouldn't have to explain this; it was too big a lesson for him to teach her. He applies the slightest bit of pressure to the bird's narrow

198

breast with the heel of his hand, thinking about fleas and mites. Worms, even. The creature is nothing but feather and bone; a tiny bowed rib cage like the hull of a toy boat. He's no idea what he's feeling for. A heartbeat? The girl is eight years old. How can she not know about death?

Annette giggles, and then puts her hand over her mouth.

'Sorry,' she says, 'sorry. Do it like that. You're doing it. Make it better.'

Tim opens his palm and lets the bird lie on it. He smooths its rumpled feathers down with his finger. Starlings were evil, pecking little things when they came in crowds, oily black and speckled with dandruff but close up and still, he sees the green and blue sheen to its feathers, the sleek tear-drop shape of its wings tucked neatly against its body, the plum-coloured ruff around its throat. Annette is holding her breath.

'I don't know if I can help,' Tim says. 'Sometimes when a body is badly damaged, there's no help that can be given.'

'You've hardly tried at all.'

He's ashamed, and won't look at her. They wait together and the bird cools in his hand.

When it happens, it feels like it always feels. Something going out of him. The skin around his balls tightens. He shivers and his hands heat up and start to sting. And after he's handed the bird to Annette, raised the sash and helped her to release it out of the window (it spirals downwards like a spinning jenny, and he thinks he's misjudged the thing entirely until, at the last minute, it finds its wings, explodes into a flutter of black fluff and cawing, then resolves itself into a dart, shoots over the hedge and away), he feels the familiar sense of shame. He wasn't supposed to be doing it at all any more. The trick at the lido was stupid. It was showing off, the beer and the sun and the gazes of all those pretty boys acting on him until he couldn't help himself. To do this now, some party trick, with the girl's mother dying in the room over their heads, well, that was the worst thing.

Annette closes the window and looks at him with the exact same air of unimpressed acceptance as she did the first time he pulled money out from behind her ear. It's all the same, to her.

'Thank you, Mr Richardson,' she says.

Is she being sarcastic? She's too young for that. She must be.

'I knew you'd be able to fix it. I knew you would, if you tried hard enough.'

'It just needed a little rest,' he says, weakly. 'It probably knocked itself senseless on the window and needed some time to come round.'

'It's flown away now.'

'That's right. Back to its nest.'

She smiles.

'Get on and play,' he says, 'I need to change my bed. Go and ask your father where the spare bedspreads are kept.'

She trots away and he busies himself by tugging at the coverlet and sheets, exposing the stained mattress ticking. He swears, bundles the whole lot up together and dumps it on the landing outside his bedroom. He slams the door.

They expect a miracle out of him. He's told them he can't give them one; that it doesn't work like that and in their desperation they haven't believed him. It's Jack's fault. The man has seen this thing he can do with his hands sometimes. How to explain? It is an event, sure, but one that makes him its victim. It happens to him. Is as infrequent as a case of bad heartburn and just as outside his control. It's not a gift, not a talent. It's not even reliable enough to be a fucking profession. He made more in his days doing tearoom trade in Port Leith with boys from the merch and had a better time doing it. No. This odd, nasty thing he can sometimes do is never going to get him where he wants to be.

He could start a church, perhaps. Ask for donations. But to be like that — to be like Candy, in her five-year-old coat and cheap patent shoes, home perms and false eyelashes, coppering up for the gas and collecting pennies for widows and orphans — Timothy Richardson was going to be something bigger than that. Nobody told the headmaster they wanted to be a two-bit purveyor of gruesome miracles, mostly fake, when they grew up. He's already got a plan. He is going to the Row and then on to America. He thinks of a huge white cruise liner powering through azure-blue waters, a measuring tape around his neck and a suitcase of samples in his cabin. Chilled bottles of beer every night, lobster for tea, and being invited to the captain's quarters to fit him for a dinner suit. The best hotels, once he was stateside. Temporary stays at

201

the Hilton, the Carlyle. A proper suite, with anonymously lavish rooms for seeing clients and an assistant of his own, to bring in the fabric swatches and take down the figures. He was no tradesman. No apprentice, no sea-front conjuror collecting a few bob in a flat cap once the tricks were over. He was on his way to something else, something entirely different. He was going to be an artist. Expenses plus basic plus commission, once he got the apprenticeship over and done with and worked up his own client list. He will never again have to settle anywhere where explanations will be necessary, only move back and forwards across the Atlantic like the shuttle on a loom, constantly in transit, existing over the water, neither in one place nor the other. The plan could still come off. The Sycamores is only somewhere he's washed up along the way.

Netty is awake. He hears her moan, as if in despair at having opened her eyes to the same day, the same place, the same roses on the wallpaper. Tim cringes, is near to putting his head under his pillow, then sets his jaw, lies back on his stripped bed and reaches beneath it for his magazine. It's *Tailor and Cutter* and he flicks it open and begins to memorise the names and patterns of the new worsteds and serges. They're advertising the major houses' spring collections already, he notes, and realises, with relief, that soon it will be time for him to leave.

17

We wait on the landing, the light changing around us. Here comes Netty, huffing and sighing her way down the stairs, her bare feet on the carpet (which needs a proper sweep) and her hand unsteady and heavy on the banister (which is wobbling). She's looking for Jack. Has been calling for him and receiving no answer. He's been bad-tempered recently. Snapping at the boy, even though without Tim in the house they'd be worse off in all sorts of ways. All right, he probably wasn't paying what he should and making more washing at a time when they could least afford to send it out, but he made the place feel like a home, rather than a collection of empty rooms with a roof stuck on the top. He doesn't treat her like she's ill. He's cheeky — even teases her sometimes, tells her to get some lipstick on and stop malingering. It makes her smile. He'd not dare speak to her like that unless he was confident it was going to be all right. He wouldn't be that cruel.

When Netty gets downstairs Jack is nowhere to be seen but Tim is sitting at the sewing machine set up on the dining table, working on Jack's shirt. Annette is tucked in so close to him you couldn't fit a piece of paper between them.

'Let me help you,' he says, and gets up, takes her arm, folds her into her little chair and tucks the blanket around her knees. 'We'll get along much better now the Head Seamstress is here, I'm sure.'

Netty tugs at the blanket. She's wearing her slippers and dressing gown. It's not her habit to prance around the house like this, undressed with the lodgers around, but it's only Tim now, and anyway, he's different.

'Where's Jack, Tim? What have you done with him?'

'Which Jack? Do you mean that handsome man standing over there?'

Netty turns. Jack is standing in the doorway, his arms folded. He won't meet her eye. She wants to ask him for fresh bed sheets but she doesn't want to do it in front of Tim and Annette (if only there were a woman — a sister or a cousin, who could come and help) so she just smiles and waits in her chair. Tim whips the shirt out from the machine with a flourish and holds it against Jack.

'Have you had any thoughts about buttons, Mr Clifford?'

Jack looks so dumbfounded that Netty wants to laugh.

'You'll not get any sense out of him where clothes are concerned,' she says. 'He couldn't tell you the colour of the jumper he's wearing without checking.'

Jack doesn't smile. The mardy sod. Tim is pressing the shirt against his shoulders; twitching at the material and removing loose threads.

'We'll get to the buttons. It's a finishing touch, nothing more.'

Jack runs his hands across the front panels of

the shirt. The pockets are on now, though the thing is still without its collar.

'I'll have to fit you again. Tomorrow maybe. There's no rushing perfection.'

'It looks lovely already, doesn't it, Jack?'

He could at least try and make an effort. Jack gently takes the shirt from Tim and holds it in his fists, examining it.

'It's the Italian style,' Tim says. 'And I'm going to do you a tab collar too.'

Jack raises his eyebrows. 'Italian?'

Tim laughs. 'We're not at war with them any more, Mr Clifford. All the big houses are in Europe now. Those American-style suits you see men in — hanging like old sacks — they're on the way out. And good riddance too, if you ask me. This is a proper shirt.'

'The work is very fine,' Jack says, reluctantly.

But is it reluctant? Netty watches Jack pore over the shirt, turning it over to inspect the way the yoke is tacked to the back panel, the precise darts and neat scyes. He's letting the material fall through his fingers, enjoying the smooth feel of it. He's even smiling.

'I can't wait to wear it,' he says, finally, looking at no one. He's embarrassed. Is that it? 'We'll have to invite someone round. A shirt like this deserves a special occasion.'

'Right. Hand it over. Those sleeves might look all right to you, but I want to pull the left one out and put it in again. Once I've finished this one,' Tim says, 'let's call it the trial run — though it will be perfect, I promise you that — I'm going to make another.'

'You've enough cloth,' says Netty, 'you should open a shop.'

He laughs. 'First, another shirt, for me — Annette can help me with the measurements, she's getting a dab hand at taking down the numbers — and then I'll do a jacket. Maybe even see if I can get a bit of silk and do myself a tie. Blue, do you think, or something a bit brighter? To draw the eye?'

'You can't go wrong with blue,' Jack says. 'Weddings, Christenings. Anything formal — a blue tie will suit.'

'You had a blue tie for our wedding, didn't you, Jack?'

He doesn't hear her, and Tim is holding the shirt against him again, checking the length of the sleeves and adjusting pins here and there.

'I'm just imagining what an impression it would make, to turn up in a shirt and jacket that I'd cut and put together myself,' Tim says. 'They're bound to be impressed. I'm thinking a slimmer fit, with narrow lapels. Up to date, but classic too. A style that says you can afford something new, but want something of quality — something that won't wear out in a few years, and will still look smart.'

'What are you going on about, Tim?' Netty asks, chuckling. Annette is handing him tape measures, the pincushion is going back and forth, there are spools of cotton rolling around the table.

'He thinks he's going to go and ask for a job,' Jack says sullenly. 'He thinks he can just turn up on Savile Row, pick the poshest-looking place, and talk himself into an apprenticeship.'

Netty draws breath. He can't be planning to leave, not yet. She's not improved enough. They've not put the sickness on the run. Not yet. Tim wraps the tape measure around his hand.

'I'm in no rush,' he says, quietly. 'There are things I want to attend to here before I go, of course. My suit will take a long time to finish. Don't fret.'

'I wish you luck with it, Timothy,' she says, mollified. She shivers and draws her dressing gown tightly around her. 'If anyone can turn up and talk themselves into a top job, it's you.'

'Your faith in me will be rewarded,' Tim says, 'not only in heaven, but by a baby pink Pringle twinset which I shall have delivered to your door as soon as I get my first proper pay packet.'

'You know what they say about chickens,' Jack says. 'Best left uncounted. I'm going to do us some dinner. Butties again, I'm afraid. You can have crab or egg.'

Annette and Tim screw up their faces: matching expressions of disgust, and Netty is still laughing at them when they are interrupted by a knock at the door. Loud and insistent, like a tallyman. She looks at Jack, who shrugs at her. Their eyes meet and she knows what he's thinking because she's thinking it too — the account at May's.

'We're not expecting anyone.'

'Someone at the door and here's me, dressed like this!' Netty puts her hands on the arms of the chair and attempts to stand up. Jack moves towards her but Tim is there first, solicitous, patting her shoulders and easing her back into her chair.

'Leave it to me, Mr and Mrs Clifford,' Tim says. 'I'll answer, and let them know that you're both indisposed, shall I?' He disappears without waiting for a reply.

'Indisposed!' Netty says, giggling. 'If he tells them we're both indisposed, they'll think we're in bed. Together. In the day!'

Jack drifts to the window and is trying to look through the nets to see who is at the front door and Netty is left to laugh at her own joke.

It's only Candy. Armoured with her belted coat, hat and gloves, carrying a covered pan in one hand and a cake tin in the other. She breezes right in and sets the lot down on the dining table.

'I thought it was high time this family had a proper cooked meal,' she said. 'No, Netty, don't even think of arguing. It's a good soup and cake for afterwards. I know you weren't expecting me, but you're in, and here I am, and I have food, and it's time to eat. So no complaints.'

She takes off her coat, drapes it over the back of the dining chair, and bustles off into the kitchen. 'Jack, where are your matches? I need to light the gas.'

'You'd better go and help her,' Netty says. She studies Jack as he folds the shirt and put the bobbins back in the sewing box. He sends Tim to hunt out the matches for Candy, as if he doesn't want to be on his own with her, and Netty begins to wonder.

★ ★ ★

208

They eat together. Netty isn't hungry. She sits still with the tray on her lap and watches Candy carefully. She's wearing a new dress — or at least, Netty hasn't seen it before. It's brightly coloured; patterned with red and orange flowers and too loud both for her complexion and the occasion. She's got lipstick on and her hair is swept up at the back in a complicated swirl, glued light with enough spray-lacquer to render it bombproof.

'You off out anywhere this afternoon?' Netty asks, with the spoon paused between the bowl and her mouth. The soup smells wonderful: meaty and thick, homemade, with real stock, not cubes. She's put effort into this. The slicing, the peeling, the sweating of the vegetables, the simmering. It's been a labour of two hours or more. A labour of love.

'No,' Candy says lightly, 'I'm in no rush to be away. Take your time, have a second helping. It'll build you up.'

Candy won't eat anything herself, but fusses around Jack, bringing him napkins and salt and glasses of water, emptying ashtrays, ransacking the kitchen for Birds' powder, dirtying pans and milk jugs, and serving doorstop-sized slices of cake, slathered in thick custard. Tim accepts a second helping and even asks if the jam between the layers of sponge is homemade. Candy clucks and rolls her eyes at that. Jack leans back in his chair, pats his stomach appreciatively.

'It's been a while since we've had a cooked meal and hot sweet in the middle of the day,' he says. 'My guts won't know what's hit them. It's

209

very good of you, Candy.'

'Anytime,' Candy says, 'it's really no trouble.'

Jack, Candy and Tim talk about Tim's sewing, about the adjustments he's had to make to the machine, about how hard he had to hunt to find the instruction manual for it. Netty doesn't join in with the conversation. Annette tilts the custard jug, dips her finger into it and hooks out the skin, which she transfers to the edge of her bowl. She's about to lean forward and remind the girl of her manners — they don't eat like pigs, not in this house, and especially when they've got people round, but before she can, Candy drops a hand onto the girl's head and pats her hair absently, approvingly. Netty forgets her words. The roof of her mouth is raw, her stomach rolling, and there's a lump in her throat that tastes like old fish and bile. Her hands tremble and she clatters the spoon onto the tray. Hot sweet in the middle of the day. That stings, that does. She can't help it. Jack was the one always telling her to get to bed, to sit down, to stay off her feet. Annette is scraping the spoon along the bottom of the bowl, collecting up every last crumb and smear of custard. Candy will think the girl never gets fed.

(The sight of her smiling daughter bent over her bowl of pudding will haunt Netty. She will sit up late and smoke in her bed with the window ajar, seeing a procession of Candys ironing school uniforms, plaiting Annette's hair, dancing with Jack at Annette's wedding, bouncing Annette's babies on her bony knees, sleeping next to Jack in her bed, Candy in all the places where Netty should be, like a paper doll cut out and pasted into a picture where she doesn't belong. Candy. Bitch. Netty will silently rage and chain-smoke until she vomits, which will wake Jack, and she will weep, and refuse all comfort as he hurries to fetch damp cloths and fresh bed sheets.)

'Will you not try a bit more?' Candy asks. 'Just the custard, if you can't face anything else? The milk will do you good.'

Netty shakes her head. 'I haven't the stomach for it,' she says.

'Shall I give you a treatment?'

Candy takes the tray and Netty dares a glance at Tim, who is lighting a cigarette and smirking.

'I'm going to have a doze instead. A sleep always does me good.'

'Righty-ho. If you're sure.' Candy puts on her coat. There's lipstick on her teeth. 'I won't clutter up your house any longer. Shall I come again tomorrow? I've got some stewing steak that will walk out the kitchen if I don't cook it up tonight. Too much for me to finish on my own.'

'That's very good of you,' Jack says. Netty wants to batter him senseless while Candy is cheerfully surveying the room, the cleared table, the stuffed drowsiness of him and Annette.

'Pre-heat the oven and I'll be round at four.' She glances at Tim and purses her lips. 'And Mr Richardson? It wouldn't kill you to make yourself useful, now, would it? Wash these pots up. Give the kitchen a wipe-down. I'm sure Mr Clifford has more than enough on his plate at the moment without extra bodies in the house.'

Tim smiles at Candy, gives her the full beam of his charm, and toasts her with the rim of his teacup.

'You get yourself home safely now,' he says, and Netty ducks her head and smiles. Candy huffs and heads for the door. Jack follows her out.

★   ★   ★

She shouldn't begrudge them the benefit of someone else's kindness. It's nasty of her, and there's no reason for it. It's this strange mood of Jack's. Discombobulating her. Candy's only trying to help. Annette and Jack are in the kitchen, cleaning up. Annette is happily singing some made-up silly song about boatmen, as if all it's taken to lift the weight of the world off her shoulders is a lousy bit of cake. Netty closes her eyes. A movement in the room, close to her elbow, startles her away from the brink of sleep. It's only Tim. He's got the shirt out again. He shakes it, inspecting the seams.

'You still awake?'

She nods. She should pull herself together, that's what she should do. Stop letting these strange imaginings take her over. Have a bit of self-control. She isn't a teenager, for God's sake.

'You better hurry up and have that sleep of yours. Get your strength back. Build yourself up and get on your feet,' he says. He's looking at her oddly now. Netty isn't sure if he's making fun of Candy's brisk mothering tone, but it sounds like it. 'You didn't eat your magic soup.'

'I'm doing my best,' she says.

'Aye, well you need to do a bit better.' Tim winks at her. 'Mrs Clifford's school report says must try harder!' He glances at the door, and drops his voice. 'Did you see what she was wearing? I know you did. She was fit for a carnival, wasn't she? And drenched in perfume too.'

There's no privacy with Tim around. Not even inside your own head.

'It was Arpège,' she says. 'Posh stuff. I couldn't afford something like that.'

'Women don't buy their own perfume,' Tim says, 'that's not how it works. What do they say? Promise her anything, but give her Arpège?'

'She's not got anyone to buy her perfume. No one else to spend her money on but herself.'

Tim laughs. 'That's the spirit. A bit of fight. They've not rung the bell on you yet, have they?'

It is shabby of her to take Candy's food with thoughts like these in her head. She's not feeling well, that's all.

'I'm just out of sorts,' she says. 'And I don't like soup.'

'Sleep,' Tim says, folding the shirt away. 'I'll close the door and leave you so you get some peace.'

He does, and we wait and watch over Netty as she dozes in her chair, drifting slowly into a thick, dreamless fever that doesn't break for three days. Jack has to carry her to her bed. When she comes out of it her ankles have swollen like balloons; the discoloured skin stretched tight. We're there when the GP visits,

213

when he draws back the sheet that covers her and presses his thumb into the back of her calf, when he closes the door gently and speaks to Jack on the landing. He says her kidneys are waterlogged.

'The nurse will be round later to give her an injection. Only morphine now, I'm afraid.' The rustling of paper. 'And a prescription for some water pills that will help the swelling.'

We hear him tell Jack he might be entitled to some national assistance and he should ask his MP if he has any difficulty with the forms.

'But it won't be long now,' he says. 'Best not to mention anything to her.'

18

She's coming. She's coming. We're there when she fiddles with the buttons for the radio, driving out of the range of her local station and into the next one along the coast. And we are there when eventually she quiets the fizz and crackle and drives on in silence. The roads are empty, the sky growing lighter. The bay is just visible through the silhouettes of stripped trees and uneven dry-stone walls: the clotted grey darkness of the rocking water and nearer, the network of tributaries and channels that knot and unknot their way across the mud and marsh, deeper than they look, unmappable, treacherous. The cockling teams and their vans are out; the lights of the battered four-by-four that carries them onto the sands and follows them, to be loaded with plastic sacks of sand-soaked cockles, glow in the morning dusk. They bend towards the sand, their thick padded jackets and deer-stalker hats giving them lumpy, monstrous silhouettes in the yellow light shed by their vehicle. It must be freezing out there.

In the summer just gone, she and Maddy had taken Tom out on the sands for one of the bay walks. Imagine living here for as long as they had, Eve said, and not bothering to go. It was shameful. There was word that the bloke employed to guide them over the sands would be retiring any time now, and they might not

215

replace him. He'd been in the same job since the early sixties, he'd said. Lost count of the number of people he'd guided, with his stick and his whistle, from one side of the estuary to the other. Had letters from the Queen and photographs of himself with famous people, including Victoria Wood. As jobs go it's not a bad one.

There was something quaintly old-fashioned about the way he'd mark the route with laurel branches sunk into the sand. They were called brobs and when asked why he didn't use something more modern, something more permanent, he'd laughed. It was traditional, he'd said. And it gives the dogs somewhere to do their business. Good for the environment, though a laurel tree on the wet Sahara of the bay is still a strange thing to see. It was nearly biblical too — him leading two hundred or so followers across the rippled grey sand, barefoot, loaded with a battered rucksack and armed with a wooden staff as tall as he was.

It was a hazy day, and all Eve saw was the misty, no-colour sky, the grey shapes of the fells and the dark shadows of the people walking with her reflected in the wet sand. They were barefooted and muddy-legged, all of them, and spread out in an uneven, straggling phalanx so as not to churn up the ground and turn it into quicksand. But it was there — he showed it to them, standing on the wobbling skin of the earth until the dun-coloured surface began to bend and buckle, so saturated with water it showed signs of cracking wide open, falling into crumbling fissures that would set and ooze

216

without warning. And that is what the brobs were for. To keep them on track because the sand pilot couldn't be in five places at once. Not with the best will in the world.

It took three hours to get over, sometimes wading through thigh-deep brown water, the Kent pushing at their legs and dragging the sand out from under their feet. But three hours was not a bad time. Sometimes the walk was six miles, sometimes as much as eight or twelve. There was no telling until the morning of. As they approached Kent's Bank the pilot paused, pointed out his farm and showed them his fluke nets, staked into the sand. He'd been lucky and there was a catch. He bent, tossing the fish into an old wire shopping basket. They flapped and curled, exposing their waxy underbellies.

'I'll have you for tea, later,' he said.

At Kent's Bank they were met by an ice-cream van and a woman in a trailer selling hot dogs and coffee. They were starving, Tom was bored, and Maddy complained about her feet: bruised and chapped they were, she said, and she'd been cut by a razor shell. Eve was quiet — bothered, somehow, by the wide silence of the bay, the way people had instinctively dropped their voices when the Arnside viaduct had faded out of view. Even the dogs had stayed close while the pilot told them folktales about the fisherman who'd forgotten the tide comes in faster than a man can run, and had watched it rush in, lick up the sides of his tractor and carry it away. The four boys who'd gone out for a stroll on a sunny day, and the one who'd had to find his way back alone.

'Distance means nothing out here; it's flat, it plays tricks on you. It might as well be the surface of the moon. I can read these sands like you could open up a newspaper in the morning and read that,' he said, 'but they say something different every day. The tide comes in, and a few hours later, when it drops off, it carves patterns into the flats. You'd never get sick of it.'

'I wish we'd gone to Morecambe instead,' Maddy said. 'We could have built sandcastles.'

★ ★ ★

It is still early when she turns the van onto the Clifford woman's street: she can pick out the house right away, the only one with trees in the front, trees visible from such a distance it's a surprise no one has wanted to do anything about them before. We see her roll the van past the gate and we watch her face change as she sees Annette, half sitting, half lying in front of the house, her dress dark with damp up to her knees, her hair flying about in the wind, her hands covered in — what is that? Blood? Eve parks the van — or rather, she gets it approximately close to the kerb and abandons it, the door jutting out into the street, the keys still in the ignition. We hold our breaths and we clutch at each other's hands as she runs.

'Miss Clifford?'

Annette lifts her head slightly, but she doesn't answer. It will be all right now. It will be all right. We're there when Eve throws open the gate and runs across the overgrown garden, slipping but not falling on the moss-spotted path.

'Are you all right? What have you done?'

Eve kneels on the grass and the dampness of it soaks through her trousers: she immediately starts to feel it in her knees: the slow treacherous throb of worn-out cartilage and overstretched ligaments. *For the love of*. What was she thinking? What would this woman have done if Eve hadn't taken it into her head to drive over here? What a mess she has made of her hands. What is she supposed to do with her? She grits her teeth. She only wanted to pop in. She'd imagined having a nice cup of tea. Maybe a little chat about the trees, or her plans for the day. She might have brought her some muffins, if the bakery had been open. Basked for a while in the warmth of the poor thing's gratitude, and spent the rest of the day feeling like a hero.

Eve tries to lift her up but Annette is weak and resistant and the rest of the day is right down the spout. She will have to call Alec and make her excuses as soon as she gets a chance. Maddy is going to do her nut. Eve puts her arm around her and with difficulty they stand, and she leads her away from the tree she's been worrying at and over the threshold, back into the house. The woman's shoulder is jammed into Eve's armpit, her knobbly shoulder blades pressing into her. She's skin and bone, starving away to nothing and rattling around on her own while the place shudders around her, the bricks gradually coming apart, the house well on its journey towards its end: a heap of bloody rubble. Eve is practically carrying her and she weighs nothing

219

at all — as insubstantial as a ghost. It's a bloody scandal. That's what it is.

We watch as Annette leans into her, shaking, rattling, almost. She's been out all night. All night. And in this weather. Her eyes are blue and watery, her hair pale and flying up around her face like a knotty halo.

'Come on then.' Eve shoulders the warped front door. She is not soft, is not sympathetic, but she is there, which is more than can be said for us. 'Get inside. What the hell were you playing at?'

The house is as cold as it is outside, and the place stinks of damp. With her own front door closing behind her, Annette finds her feet a little and Eve follows her down the hallway towards the little kitchen. She's been thinking of her as a frail, doddery thing, but she sees that she's not old, not really. Can't be more than ten or fifteen years older than she is herself. It must be living alone. Neglecting herself. Where was her family? Shouldn't she have a home help, if she's not up to looking after herself properly? It's a scandal. That's what she thinks. We know she does. She must blame us.

They're in the kitchen and there are drops of dry blood on the floor, smears of it around the taps and sink. She's tried to sort herself out a bit (there's a tea towel marked with rusty stains lying on the cooker — and that's a fire hazard for a start) and then, Eve realises, after dabbing at her hands Annette went right back out there with her saw. The front of her dress and her sleeves are smeared with blood. Eve is starting to wonder if she should call an ambulance, or even drop her off at the hospital herself, but when she holds Annette's forearms and examines her hands in the light from the window she sees they are raw and scraped but they are not cut. She's lost a fingernail and most of the skin from the palms of her hands, but she has not done any serious damage to herself.

We wait in the kitchen with them as Eve runs a sink full of warm water and eases her hands into it. We watch as Annette shudders and weeps like a child. We see Annette lean into her helplessly as Eve holds her wrists and moves her hands around in the water, trying not to touch the places that hurt.

'What do you think you were doing?'

Her voice is a little bit softer. That's good. But she doesn't wait for Annette to answer. We know she doesn't want her to answer. Eve gets it — Annette had not wanted to wait for her, not wanted any delays, had picked up on Eve's uncertainty about the job. So she'd tried to take matters into her own hands.

Well, there's no point her blaming this on me, Eve thinks. It isn't her fault. It just isn't. She can't be responsible for everyone that crosses her path. Every single mad idea they might or might not have. It's ridiculous. Maddy is going to have a field day over this. Eve can hear her already. Annette is mewling and shaking, and Eve props her on a kitchen chair and starts opening and closing cupboards and drawers looking for a first-aid box. She's hardly any food in the place. A packet of crumpets. Some basic-label tea-bags.

A box of eggs. The nearest thing to a bandage she can find is a pair of clean tea towels folded in a drawer, and Eve wraps them firmly around the woman's palms then stands back to look at her properly. She is hunching dumbly over her hands, bound up into little fists.

'Miss Clifford? Annette? Have you family nearby? Children? Any brothers or sisters?'

The woman shakes her head. Says something that Eve doesn't fully hear about nuisance birds and black mud. Eve thinks she might be laughing.

'Have you anyone I can call?'

Eve resists the urge to shout at her. To grab her by the shoulders and give her a little shake. What's she been playing at?

'There's nobody.'

Eve is hoping she can get Annette to remember the phone number of some friend, some niece or nephew perhaps, anyone, anyone to get the woman off her hands. She won't believe she's entirely alone. Not in this day and age.

'Pull the other one,' she says lightly, trying to make Annette laugh.

Annette doesn't smile. She's shivering — no, it's past that, she's shaking so hard her jaw is rattling. She's freezing. Shit. Eve should have thought of that earlier. Pneumonia. Hypothermia. Whatever it's called. That might be serious. And if it is, how would she tell? Maddy would know, she supposes. But even if it's not, she's not going to be able to cook for herself. Nothing. Not with those hands. For a week, maybe more?

For God's sake. She looks at Annette's clothes. The mud and blood on her dress, the bottom of it soaked where she's been sitting in the grass. Eve can't change her clothes for her. It wouldn't be right. But she can't stay in them either.

She thinks about cures for hypothermia. You're supposed to take their clothes off, take yours off. Skin to skin. Like a mother and a newborn baby. She thinks about orange survival bags. Wonders about central heating. There's no way she's taking her clothes off. Annette's still shivering. Her eyes watering. Eve pulls off her jacket and drapes it over Annette's shoulders. She won't unclench her fists and whimpers when Eve tries to bend her arms and feed her hands down the sleeves. So she gives up and tucks Annette inside the jacket, zipping it up over her folded arms. She looks at her, then flicks the hood over her head. Like trying to dress a toddler.

Hot water. Tea. The cooker is working at least. Eve could make her a tea. Warm her up from the inside. But she's going to have to hold the cup to Annette's lips. Try and get it down her without scalding her. Eve sighs and looks around her. The kitchen ceiling is speckled with mildew. There are actually plants growing through the cracks in the window frames, a persistent tendril of ivy heading towards the light fitting. Eve makes a decision. Pulls her mobile phone out of her pocket and calls home, imagining the handset rattling on its hook in the overheated kitchen.

Maddy will be in her cubby-hole office under the stairs typing numbers into a spreadsheet with her glasses hanging off the end of her nose.

223

Cursing the suppliers, their clients and the whole arsing world with every heavy-handed keystroke. Why people leave it to the last minute (less than three weeks to go, and she is neck deep in orders and enquiries) to decide they'd rather have a sixteen-pound bird than a twelve-pounder is beyond her. Why she's got village shops ringing her and asking her about giblets when the information is clearly printed on the label along with the cooking instructions is beyond her too. If she gets one more phone call asking how big a bird to order for twelve when the guide on the website couldn't be clearer, she will lose it completely. She swears she will. The phone will have to ring four or five times before she even registers it. Then she will tut, push at her glasses with the back of her hand and stride into the kitchen. There's something in the slow cooker already. A nice curry, maybe, for a hot lunch. Anything but turkey. She opens the window a crack before answering the phone, muttering under her breath in annoyance, reeling off her name with her distracted, irritated voice. Just the right shade of polite, in case it's a client, or Tom's school, or someone from the plant wanting to check an order with her. But it'd better not be. Not after last time. Not after the mock-ups and the memos she'd sent out. Why these people didn't bother checking their email before harassing her with moronic questions when she's trying to —

'Hello, love?' Eve sounds tentative. 'It's only me. Listen. You're not going to like this, but . . . '

19

She leaves in the tree surgeon's van. Takes a little bag and abandons the rest of her things in the attic. We wheel, senseless as drunks, around the empty rooms of the house, calling for her even though we know she is not here, and will not come. We pat our hands against the wooden doors and flaking plaster, looking for something else — we don't know what, some comfort, perhaps? — but hear nothing except the long echo of the front door closing, the gate clattering shut a moment later, the engine starting, the pair of them going. We hear nothing but that until the sound eventually fades, then even we grow tired. We sit on the roof ridge and hold onto the wiry stems of the sapling growing out of the chimneystack and listen to the gaggle of starlings perched along the gutter gossip and complain. And we watch. What else can we do now?

Jack leaves the house in a worn-out shirt and his second-best jacket. He slams the door behind him and hurries along the street towards the bus stop. He waits with his eyes closed, and when it arrives, throws his money into the tray wordlessly and climbs the stairs with his guts churning.

It would have to be something urgent to get Jack onto a bus — he's never got over his childhood tendency towards travel sickness. And today the bus is rumbling noisily out of Grange and Jack rattles about queasily on the top deck, trying the special method his father taught him to use on occasions like this. You have to keep your eye trained on the most distant point you can see. Fighter pilots do it: it doesn't matter how the horizon bucks and tilts, so long as you keep your ears straight and your eyes stuck to the place where land meets sky, you'll hold your breakfast down. (The familiar dead voice gives Jack the old instructions so clearly that the hairs on the back of his hands prickle.)

When Jack was young he was always made to take barley sugars and a paper bag on the train with him. If sucking the barley sugars didn't work then he was permitted to vomit quietly into the bag. His father would wait until the train was going through a bit of empty countryside before twisting the top closed and throwing it out of the window. No paper bags today, though. We watch as Jack takes deep slow lungfuls of the diesel-scented air and stares hard at the vanishing white lines in the middle of the road. Mind over matter. He has a newspaper with him and he rolls and unrolls it, feeling the paper dampen under his palms.

Netty. Yesterday the nurse had managed to get her temperature down properly and they'd got the water tablets down her. Whatever it was that had hit her had galloped through her reserves like wild fire. He thought she'd had it. But this morning she'd opened her eyes at first light and tried to get up. She didn't want Candy doing breakfasts as well as dinners, she said. It was humiliating. She was almost rallying, but getting herself down the stairs was all she could manage.

226

She sat at the kitchen table with her head in her hands, sweating and panting. There was nothing for it. Jack carried her back to her bed. 'Try again tomorrow, love,' he'd said. 'You just need a bit more sleep, that's all.'

He'd made his own breakfast. The dining room was a state again, the table strewn with oddments of material, the sewing box open and on its side with the contents spilled all over the place. Richardson was nowhere to be seen. Jack had taken his eggs (rubbery, greasy and almost certainly not as fresh as they should have been) and eaten them standing up in the kitchen. The boy surfaced only after ten with some red-headed girl in tow; she was all smudged eyeliner and laddered stockings. No prizes for guessing what they'd been up to. She was a looker: God knows where he'd found her. At a dance or a party, he supposed. The little thing was dressed for a night out: she had on a pink sheer blouse and a short skirt and she pranced down the stairs in high-heeled shoes making a racket and not caring who she was disturbing. She must have thought the place was some kind of hotel. Tim followed along behind, still buttoning his shirt and grinning like it was everyone's business what he'd been up to. Jack sent Annette into the sitting room and closed the door behind her.

'Morning, Mr Clifford! You're having a late breakfast too, I take it? Bad night, was it?'

The boy was getting bolder, no mistake about it: he actually kissed the girl at the door before sending her off to the bus stop, the sound of muffled giggling compelling Jack to slink back into the kitchen like a bloody tradesman. He left Annette with the television and strict instructions not to touch the cooker, answer the telephone or, under any circumstances, the door. She'd cried. Not wanted him to go out.

'I want to come with you,' she said.

'I'm just popping out to pick something up.'

Best to keep it nice and vague. There wasn't any need to go into detail. She was still in her nightdress and tried to hold onto his hand, to tug him back from the door. Said she was worried about being all alone in the house.

'It's all right,' he said. 'Mr Richardson's around, and your mother is only up the stairs if you need her.'

Having shaken off his daughter, he had left late and had to run for the bus, fearful that he would miss his appointment. He was stiff with anger. In the old days none of the boys would have dared: Netty herself would have run them off fast enough to make their heads spin, but now Tim had both feet under the table he knew full well he could do what he liked and there was nothing Jack was allowed to do about it.

The bus rounds a corner, the big Glaxo chimney comes into view and Jack fastens his jacket. Not long now.

★ ★ ★

The horizon becomes invisible: the furthest-away thing Jack can see is the end of Ulverston high street, clotted with traffic. He swings himself out of his seat and presses the bell: when the bus

228

slows he tucks his paper under his arm and picks his way precariously down the stairs. He's no idea what the boy is doing now. More shirts, he supposes, or poring over those books of his. *The Gentleman Cutter. A First Course in Cutting Block Patterns.* Helping himself to tea and toast and the last of the bacon. Winding Annette up with ridiculous stories and magic tricks and, worst of all, not giving Netty the treatments he'd promised.

The town is unfamiliar and though he has written down the address of the office he's heading for he needs to show it to three people before he can get clear directions for where to go. The centre is a cobbled warren and there's a street market on so he has to thread his way between crates of apples and carrots, rainwater dripping from green and white awnings onto his jacket, before he can find the right place. Because of that, he gets there late, bedraggled, sweating slightly and red in the face. He gives his name to the receptionist.

'Mr Prentice will be with you in a minute, sir. Will you sit and wait?'

But there's no chance to sit and wait. Less than a minute after arriving and before Jack can pretend to flick through his paper and steady his nerves a bit, he is ushered into a narrow windowless room, divested of his jacket and asked, without ceremony, to read the letters on the familiar black and white chart on the wall in front of him.

The optician — Mr Prentice, presumably, though he starts the test without introducing himself — is a neat, womanly little thing with a tiny moustache and a low round belly. He keeps pulling impatiently at the end of his tie as Jack reels off the rows of letters with ease. He is squinting but he knows already that is only an old habit, ingrained since childhood.

'Who told you that you had a problem with your sight, Mr Clifford?'

Jack shrugs but before he can think of a reply, the optician has snapped off the overhead light, plunging the room into darkness. He advances, taking a pen torch from his shirt pocket.

'Look at the ceiling, please.' He shines the torch into Jack's left eye and then the right, standing so unpleasantly close to him that Jack can feel the man's minty breath on his cheek and can practically taste his hair cream. Jack shrinks backwards, temporarily blinded by the yellow orb of the torch shining right in his face.

'You've a regular optician, yes?' Prentice is still peering into his eyes. Jack keeps them turned to the ceiling and sees a network of his own red capillaries as if projected onto the plaster. 'Someone who usually does your tests? Am I providing a second opinion?'

Jack hesitates then shakes his head, thinking of the NHS glasses sitting abandoned on the top of the medicine cabinet at home.

'No, I've never been tested before,' he lied. 'Not since school, anyway.'

Better that, he thinks, better a small lie to keep things clean. He has a vague idea that he wants the man to be working on him blind, so to speak, with no access to his earlier records. No prior information about his chronic myopia and childhood astigmatism to cloud the issue. Peter Jackson's insinuation in the pub has stung him more than he can admit. It can't be possible that his eyes were all right all along, can it? That his short-sightedness was a singular piece of self-protective attention-seeking, the deception so perfectly miraculous that even he himself was taken in by it?

He will tell Prentice nothing. The process will be more scientific that way. The test will be more likely to yield reliable, verifiable results. Ideally, he will return home with a proper piece of paper to show Netty. It will prove that there is something medical and not mysterious going on with his eyes. Prentice replaces the torch in his shirt pocket and puts on the light. Jack rubs at his eyes, blinking, still seeing the ghostly after-impression of the torchlight sliding up and down the walls.

Maybe they hadn't got better at all. Maybe the fix was only temporary. It might not have been Tim, but something else, something that (Jack gropes around for this as the optician slots test lenses into a visor and instructs Jack to read the chart again while wearing it) he'd eaten or drunk, an infection, a bang to the head he'd forgotten about. He'll leave the matter of his ears to one side for the minute. Isolate the variables in a scientific way, and think about things one bit at a time. And anyway — he'd have to go to the GP to get his ears tested, and he's had too much to do with the GP lately. The man is never away from the house. It wouldn't feel right to take time from Netty in asking the man to shine a torch into his head and investigate what most people would hardly be calling a problem in the first place. Eyes first. Then he'll consider his next steps. He'd read *Reader's Digest* articles about hypnosis, about the power of the mind to play tricks. It is almost certain (the optician takes away the visor, removes the chart from the wall, turns it over and replaces it; the letters on the other side are even smaller, as fine as newsprint at the bottom) to be one of those things, and the optician will root it out, and diagnose it, and give him back the familiar blur of his myopia and then he will go home, show Netty the prescription card (Jack ploughs down the chart flawlessly, with despair) and the pair of them will sling Tim out on his ear, together, and get her back to the doctor for a transfusion (he'll give her his own blood if he has to: pints of it) and after that a third or fourth opinion. He'll drag her to London. Whatever it takes.

'All done,' Prentice says. He sits at his desk, his neat little feet tucked under the stool, and scribbles his findings onto a clipboard. Jack plucks at his jacket and awaits the verdict. We wait with him, fluttering, anxious as birds.

'Nothing wrong with you. You could fly planes with eyes like that,' he says frankly — irritated, Jack can tell, with the waste of his time. 'You have perfect vision. Which is very rare, especially for a man in his forties.'

'Are you sure? There's nothing wrong at all?'

'Any headaches?' Jack shakes his head. 'Problems reading the numbers on the front of buses? Recognising people from across the room? No? Of course not. Your eyesight is perfect.' Jack is handed his hat. He realises he is being turfed out and stands. 'Come again for a test in two years, or before, if you're having problems. Blurred vision or headaches, trouble with the newspaper — that sort of thing,' the little man says. 'If you give your details to the receptionist she'll send you an appointment card through the post when the time comes.'

Jack shrugs himself into his jacket as he goes and rushes past the biddy at the reception desk without stopping. She calls out after him — 'Mr Clifford?' — in a tremulous, high-pitched voice, and he turns back, catches a flash of a frown, scraped-back hair and a yellow blouse with sweat circles under the arms then turns away and hurries out of the office. The door clatters shut behind him and he carries on, even though he's out of breath now, right down the street with his jacket flapping behind him, old ladies out on their errands pressing themselves against walls to get out of his way. Finally, he can run no further and he bends in the street, his hands on his knees, breathing hard and gasping for a cigarette.

Perfect! Was that what Prentice said? Vision so perfect that it's rare in a man his age. And Peter had accused him to his face. *They stuck you in with the C.O.s and the queers, did they?* Digging spuds like a land girl. He should have shoved his darts where the sun don't shine. Perfect! His eyes are so good he's one step away from being a fucking curiosity. Before he knows what he's doing Jack is battering at his temples with both fists. His eyes. His bloody stupid useless fucking eyes. We see him pounding until the tears come, until he is able to collect himself, until he realises that people are staring. Someone asks him if he's all right. He straightens, nods curtly at no one and buttons his jacket. Trembling, and still numb with rage, he walks unsteadily in the direction of the bus stop and home.

20

While Jack is waiting, almost tearfully, for the bus back to Grange to arrive (noting dismally that no, he has no problem at all reading the numbers on the front of the vehicles, thank you very much) Annette and Netty are out walking. We follow them, feeling the salty breeze on our hands and faces. Annette is holding Netty's elbow instead of her hand because it's tucked inside her coat and is clutching hard at her belly. Annette chatters and smiles while her mother stumbles along, moaning slightly and sweating heavily under her headscarf.

This is better, Annette thinks. It has been ages since they've gone out on their own. She remembers the times her mother walked her to school. The times her mother pulled at her arm and shouted at her for walking too slowly or scuffing her shoes on the kerb or not looking where she was going properly. But they're not going out to school today.

Mister Richardson is out at the haberdasher looking for mother-of-pearl buttons for the new good shirt and Dad is out somewhere else probably looking for medicine or jewellery. She knew it would be another boring morning at home until Mum came down the stairs in her outside clothes and said she was going stir-crazy with cabin fever, which is not the name of what is wrong with her but a feeling you get if you're not allowed out to the park or to the shops for a long time. So she said the pair of them had to get their coats and shoes on and get out quick before Dad came back. Otherwise he'd make a fuss. She wanted to use her legs while they'd hold her. Take the benefit of the air, and seize the day. So they put their coats and shoes on and got out.

But it isn't quick. There's something wrong with Mum's legs and she has to walk slow on the edges of her feet, like she's got little bits of grit in her shoes and socks from walking on the beach.

'Where are we going?'

'You'll see when we get there.'

It's not even that far to the shops. Less of a walk to the duck pond and gardens. They've not brought bread though. The bandstand? But they pass it. They might go over the footbridge to the tea shop and the swings on the promenade. Annette likes this strange walk because Mum is letting her go more slowly than usual. She is often stopping to hold on to the railings and letting Annette have as many rests to look at things as she wants. A stray dog walks past with a brown patch over its eye and a big bushy tail and Annette is allowed to stroke it and today it isn't dawdling.

At the top of the little hill there is a clock tower and a church with a garden and a low wall around it. Mum pulls Annette's hand and they start on the path that leads through the garden to the church doors. The clock is chiming, eleven for eleven o'clock which means biscuits and milk and a morning cup of tea and maybe a bit of cake if Candy's been. It has a steeple and big

236

windows and there are old bits of confetti caught in the grass from a wedding. Annette has never been inside here before. She doesn't think it is a Sunday but it might be.

'Are we going in?'

Mum doesn't answer, probably because she's concentrating so hard on walking, her head down like she is going into a strong wind, a proper sea-wind, so Annette runs up the path and peeps through the door and waits for her to catch up. She can't hear anything inside. There's supposed to be people singing in church and talking about the Bible but maybe it is shut or perhaps they have come too late for whatever it is Mum wants to see.

Finally, Mum gets to the top of the hill and pushes the door open. Smells like doormats and old grates in there. She's frowning. She's gone all white. The skin around her eyes is pink and scaly like that time Annette had eczema on the insides of her elbows. She should have put more make-up on for going out, especially if she wants to keep being ill a secret. Mum points a finger.

'You be as silent as a mouse,' she says. Her breath is really crackly. 'People come in here to have a quiet think. Not to listen to you running up and down in the aisles or clattering your shoes on the kneelers or dropping hymn books. You just sit nicely and do as you are told. Do you hear me?'

Annette says yes because she knows if she doesn't she won't be allowed in and she wants to see what aisles and kneelers are. She shoulders open the door. It's quite dark inside even though

237

there are lots of windows because the windows aren't made of ordinary glass but coloured glass. This might be the church where Candy goes and they might be coming along to hear her singing. But all the seats are empty, no one is here, not even for a quiet think, and Mum is walking right up to the front, hanging onto the edges of the wooden benches as she goes. Annette tiptoes behind her, making sure her feet don't make a noise on the flags. The ceilings are dead high. You could hoot like an owl and hear an echo but she wouldn't dare.

'Come on. It's the lady chapel we want,' Mum says.

Annette doesn't know what that means. Maybe there is a separate place for boys and girls to go like the toilets at school, but she keeps quiet and follows Mum into a separate bit of the church, with its own seats and windows. There's a statue of the Virgin Mary and some big silver flower vases with white flowers in them. Some of the petals have fallen off and are lying on the floor like little overturned cups. The main thing to see here is not the chipped plaster Mary, but the window. It's all done in bright colours and there are loads of things on it. Scrolls with fancy writing on, angels and trumpets, a sheep lying down in a hedge, an anchor, and a giant bird standing on a big round pile of sticks with its wings spread out like a show-off. There are some people in capes and some writing, and the sun shining through from behind makes everything glow, and melty patterns show up on the floor. It's brilliant.

'Is this where Candy comes?'

Annette, in her amazement, forgets to use a very quiet voice and though she really isn't shouting it sounds like that because it's so silent in the church. Her voice echoes and Mum makes a hissing noise between her teeth. There are wooden folding chairs in two rows in front of the statue and Mum sits down, so heavily that the legs of the chair scrape across the flags and make their own loud noise, which Annette can't be blamed for.

'Look about you,' she says. 'See if you can find candles.'

'What for?'

'You're supposed to light a candle.'

'What for?'

'Never mind what for. Just do as you're told and look about for me, will you?'

Annette looks around without touching anything and although there is a metal tray on legs in front of the Mary statue and in that tray there are little candles, one or two of them lit, the tiny flames bobbing and fluttering but not going out, most of them are burned out in white puddles of hard wax and she can't see any new ones. Perhaps you're supposed to bring your own.

'Never mind. It doesn't matter.' Mum leans back in the chair, unknots her headscarf and uses it to wipe her face and neck. Her hair is damp and flattened.

'Is this where Candy comes? Is she going to meet us? Will she show us what to do?' Annette asks.

'I don't want to hear any more about Candy,' Mum says, her mouth going all small like a letterbox. 'We're not meeting her. You're out with your mother. We're here to get better. Let's just sit and wait for a while. Nice and quiet.'

We watch as Annette sits on one of the wooden chairs, folds her arms, and waits. She is supposed to be getting better at something. What, she doesn't know. Sitting quietly, probably. Mum has closed her eyes again and Annette studies her closely. What is she getting better at? Sitting there and doing nothing. Staying in bed, that's all. Shutting her eyes in the middle of the day and weeing in the bed. The church is chilly, and even in her coat and tights, she shivers a bit, with her teeth held together to stop them from chattering and disturbing Mum while she has her Quiet Think to make her better.

And we wait with Netty too, as she trembles, uncomfortable and feverish on the hard chair. We watch her stare at the stained-glass window until her eyes start to stream. She's no idea what she's supposed to be doing. She'd imagined lighting a candle or saying a prayer. She girds herself and mentally rehearses half of the Our Father before getting confused and giving up. She had some idea that forcing herself out of the house would get her circulation going and clear her head a bit. The swelling in her ankles went down once she started taking the water tablets but they're throbbing now. It must be building back up again. She should put her feet up but you can't do that in church. She's not sunk so low that it's time to make a show of herself by

240

stretching out on the pews like a vagrant.

Try harder, that's what he'd said to her. Well, she was trying. But he didn't say what to do. Didn't give her any instructions about diet, or exercises, or anything. So she'd come to St Paul's to light a candle and couldn't even do that properly. She tries again with the Our Father Full of Grace and realises she's mixing it up with the other one, both of them relics from her school days.

She stares at the window and the pelican starts to twitch, the stained-glass feathers ruffling as if with a strong sea breeze. Netty is used to this: these aberrations in her senses and her understanding. It's the pain relief she is taking, nothing more. The remains of her fever and her body's way of protesting about the walk and telling her she should be back in bed. Annette is swinging her legs and trying to read the inscriptions on the brass plaques mounted on the far wall. Memorials for those gone in war, or lost at sea. Morbid, they are. When she goes, she doesn't want a plaque. Doesn't want some letters carved into a bit of stone. What's the point in that? A few words don't add up to a person. They're no compensation at all.

A movement on the edge of her field of vision draws her attention and she looks, once again, at the pelican. It stands proud on an unruly mound of sticks and twigs, its enormous beak lowered to its own breast. There is blood too, three diamond-shaped drops, caught in the act of falling downwards to the chicks, who have their heads flung back, beaks wide open. It's a

241

gruesome thing to have up in a church; distracting, too, but no doubt it will mean something or other. The pelican blinks, and Netty grits her teeth and pours all her will into keeping herself upright, and sane. Mind over matter. Candy will know what the pelican stands for. No doubt she'll have a ready explanation for all of these things.

Netty considers the lamb hotpot, the apple pie, the sponge cakes. All the food that looked like kindness. But now Candy has decided that Netty's light really is going out, she's stopped offering her funny little treatments and poured all her energy into feeding Jack and Annette. The way to a man's heart, was that it?

The pelican opens its beak and caws; not a song (Henet! Henet!) but a croak. Then it lifts off from the window, peeling away like a piece of tissue paper and flexing its huge black and white wings.

Netty finds herself thinking, stupidly, that it must be nice to have a good long stretch after all that time standing still, and gets to her feet. The bird is circling above them now, its great wings outspread. Netty can actually see the wind from its beating wings disturbing the cobwebs hanging from the exposed beams. It flies across the church slowly, towards the sanctuary, and as Netty turns to see what it is going to do next her knees give way and she falls back, first against the chairs in the lady chapel, which fold and scatter and slide away from under her, and then onto the cold floor, which is as hard as it looks. Her hip and elbow take the impact, and she cries out in pain. The noise in the wide dusty hush of the church is humiliating, and it is that, rather than the pain, which brings the tears to her eyes.

Annette is beside her quickly, pulling at her coat and saying something, though Netty can't make out what, and she realises she's going to wet herself if she doesn't get up soon but she can't make her arms and legs work, can't catch her breath, can't do anything except lie there, flapping like a bloody fish. Jack will have something to say about all this. There'll be hell to pay. She tries again to sit up, falls back against Annette and feels her skirt ride up around her knees. The bird circles again, then drifts lower. It alights heavily on her abdomen. The solidity of its weight and the cool pressure of its huge black webbed feet against her belly are undeniably real. It stinks of tar and fish.

She tries to call for Annette, to tell her to go out into the main church and find help. There must be a priest about somewhere, they wouldn't leave the building unlocked and unattended as a matter of course — would they? — but Annette is right next to her, her hand on her shoulder, her fingers twisting into her hair. Netty's voice gurgles in her throat and she tears her eyes away from the bird to look at Annette. She's staring at the pelican, pale-faced and open-mouthed. (Henet! Henet!) The noise it makes bounces around the church and into her skull and the loudness of it is the last straw for Netty. She closes her eyes and lets herself go limp, aware of nothing but Annette screaming, and finally, thankfully, the sound of footsteps hurrying towards them. There's nothing we can do but wait with her, with them both. So we do.

21

And we go to Jack too. We hurry, insubstantial and trembling: as useless as feathers. And here he is, on his way home from the disastrous trip to the optician. Only one thing to do now. He hasn't time for it but he'll do it anyway: Gregson's. There's a man having a cigarette outside the chain curtain that protects the doorway of the shop. Jack sees he's being observed as he walks towards him and suffers the agonising awkwardness of having to avoid eye contact with a man he is still too far away to greet. Never happened much before, not with his eyes the way they were. It must be Gregson himself. The apron, wellington boots, the white hat — didn't take Maigret to figure it out.

The man nods but Jack is guilty, furtive. Conspicuously wifely with his bloody shopping bag. Ridiculous. He has money in his pocket, doesn't he? He's entitled to go in and buy a few links of sausage, same as anyone else, isn't he? When he draws up, the butcher throws his cigarette into the gutter and holds the curtain aside so that he can go in.

We go with him, thrumming with impatience.

Go home, Jack, we want to say, but we can't.

'What will it be, sir? We've some fresh lamb in today. A half-leg for your Sunday roast?'

Jack clocks the pink and red cuts of meat and links of sausages lined up in white trays under the glass counter. There are pheasants strung up by their necks in the window, their wings hanging limply, slightly spread. Their eyes are dull. Jack has never tasted pheasant. Wouldn't know what to do with it.

'Take your time.'

Jack browses the offal. There's a radio on, very quietly, but of course he hears every single sodding word. Crystal-clear reception, his side of things. He listens without wanting to. They've got another one of those robbers. The Cheddington mail raid lot. Picking them off one by one, and hauling them away from their wives in handcuffs, blankets over their heads. They're no Robin Hoods, Jack knows that. He's seen the wives on the television — all beehives and eyelashes, expensive furs and short skirts. It's not hard to see what the money — the estimate of the total amount taken rises every few days — is going on. They're even paying their barristers in cash, apparently. It's not like they're giving the loot to charity. But all the same.

They're going to throw the book at them, that's what people think. Give them ten years apiece, or even more. And no one got hurt. They've had a picture of the driver in the paper, black eyes and a swollen jaw, a great big bandage on his head, looking all aggrieved and with a baby on his knee as well. But he was all right. He was going to be fine. It was only money.

'We've bacon. Back, streaky, smoked. Whatever you like,' the man says pleasantly. Jack realises he's been wool-gathering, and pulls himself together.

246

'Is it Mr Gregson?' he asks.

'George Gregson, yes.' The smile has faded from his face. He clasps his great raw hands in front of him. 'Our rates have been paid.'

Gregson thinks he's from the council. It could be a compliment. He's never had an office job in his life, but Netty had always said he was capable of it, if he put his mind to it and put himself forward.

'Have you a minute? I'd like to check a reference. One of my lodgers gave your name.'

He has prepared this line. It comes out in a rush, but sounds right enough. Jack expects Gregson to relax, but apparently some things are worse than business rates and health inspections.

'Richardson,' he says. 'The Scot. Is that your man, by any chance?'

'That's the one.'

Gregson crooks his index finger and Jack obediently follows him behind the counter and through a side door. It's all white tiles and stainless steel in here — the floor is scrubbed spotless; he'd half expected sawdust. The place smells — bleach and blood, probably — and there are cleavers and knives in a wooden block on a central island. There is nowhere to sit so they stand either side of the island, facing each other. Gregson places his hands flat on its surface and leans forward.

'Landlords usually write for a reference.'

'I was passing,' Jack says, 'it seemed easier.'

'What do you want? Confirmation of salary? I'm not paying him any more. He left.'

'He told me,' Jack says.

'So it's a character reference you're after?' Gregson pulls a cloth out of the pocket of his apron and begins to wipe. 'He wasn't here long.'

'You found him reliable though? No funny business?'

The hand holding the cloth stops moving.

'If he's already living with you, you'll know for yourself. He was an odd sort. Friendly enough.'

'He was honest? You could trust him?'

'Never caught him with his hands in the till, if that's what you're asking. He turned up when he was supposed to. Didn't sneak out early.'

That's all Jack needs to know. He's asked all the questions he planned to ask. The man has answered. So he should get some sausages, for politeness' sake if nothing else, and he should go to Netty, who will be needing water, or the toilet, or a cold flannel. He should be at home with her instead of wasting his time here on wild-goose chases. The thought of her tossing and turning in her bed, Annette floating around downstairs alone, moves something in him.

'I don't usually go to such lengths. But my wife is sick. The boy — Richardson — says he can help her. The arrangement is . . . irregular.'

Gregson frowns.

'I'm not making sense. I know. I'll leave.'

'You got kids?'

Jack nods. 'Just the one. A girl.'

This information seems to matter to Gregson and on hearing it he appears to make a decision and having made it, his manner changes and becomes easier and more purposeful.

'Wait,' he says, and goes back into the shop.

Jack hears the door close, the click of the latch as he locks up. He's back in seconds.

'What you're asking me is if I think he should be living under your roof. With your wife and daughter,' Gregson says. Jack nods. 'I'm not married so I can't say what I'd do in a similar situation. But put it this way. He was the best apprentice I ever had. Picked up in six weeks what it takes most of us three years to learn. The customers loved him. He could sell veal to a vegetarian. And when he sodded off me and Trevor — he's the other one that works here — felt like throwing ourselves a party.'

'What did he do?' Jack already knows that he doesn't want to hear the answer to this question. What difference is it going to make now anyway?

'See that saw over there?' Gregson points at a freestanding machine, made, like the rest of the counters and equipment, of dull stainless steel. There's a single straight blade jutting upwards from its base.

'We use that for the ribs, the steaks. Chops, sometimes.'

Jack decides to leave now and vows to buy a dozen best sausages the next time he's passing. He can give them to Candy; she's been providing too many meals for them recently and would probably appreciate the gesture.

'You must be very busy . . . '

Gregson ignores him.

'I had two of them working under me. Your man, Richardson. He was my junior apprentice. Trainee, if you will. Trevor, who's been with me three years. A couple of months back, Trevor was working at the saw, doing chops for me. We'd had a pig come in three days before we expected it and it was all hands on deck. You can't just leave pork, it isn't like beef. You've got to get it cut and get it sold quickly. Trevor was in a rush. He was supposed to be wearing these gloves.'

Gregson points at a pair of oversized, overlong gloves.

'They shine like that because they aren't knitted with wool, they're knitted with steel threads. Try them if you like.'

Jack doesn't move.

'They won't protect you if for some reason you press your hand down over the blade while it's moving,' he says, 'but if you slipped while you were running a rack of ribs through, wearing a pair of them would stop you going home with one less finger than you came out with. It's called a bone cutter and that's what it does.'

Jack swallows hard. Gregson is speaking quickly, as if this is the first time he's been able to tell a story he's been rehearsing for weeks.

'Trevor wasn't wearing his gloves. No idea why, the stupid sod. I know we were busy, but how long does it take to get the proper equipment? Ten seconds? I was in the shop, dealing with a customer, when I heard this scream. Never heard anything like it before in my life. I went through, and Trevor is holding his arm, like this,' Gregson wraps his left hand around his right wrist, 'and there's blood shooting out of him.'

'Did Richardson do it?' Jack asks. 'Fiddle with the machine, or distract him? Something like that?'

250

'Richardson was there all right. He was jointing chicken — it's one of the easiest jobs, and he was still new, so I always got him to do it. He turned around, saw what was happening and went over to Trevor. I didn't see what he did. Grabbed his wrist, maybe? Trevor sat down on the floor — like his knees had given up on him — and I was picking up the phone. You don't get long with a wound like that. Not with that sort of bleeding. But before I had a chance to dial, it had stopped.'

'I see.' Jack can't think of anything else to say.

'Trevor was still screaming. Richardson said something and I couldn't hear it, so Trevor must have been making a right racket, but I did see him hold up his wrist. His sleeve and his coat were covered in blood. His hand, where he'd been holding onto it. But the wrist itself. There was nothing there.'

Jack realises he is supposed to say something. To make some protest, perhaps, or enact a performance of disbelief.

'Richardson had fixed it. Is that what you're saying?'

'No. That's not what I'm saying.' Gregson is abrupt, almost offended. He shakes his head, as if he's being accused of something. 'I didn't see that happen. I didn't see anything happen. I'm just outlining to you, as plain as I can, what I did see. Which was blood shooting out between Trevor's fingers. The machine was puddled with it,' (Jack wills himself not to look, but can't resist, and sees the gleaming teeth of the saw blade afresh) 'and then the bleeding stopped and

251

there wasn't a mark on him. I said something — I don't remember what, probably asked them what the hell they were playing at — but Richardson acted like I wasn't there. Trevor was still shouting and bawling. I don't think he realised that there was nothing to be screaming about. Shock, maybe? I don't know. But he wouldn't shut up, and then Richardson put his hand up,' Gregson makes a fist, 'and I thought he was going to hit Trevor — a slap, maybe, to get him to be quiet, like you do when women are hysterical?'

Jack nods, encouraging Gregson even though every bit of him is desperate to get out of the door and away.

'He didn't slap him. What he did was slam his fist down and punch the side of this crate of rabbits we'd had delivered that morning. Nearly knocked it flying.'

Jack is puzzled. Gregson seems to be making more out of the punch than he is of whatever the boy did to Trevor. He pictures the scene: Tim leaning over his chickens with the knife, working carefully, methodically, with those slim white fingers of his. Then blood and noise, and Tim being forced almost against his will to intervene and to act in a way that he didn't want to. Not doing it would be murder, pure and simple. That was why he was angry. Whatever it was that he did — this strange ability (the word Jack thinks of first is power, but he pushes that one away quickly) — is more of a burden to him than a talent. He resents it.

'Have you ever heard the noise a rabbit makes

when it's really frightened? When a fox is on the prowl? They squeal and mew like kittens. And that's what they started doing. They'd been delivered bound up, feet together. That's usual. Makes it easier for the gun to carry them off the field and into the van. I'd not got round to dressing them. They were dead though. I'm sure of that. Our man shoots them outside Cartmel and brings them in for me twice a week. Their necks were bloody. But they were starting to wake up. Those rabbits started twitching in their crate. Making a god-awful racket. Me and Richardson just looked at each other, looked at the box. 'What the fucking hell is happening here?' I says. I started to think it was some sort of prank he was playing on me. The pair of them in on it together. The boys get lively sometimes. I can take a bit of horseplay, so long as the work gets done and no one's arsing around with the cleavers. It's happened before. I've had lads fill sheep bladders full of pig's blood and stuff them in their top pocket so they can kid on they've been shot. They mess about with lambs' tongues. Slip eyeballs into your tea when you're not looking.' Gregson laughs. 'You get used to all sorts here. It's the novelty of the work. They settle down soon enough. If that were the case, if it were just a prank, it would have been no bad thing. The pair of them had never really hit it off, and if this was a sign of them finding a way to get on together, at my expense, well, I could wear it. Do you know what I mean?'

Jack nods.

'I kept looking at Trevor's wrist. Wondering

how they would have got hold of the rabbits. I even started to think our man in Cartmel might have been in on it. Trevor was still sat on the floor, white as a sheet. He kept looking at the wall. You'd think we'd all be used to the sight of blood, but this was different. It had shot out of Trevor and sprayed a line three feet high. Looked like someone had been murdered in here.'

'An artery,' Jack says. 'That's what they do.'

'Aye. He'd have been dead if Richardson hadn't stepped in. That's what Trevor thinks. The thing is,' Gregson says, 'you'd think he'd be happy, after doing what he did. But his face was like thunder. He pointed at the box of rabbits and booted Trevor up the arse. 'Get up and get rid of them,' he says. He was fuming. Trevor was in no state to do anything. Just sat there. Not a scar, not a mark. Nothing. He was pacing about here. Right round here, like a cat. It can only have been a minute or two. Not even that. But the rabbits were moving about. I swear to you. The crate was lined with newspaper and you could hear it rustling. 'You'd better dispatch them,' Richardson says, calm as anything. You'd better dispatch them! They were screaming. I didn't want to go anywhere near them. He laughs at me. 'You're not sentimental, are you?' he says.'

Gregson leans towards Jack, drops his voice.

'I just joint the carcasses when they arrive, do the sawing, boning, trimming, the tying off. Sometimes a bit of skinning and gutting, like with the rabbits, and any game birds we get in.

I've never done the abattoir side of things. It's a totally different type of work. Like an assembly line. I've never killed in my life. It's a skill, to put them down quickly, not cause them too much suffering. Not make a mess of the meat. People have training for it. I didn't know what to do. But the longer I waited, the more noise they made. The box was jumping.'

'What did you do with them?' Jack's throat is dry.

'Richardson did it. Sparked up, got the crate and took them out the back. He wrung their necks. Brought the crate back in and started mopping up the wall tiles. I sent Trevor home and closed up the shop. Wasn't feeling up to dealing with them. It didn't seem right — skinning and jointing them for the pot. He didn't come back. No notice. No forwarding address for his last wage packet. He just,' Gregson flicks at the air with his fingers, 'vanished.'

'But you weren't sorry to see the back of him?'

Gregson laughs humourlessly.

'He came back.'

'To explain himself?'

'We never saw him,' Gregson says. 'But I know it was him. He must have come in the night and lifted some of the stock — steak, sausages. The rabbits too. His rabbits.'

Jack thinks of the meat the boy arrived with, the way the limp, dull-eyed bodies dangled from his fist.

'You didn't report him? You never told anybody about this?'

'What do you think? No fucking way. No way.'

Jack might as well ask himself the question. The matter of his eyes was indisputable now. He could write to the BBC. *Panorama* could cover it. Maybe there was a professor somewhere who could do a study and make sense of it all. Getting the news out there was almost a public duty, if you thought of it that way.

'The police? A newspaper? Who would believe me? Trevor won't talk about it. I wouldn't believe it if my own mother told me. Don't blame you if you don't.'

'I do. I know.'

Jack moves towards the door, nothing but silence and awkwardness between him and Gregson now. He won't return, but he does understand. Jack knows he could no more tell someone that Timothy Richardson had touched his face and cured his sight than he could take a running jump off Jenny Brown's Point and fly to the Isle of Man.

He heads towards the promenade. The tide is out, and the greyish rippled sands are dotted with people sitting on blankets enjoying the late sunshine. There's the faint blast of pleasure cruisers sounding their horns as they trip over the bay. The wind is cool-ish and damp on his face and neck and he is glad of his jacket. Richardson lit out of his job because of a box of fucking rabbits, that's all. Ran away. Performed a resurrection then scarpered in what — embarrassment? You can't judge him by normal human standards. Jack does not envy the boy but he will not let him run away from Netty.

When he turns the corner onto his own street,

he sees a car parked in front of the house. A man in a black smock — a priest? — helping Netty out of it. She can't stand and he's having to hold her up.

He breaks into a jog and gives a desperate, wordless shout as he approaches, grabs at her arm and finally lays a hand on the side of her face. He feels what the district nurse has told him to watch out for; the thing he dreads the most: his wife is burning up with a new fever. She's wet again too, slurring nonsense about birds, cats, dust, and the water she's convinced is coming through the roof of the car. She's lost one of her shoes. Her ankles have swollen up again, the skin on her lower legs mottled, like she's been sitting too close to the fire.

'All right, love,' he says. 'Let's get you in.'

He lifts her into his arms and carries her, wet clothes and all, up the stairs to her bed. He pulls the blankets over her. Please God, let the nurse come along soon. Annette sneaks away into one of the empty bedrooms and rolls marbles along the skirting boards until Jack barks at her to stop. The priest — he forgot about him — has been waiting in the kitchen. What did she want with a priest? Did she have something to get off her chest? Jack asks what went on but the man doesn't comment and only asks Jack if he can say a prayer for them. Jack doesn't know if he's supposed to address the man as 'Father' or if that's the other lot, but throws himself onto a chair, puts his hands over his face and nods, dry-eyed and numb. The nurse is due at five but she won't arrive until seven.

22

It's still strange to see ourselves like this. Unpleasant to have this time returned to us. It's not what we would have wished for, if anyone had asked. With Annette gone, we'd rather sleep now — go back to the blankness of the no-time before she arrived, when we were aware of nothing. But our eyes are bright and dry and we are trapped in our wakefulness and there's nothing we can do but watch over Netty as she slowly recovers from her second fever and wait, helpless, as Jack locks up The Sycamores and pockets the keys.

Tim is caught. Contained, like a strange butterfly in a jar. He's determined not to feel like a prisoner and, as the days unspool like thread from a bobbin, he makes himself content with the sewing machine and the television set. For days we sit with the boy as he concentrates on the shirt, unpicking the box pleats from the split yoke and re-stitching them over and over again, hand-felling French seams and adding buttons to the sleeve plackets. The old man barely speaks to him: spends most of this time sitting with Netty, willing down her temperature. Tim knows this recovery of hers is only relative and she's on the downhill slide. He's seen it before and it is worse for him to stand and watch with his hands in his pockets than it is for most.

He resolves to wait until Jack's fit of temper

burns itself out and pretend he hasn't noticed the locked doors and the missing keys from the board in the kitchen. Whatever he thinks he knows, whatever his fucking plan is (there will be a plan, he's sure of it) Jack can't just keep him locked up forever until he performs. He'll leave the door unlatched after one of the nurse's visits, or Candy will come, or Jack himself will have to leave to go and buy food. Tim runs out of cigarettes, does all the crosswords in Netty's magazines and teaches Annette to play canasta. He ransacks the missus's bedside table while she's sleeping, hoping for drinamyl and finding only a packet of menthol cigarettes, which he claims. It's the principle of the thing that starts to chafe at him. He's supposed to be a guest. A guest.

★   ★   ★

We lose count of the hours — we have never been very good at keeping the clock straight. It is easy enough, in our position, for the days to pool into each other, for events to get muddled. Perhaps it is on the seventh or eighth day of this confinement we realise we are still with Tim. He is lying on his bed working his way through *Noblesse Oblige*, a stub of a pencil in his hand. Underlining the ways he might better himself. And Jack opens the door to his room.

'She's awake and asking for you.'

Even though he didn't knock before entering (Tim knows he is supposed to notice this invasion of his privacy: Jack is making some point about his rights, about which parts of the house belong to whom, and about what privileges prisoners can expect as opposed to paying lodgers, as opposed to real, invited guests), Jack's tone is almost respectful. Tim rests the Nancy Mitford on his chest, gazes at Jack for a moment, then gets up from the bed.

'I'll come up. What is she wanting?'

'What do you think?'

Tim nods and stows Nancy away. Tucks in his shirt and straightens his sweater.

'All right then. Lead on, Macduff.'

It'll come to nothing. It isn't the sort of thing you can try for. It comes, or it doesn't. But who is he harming? It costs him nothing to visit her.

He follows Jack up the stairs to the attic.

Netty is sitting up in her bed with a nightdress and cardigan on, her hair combed and her face pink with scrubbing.

'You're looking better than you did when I saw you last, Mrs C,' Tim says.

'I'm doing my best to get it on the run, Tim.' She makes her big eyes at him. 'I think I'm all right to get up and out of bed today. If you could see your way to . . . ?'

'Don't say another word, Mrs Clifford. Not one word. We have a perfect understanding, don't we?' He unbuttons his cuffs, stooping against the sloped ceiling of the room. He's never stopped being amused by the Clifford peculiarity: a great house like this, and they stash themselves up in the servants' quarters like scullery maids. 'Your wish is my command and I am here to serve.'

Netty smiles weakly and Tim helps her get up, pretending not to hear the tell-tale crackle of the mackintosh sheets on the bed as she gets out of it. He holds her elbows and lowers her into her chair. She weighs practically nothing — he could carry her with ease — but still he goes slowly, and Jack hovers, managing both to remain utterly silent and to fuss around them until Tim is tempted to bat him away like a bluebottle.

'Right you are, Missus.'

With Netty settled, her head dropping forwards and her eyes half closed — stoned out of her mind, she'll be, on the poppy juice — he moves behind her, kneels on the linoleum and clasps his hands over her abdomen.

'I'm ready,' Netty says, and giggles. 'Ready for anything.'

Tim pulls his hands towards himself and feels Netty whimper and squirm at the pressure against her swollen gut. It can't be pain. She's on so much morphine these days he could probably cut her in half with a knife and fork and she wouldn't notice. Jack is standing at the door with his arms folded, just daring him to stop — his glaring is burning a hole in the back of Tim's head. She stinks. It isn't pleasant to say so, but she does. Underneath all that rose and lavender and lily of the valley there is something else — something rotten, like a bad tooth or a wound gone septic. He turns his head, tries to breathe through his mouth, and pulls.

'Do you feel anything, love?' Jack asks.

'Oh yes,' Netty says, dreamily. 'It's running right through me. Like a current. Like a river. It's lovely, Jack.'

Tim could tell him to shut up. Could get right

261

up and push him out of the room and lock the door and make some claim about needing privacy and silence in order to work. He could say Jack's fretting and hanging about was putting him off. What would Candy say? Disrupting the air with bad energies? Something like that. He can say what he likes, he always has, but the locked doors suggest Jack knows something (and he can't catch what it is — he's usually good at being able to dig out things like that, but the man is a blank to him) and he's pushed his luck here hard enough.

'That's good, Mrs C. Just you sit quiet now, eh?'

He closes his eyes and strains — though at what, he doesn't know — and feels nothing at all. He waits for — hopes for — the heat to gather in his hands, his tongue to prickle, the usual stinging sensation (unpleasant, it is, and nearly painful) to begin in his wrists and finger-tips, at the small of his back. But there's nothing. He applies more pressure and Netty yelps, leans forward in her chair and gags. Vomit splashes onto the lino.

'Let it out if you need to. We're old hands at this now, aren't we? Nothing to be embarrassed about,' Jack says.

Tim rests his forehead against the back of the chair. A fucking performance. He's faking, he knows it, and Jack knows it too; but he has to carry on the show now, out of hope and kindness and the knowledge that his stash of money is all but gone and he's not likely to find a landlord as flexible as Jack again. He tries again, and waits for the throbbing of the veins at his throat and temples to become painful. But once more, nothing.

'Don't hold back, Tim. Don't worry about me. Strong as a horse. Get it. Get it on the. On the run.'

Can she tell that there's nothing doing? He's always been curious about what being on the receiving end of these hands of his feels like. It must be a strong sensation: his patients blush and shudder and flap about. He's seen the hairs on their arms lift up like the temperature in the room has dropped to freezing in the space of a heartbeat. It drives them a bit mad. Even our Jack here, the daft gink, is half in love with him because of it. The missus is crying.

'Shall I clean the floor?' Jack is tentative, his voice low and sober. Tim withdraws his arms and sits back on his haunches.

'I'll stop for a minute,' he says, 'give her a rest.'

The room doesn't smell like vomit — not like the thick, rancid stuff she normally brings up into a bucket in the afternoons. And thank Christ for that. But then again, over the last few days she's eaten nothing, not even soup. The skirt of her nightdress is wet and there is a puddle of water on the lino between her feet.

'How are you getting on, Mrs Clifford?' Tim raises his voice. You have to, now. Sometimes she's so out of it you have to shake her awake to get an answer out of her, or bellow your question into her ear, as if she's at the other end of a long-distance telephone line.

'Salt,' Netty says, and Tim doesn't know what

she is talking about — whether she is signalling an observation, or a craving. Illness causes them sometimes. There was a woman back in Stockbridge who'd lost a baby and spent the months afterwards scraping plaster off the walls in the cupboard under the stairs and eating it, her useless milk weeping from her nipples and running down her slack belly. He could do nothing for her. Her husband brought her sticks of chalk to chew on, asked Tim if it was all right, and, short of anything else to say or do, he'd promised the man there was probably no harm in it, if that's what she really wanted. They'd given him a car, just for that, though he'd lost it a month later in a game of darts.

Netty retches again. She brings up more water — a great amniotic gush of it. It is seawater. It can't be, but it is. The fishy, muddy smell of the bay is unmistakeable in the stuffy attic room. There is sand, too, wet and grey — Netty leans forward and spits between her knees and grains of it crunch between her molars.

Fuck.

'Netty?'

That's Jack, hanging back and afraid to touch her but she can't answer him anyway. She only groans helplessly and retches again, another rush of brine, thickened with sand and silt, some tiny grey pebbles and broken pieces of cockleshell and finally, a long, muscular string of dark, bubbled seaweed — bladder-wrack, it is — which she plucks from between her lips, tugs out of her throat and flicks away.

Tim gets up and turns from her, walking

264

around the chair. Fuck. Fuck. Fuck. His mother, catching him twirling back the hands on the kitchen clock one morning, his hands in his pockets (she'd tried to shake the truth out of him but he couldn't tell her how he did it — was even less able to describe why he'd want to), had warned him about himself. *You'll attract attention*, she'd said. *End up in the big house, if you're not careful.* Or worse. (She'd pointed meaningfully at the floor with her thumb, the universal sign language of mothers all over the country for the destination that dare not speak its name: *the bad fire*.) Was she right? Had he attracted this to himself? Were his antics worse than playing with fire or drinking the water out of the taps in public toilets? And had he infected Netty with something much worse than the malignancy that was galloping through her system and devouring her?

She whimpers and spits. The fluid — more than is possible to fit in her stomach, even if Jack were in the habit of feeding his sick wife water dredged up from the channel — runs over the uneven floor and soaks into the rug that covers the cracked lino by the side of the bed. Tim steps aside quickly, superstitiously, but it hasn't touched him. He feels contaminated anyway: the nearest he ever liked to get to the sea were the Leith bars where he'd meet his sailor friends and ply his other trade. And now here he is, washed up in a place that's all sand and water, locked into a house with a woman puking up the fucking ocean. He wipes his hands on his trousers, checking his shoes for spots. His knees

265

are rattling and he's glad he's not got on his slim-cut trousers today or the both of them would see it.

'It's all right, Netty.' Jack's doubt is audible. 'Nothing to worry about.' He turns to Tim. 'I'll pop down and get a fresh nightdress, shall I?'

Tim nods. Netty retches again. Jack glances at Tim fearfully then leaves, closing the door quietly behind him with something like relief. Can't blame him for locking him into the house. Tim wouldn't want to be here on his own with her either, running up and down the stairs with buckets of water and clothes. It's like having a baby in the place, and Jack here gets to be mother and washerwoman. Netty gets through two or three nightdresses a day. Candy collects some of the laundry and takes it away to her flat where she boils it up in a Baby Bunco on long loan from the Women's Union. She'll do shirts for Jack, towels and sheets, and Annette's clothes too. But she won't do a thing for Tim. On principle, she says. *The idle get can fend for his self.* He hasn't had fresh sheets on his bed for weeks now.

'Tim, love? I'm so sorry, Tim. Please.' Netty's face is pinched and her eyes bloodshot, wide with shock. She follows him around the room with her gaze and only then does he realise he is pacing. 'Was that the treatment working?' Her voice is so raw and broken, either with hope, or the vomiting, that Tim can't stand to listen to it. Can't bear to feel her eyes sucking the life out of him for one minute longer. 'Is that it all out now?'

He doesn't answer. He pulls open the door. The girl is waiting behind it, her head on one side, dark, uncombed hair falling over her face. How long was she there without him knowing? Could he blame her for eavesdropping? He couldn't, he decided.

'Your mother needs a hand.' He passes her on the landing without stopping. Netty is calling him, screaming now, and near hysterical, but he takes the stairs downwards two at a time, leaping into the hallway. 'Mop and bucket,' he calls over his shoulder. And look — here's Jack in the hallway with a blue and pink nightdress draped over his arm. Tim advances on him.

'Key.' He makes a fist. 'Give me the key. Open the fucking door.'

Jack tries to protest, but Tim takes another step forward, as if to emphasise the height difference between them. There is heat in his hands now, all right, and he wonders what would happen if he were to reach out and put them around Jack's neck. Clamp a palm over his mouth or rub his thumbs over the man's thin, putty-coloured lips? There was no way to tell — no way to predict it. Hadn't he warned them about that? He had. They couldn't blame him for it being exactly as he said it would be.

'You can't leave her in this state. We had . . . we had a deal.'

The word 'deal' hangs between them. Is embarrassing.

'Deal? This is what you get when you sign me up to a deal, pal. This,' Tim gestures towards the ceiling, 'is what you get when you lock me up and force my hand. Did I not say? Did I not say?'

Tim flexes his fingers once, twice and Jack twists the nightdress between his fists.

'What choice did I have? You do it for me, don't you? You dare do it for me and not for her? What else was I supposed to do? What would you do?'

This is a question Tim cannot answer. Is singularly incapable of — forcing himself into the ordinary shoes of an ordinary human being and guessing, constricted in this way, what he might make of the experience.

'Give me the key.' Tim raises his hands, not to hit the man, but to show him his palms, show him he's in no danger if he'll just . . . but Jack, seeing the slim fingers and neat fingernails approach him, drops the nightdress, fishes in his back pocket and produces the key. Tim is out of the door in a shot.

'You'll come back, won't you? All your things are here. Your clothes. You can't just — '

Tim lets the door slam hard behind him and sets off running. Annette does as she is told and starts to run the hot water into the mop bucket. We are torn. He gets as far as the duck pond while she's still looking for the Omo and while she is dragging the bucket up to the attic, sloshing water and wetting the stair carpet as she goes, he is turning off the main road and finding, over a stile and a grey stone wall, the path that leads fell-wards through Eggerslack Woods. Annette struggles with the bucket and Netty calls for him (we know it is always for him and never for her — we know that, we do know that now, we get the picture much better now) and Tim clambers over the stile in his second-best trousers. He trips over the tree roots in the path. The chill of the approaching winter hangs in the still morning air.

23

We're still alone. But what can we do? Only cast our attention wide, across the fells and down to the little house with the fairy lights in the window, the one with the gravel drive and the box hedge in need of a little attention.

Annette sits in this house on a comfortable sofa, trying not to get blood on the upholstery. They're talking to her — Eve, and Maddy — but though she's stopped shivering she can't take in what they're saying to her. They come into and out of the room with hot water bottles and bowls of soup that she can't eat. She dozes, dreams about birds and storms and floods, and wakes as they are conferring in whispers in the kitchen. Social services won't help. The woman obviously isn't homeless. She isn't seriously ill. A GP might come and see her, but there's no chance they'd actually section her and take her away unless she was actively trying to hurt someone, or herself.

We sit on the carpet with our backs against the nice fitted bookcases and watch Annette drift back off to sleep. It's like she's trying to find her own no-time, dark-time, her own silence — it's like she's trying to go to the place we were in before she came back to the house and jangled us back to the trees.

It's Maddy who gets Annette speaking first. She used to be a nurse and she's seen this kind of thing before. The glassy-eyed wonder of those who walk away from car accidents unscathed. In the late afternoon while Eve is out collecting Tom from school, she brings a tray with a bowl of warm water, a glass of orange juice and dressings for the woman's hands.

'I know Eve patched you up a bit. But if it's not done properly you're going to really suffer. You ever seen a proper wound infection? No, you won't have. It isn't pretty. It's the surgery or me and I'm right here so it might as well be me. Are you going to let me help you?'

Annette nods. Maddy closes the curtains and unbuttons the woman's filthy dress. She's brought clothes for her: a shirt of Eve's, some jeans that would probably fit.

'Is the pain very bad?'

Annette nods again. Maddy has put a box of aspirin on the tray and she gets up to fetch it. Annette needs help with the blister pack and handling the glass of orange juice. More than a bit of this, Maddy thinks, is the tail end of a hangover. The stranger still smells of alcohol.

'Your head hurt?'

'A bit.'

Maddy nods briskly. 'So you can speak. Well, drink that juice slowly. It'll make you feel better. When did you last eat?'

No answer. Maddy purses her lips and turns her attention to the woman's hands.

'Let's get this done, then you can have a proper meal. Soak up some of that booze. Eve thought you had hypothermia, you know. You're lucky not to. You scared the shit out of her.'

She unwraps the makeshift bandages. Annette

winces as they peel away from her raw skin, and winces again as Maddy eases her hands into the bowl of water. Maddy's thinking about Tom and about how Eve is going to explain this to him — is probably explaining it to him right now, in the van on the way back to the house. And what is he going to think about coming home to find the junk room being turned into a guest room, a stranger holed up in it without explanation? Because that is what is going to have to happen here. Eve has left the decision to her, Maddy realises. She sniffs. This woman smells as if she'd been living in a hedge and there's something, even disregarding the circumstances of her arrival, there's something just *odd* about her, and Tom is going to be unsettled and that's the last thing they all need, but . . . Maddy works in silence, patting Annette's hands dry, then gently presses the new dressings into place. She begins to bind them, first against one palm, then the other.

'Eve says there's no one we can ring for you.' It isn't a question, but the woman treats it as one. Raises her eyes to meet Maddy's. She's not crying, not quite, but there's sadness there all the same.

'That's right. I'm sorry.'

'No need for that,' she sighs. 'We've made up the spare room.'

Maddy wants to ask her what went on in her garden last night. Because if she was going to get boozed up and start hacking at stuff in this house, well, she could think again. But she presses her tongue against the roof of her mouth and swallows, hard.

'Eve will be back in half an hour. With Tom. She tell you about him?'

Annette shakes her head.

'Our little boy. Well, he's twelve now. Thirteen in a month.' Maddy smiles. 'We'll ask him not to bother you. But — '

'No,' Annette croaks. 'No, you mustn't do that. This is his house. I won't do . . . ' she seems to be groping for her words, as if they'd gone missing in the night. 'I won't do anything to upset anyone.'

'Good. That's actually what I meant, you know.' There's a brief moment of silence, during which Maddy examines Annette's face carefully. Her eyes are still glassy, but there's something else there too — some spark flickering. Yes, she'll be all right, Maddy thinks. And the two women understand each other. 'But I will tell him to let you rest. You look like you need it.'

Maddy pats at Annette's knee awkwardly then stands, bundling the dress up and holding it against her chest.

'Stay tonight. See how you feel. If you're here longer, you must feel free to help yourself,' she says. 'Tea. Coffee. Breakfast things. The cupboard over the kettle in the kitchen. You mustn't think of us like a hotel.'

'I don't. I wouldn't.'

'Good.'

Maddy takes the dress away into the kitchen to be washed. Annette hears the front door open and voices, arguing over something. Something about a lost letter, a signature, a cheque. Annette sinks back into the sofa, dumb and humiliated by gratitude, her palms throbbing. Later, she'll sit in the junk room Eve and Maddy will have to learn to call the guest room and she will think about the lodgers we took in over the years. About Mr Richardson's tricks (she'll never remember his first name, not now, not unless they wrote it down somewhere — and they won't have, she's sure of that) and how he must have looked like hope to her parents. Distraction, at the very least. Could she still find it in herself to blame them? She doesn't know.

24

The saying goes, if you stood in the middle of Grange, pointed a shotgun into the sky and fired it, the bullet would sail over the houses, the woods and the fields and land right at the top of Hampsfell, where the old hospice is. Tim runs after this bullet like the devil is after him. How does he know where to go? This guest, this foreigner, finding his way to the highest spot in the town?

We see now. Netty describing the route to him herself. We know she worried about her last remaining lodger; in her opinion he was too young to remain in a town like Grange for long without diversions.

Climb up and have a look at the view, you can see for miles — right out over the bay.

She was thinking wistfully about the bay walk she'd never made the time for and the view she'd not get the chance to gaze on again. And showing off, just a little bit. Her ego was hanging on. The hospice up top had been on the television last winter, the bad one, because the farmers had taken the chains down and sheep, their wide yellow coats clogged with frozen sleet, packed themselves inside, cheek to jowl, warming and saving themselves with their own mould-scented breath. Grange, on the telly. Netty couldn't help herself. Always the hostess.

He runs off his fear and his disgust and his

anger, shaking the heat out of his hands. He turns from the road into the woods. Most of the trees have already dropped their leaves and there's a thick black mulch underfoot. He slides and skids through water-filled ruts, climbing slowly upwards. The grey and white branches sway and creak; the only greenery is the dark moss and the damp ferns which spring away from us as we push by them and follow him.

The woods seem to last forever. He finds his pace and continues upwards, tripping over roots and slipping, sometimes, on exposed slabs of limestone, greasy with moss. All the while he is relishing the cold muddy smell of the first fresh air he's had in days. Netty is rotting; she stinks, and there was no way to cover it up any more. In the spring these woods will reek of bluebells, wild garlic and fox bitches in heat, but there's nothing in the air today except the scent of musty leaves and stagnant pools of rainwater. It's still early: a hard bluish light shines between the stripped boughs. The fell slopes steeply upwards, covered in close-cropped grass and heather. The sky is low and almost white. No one would put this on a postcard; no wish you were heres, come and breathe the sea air, it's splendid, a bit of this'll cure what ails ye! Bleak is the word for this place.

Tim knows (he just does) that Netty and Jack used to be regular walkers before they were married. He sees the way they'd come up here in the summer with canvas rucksacks full of sandwiches wrapped in greaseproof paper, boiled eggs and bottles of beer — like a pair of kids on an Enid Blyton adventure. Maybe it's what passes for taking a girl out in this bloody place. It is in this hospice, apparently, resting in the shade after their climb up Hampsfell, that Jack tells Netty about the dropping-apart house his parents have left him. He's got no idea what he is going to do with it. But he needs to tell her that he's thinking of moving away, looking for work somewhere else, though what, he doesn't know. It might be hard, he says, to carry on seeing so much of each other if he has to be somewhere else for work. He's thinking of going to a city, and feeling choked and lost whenever he does. Tim inserts himself into their most private time and watches, hungrily gobbling this most ordinary and untouchable thing.

'Do you want to go? Spread your wings a bit?' Netty is a Meathop farmer's daughter and has no plans to move away. She always describes herself as a right homebody and it is true: there isn't a bit of wanderlust in her. 'Only you could let the rooms out,' she says. 'You'd make enough to keep yourself on if you did it properly. And a wife. Kiddies too.'

She winks and he looks at her in surprise and delight and she stares back, fresh-faced and unembarrassed. Why should she be? She smiles, showing the gap between her front teeth. He wants, very much, to put his tongue into that gap.

'Kiddies, eh?'

She nods. 'If they come.'

Netty's hair is blowing about in the wind that, even in the summer, slices over the bay like a blade, hits the fell and races over its slopes, scouring it raw. Tim sees her pull a headscarf out from her pocket, put it on, and start to knot it up under her chin, trying to tuck the loose hair away. Jack wants to tell her to leave it, to let it blow about, to say that he likes her looking untidy, like she's just got out of bed.

'It'd be a lot of work to get the house ready,' he says. 'The bathrooms need doing. And there'll be cooking. Laundry.'

'We could send the laundry out,' she says. He notices that 'we' and smiles at her tentatively. She goes on: 'I've got a bit of money from my mam and dad. It's sitting in a Co-op account doing bugger all for nobody. I could put it towards the bathrooms.'

His nose is sunburned and the sweat on his face is making his glasses slide downwards. He takes them off and tucks them into his shirt pocket. Her outline blurs and his sight of her is reduced to the pale shapes of her face and hands and the bright yellow of her summer dress. The black and grey of her headscarf disappears into the wall behind her. He puts his hand on her knee and rubs the material of her skirt against her thigh. Tries not to squint.

'It would be nice to fill up those rooms again. It's been too quiet,' he says.

She nods, and parts her legs slightly. The thrill he feels then, in his guts!

'That's it decided then,' she says.

He is delighted, of course he is — and relieved too. He'd never even thought of getting the house to pay for itself; she'd come up with the idea, just like that, as if it were the most natural thing in the world. He'd been thinking if he wanted to keep on in Grange, available to see her, he'd have to get out on the sands, get someone to sell him a riddle and cramb and teach him how to use a jumbo. Him! With the sea-spray all over his glasses and no family history of that type of work, he'd probably end up drowning himself in his first week. But the house. The house! Of course. It could shelter and feed them both, as well as anyone else who came along. The woman was a genius.

'As soon as we can,' he says. 'Let's not hang about.'

She invites him to her aunt's farm for Sunday lunch. There's no mother and father to ask — she's been left on her own the same as him, but it would be nice manners to come and speak to what family she does have, wouldn't he agree? There'll be no objection — they've been looking to get shot of her since she left school. But they may as well do their bit to keep them on side. Doesn't he think so? Jack laughs. He does. He does! They climb the little metal steps up onto the flat roof and toast themselves with the last of the beer.

The woods start to thin, the ground a little easier to cover. Tim gets these glimpses now and again — he always has done — but this, the full kit and caboodle of someone else's history, it's never been like this before. His stomach lurches and he has to stop, lean against a lone tree, and spit. His mouth fills with saliva and he spits again. He's lost, he thinks, leaning there, his hands so numb he can't really feel the texture of the bark against his palm. He's lost, and is just a vacancy now — other people's thoughts and feelings and memories pouring into the gap where a man should be. He retches, wipes his mouth and carries on walking upwards. And still he sees.

★ ★ ★

When they were married, she gave up her job at the razor-blade factory and the two of them were in the house, full time. She gave the place its name, after the great big scraggy trees in the front garden. More businesslike than romantic, she was. A house isn't a home until someone's named it, she'd say, and if it feels like home, our guests will want to come back. They'll tell their friends. She turned the attic bedrooms into a little nest, just for them, and even when they filled up the place with lodgers and couples on walking holidays, they could still go up to bed whenever they liked.

Jack will always remember her laughing against the side of his neck, her bare feet finding his, her hands holding tight to his hips. It had been lovely. He'd expected things to settle down in the bedroom department: men always talked about the difference in willingness between girlfriends and wives, but the tales never seemed to apply to Netty and it went on being good between them right up until Annette came along.

They'd been married more than ten years, Netty approaching her mid-thirties, before the baby had arrived. It was almost a surprise. Netty had stopped mentioning her disappointment when her monthly visitor reported for duty, and Jack, who tracked the weeks and days privately, worried he might have been a jaffa. When he and Netty were out and about together he imagined other men looking at him sideways, and wondering what was wrong with him. Was it just imagining, or might there have been something to it? He'd want to shout sometimes, to declare loudly in crowded rooms that here was a man who knew how to fuck his wife, and did so often. It was such a relief when Netty eventually fell pregnant that he didn't mind the bedroom aspect tapering off a bit. It was natural enough; the pair of them living and working together. They were in each other's pockets and the only surprise was that it hadn't eased off earlier. You can't want what you already have, after all.

Tim sweats and skids in the mud and toils upwards, panting, more anger left to spend.

★ ★ ★

We can be at home with them too. Jack is easing the mop out of Annette's hands. He sends her down the stairs.

'Go and play. Stay out of the way, will you?'

Netty is back in her bed, tear-stained and angry, blaming him, of course, for sending Tim out of the house.

'What if he never comes back? What are we going to do then? How could you live with yourself if that was him gone, after we started to

281

make some progress!'

He shouts at her. 'He'll come back. Where else would he go? Who else'd be daft enough to put him up?'

'You've ruined it, Jack. You've gone and ruined it.'

Jack mops, chasing the salty water across the floor.

'I got a letter back from your consultant.' The letter — the long-awaited reply — is tucked into his back pocket. He retrieves it. Throws it on the bed. She doesn't reach for it. 'He says you can go back in. They won't give you the radium again but he's said a transfusion might help. Top you up. Give you some energy.'

Netty shakes her head. 'Not a chance. No need for it. Tim is helping me.'

Jack twists the mop. Rinses it. Twists it again and starts to go over the floor one more time.

'Yes, it looks like it too. Looks like he's really helping you.'

'He was, Jack. How would you know?'

'What harm would it do to go back to hospital for a bit?'

She only looks at him then, shakes her head and refuses to answer. If you're so stupid you don't know the answer to that one, she's saying, well then I'm not going to tell you. 'I'm not having someone else's blood inside of me,' she says at last. 'It's gruesome. I don't care if it's medical. If they do it all the time. It isn't right.' She shudders.

'You've no right,' he says, scraping the bucket across the floor. She winces at the noise, at his

282

raised voice. 'You've no right to decide that for yourself. You're my wife. You're — '

'I'm not going back. I am not going back in there. You're going to go out and find Tim and get him to come back and finish the job. Go and get him!' She's screaming now, her hands in her hair, her fingers outstretched.

Hysterics. This is what this is. He should slap her.

'You silly bloody cow, you're making yourself worse. Lie quiet!'

Jack clutches the mop handle and wonders if he is going to hit her with it, or put out the window, or swing it round his head and sweep the pictures off the walls like a maniac. He could laugh at himself. They've not had a proper ding-dong like this in ages. It wasn't allowed any more, somehow, even though she was winding him up now more than she ever had, and more than once he'd thought about belting her. Of beating this nonsense out of her once and for all.

'I won't lie quiet if I don't want to,' she says, and sweeps her arm at her bedside cabinet, knocking off a couple of water glasses and teacups. The pair of them watch them roll and shatter on the floor. It is wrong of him, he knows it, but he wants to get into bed with her there and then, pull off that horrible, sweat-stained nightdress she's wearing and push himself against her until there's no space between them. Get her hands and put them on his cock and make her do him whether she wants to or not.

Instead he fetches the brush and sweeps everything up. He mops. He dries the lino with

283

an old towel on his hands and knees. And when that is finished he loiters in the bedroom, tidying the bottles on her nightstand until she gives up and goes to sleep. He gets in with her then, and gently presses his forehead against the sharp ridge of her shoulder blade. He isn't certain of her any more and that's why the wanting has come back. You might not be able to want what you already have, but if a woman he's lived with since he was twenty-two years old can start dissolving from the inside out, her body eating itself, her stomach mysteriously discharging the contents of the bay onto her bedroom floor, then he doesn't have her at all. Maybe never has.

★　★　★

And here's Tim. He passes a hawthorn tree, thorny and leafless and grown crooked in the lee of the wind. There it is: the squat, square hospice appears on the flattened high point of the fell. To him, it's nothing much to look at; a little grey folly with a chain over the entrance to keep the sheep out. He approaches it slowly, calmer now and out of breath. Some place to make love to a girl: it's characteristic of Jack that he'd bring her here and make things harder for himself.

He's been a few days without his cigarettes and hasn't missed them much, but he fancies standing up there, on the roof, leaning against the railing and enjoying a good puff. So he leaps up the stairs quickly, the cold of the metal rail burning his palms. Only seven or eight feet off the ground, if that, but the wind is almost

284

enough to push him off his feet. He leans in and hangs on tight. There is an old viewfinder on the top, the names of the fells and peaks written down on a board attached to the railings. Tim ignores it, holds on and lets his eyes wander over the landscape. There's scrub, ferns and eyebright. Sheep shit, all over the place, and wide limestone pavements, the clints rent with fissures full of black pools of still water. Far away, the crack of a gun. Someone out rabbiting, perhaps. Or testing the theory about the hill being as high as a bullet can fly. The bay shimmers, brown and grey and silver, wet mud and sand-coloured ice.

He's going to have to do something. Find some way of getting money. Jack and Netty haven't got a pot to piss in. He was so sick of the pits, the factories, the farms and boiling sheds and fish markets. The shipping yards, the docks and railways and garages, all of that dirty-fingernailed, cloth-capped business. He'd tried them all. And the pubs and nightclubs, white jeans and Breton stripes, whizzing about on a nicked scooter, pilled up for an all-nighter and dancing like a madman. Arguments with his dad for looking like a poof. His mum crying because he'd broken the windows without touching them and wouldn't admit to it. Telling him to simmer down or get out. He is sick of the sex — having to do it with anyone who wanted it, for a roof over his head, for a meal, for a round of drinks or a lead for a job or a train ticket or because — most of all — there didn't seem to be a good enough reason to say no. As if the effect he had on people (if he is honest, the effect he wanted to have on people, found useful to have on people sometimes) was his responsibility. As if he had to give them what they wanted because something about him made them want it.

He had toyed with the idea of facing up to this, whatever it was, this charm of his. Getting in control of it. Setting up a clinic, maybe. He'd be able to charge what he liked. A travelling surgery. People like him were common in some parts of America. Unremarkable. He could go there. The newspapers would get involved. Probably even the television. He could fake what he couldn't control and beef up the showmanship of the thing. Girls fainting and shaking, people talking nonsense and rolling their eyes into the back of their heads. He'd seen a documentary about a man who drove a Cadillac around from town to town, casting out devils and curing women who couldn't get pregnant. The man had one of those brains that could record everything and when nobody wanted healing, he'd stop off at a casino and count cards at the blackjack tables until he'd won enough cash for a change of air. It was classless and gaudy and Tim wanted such things to be beneath him, but it would be easy enough to do. He could earn enough to pay people to help him out. Stooges on their own cut.

The wind up here is something fierce: it rips at his hair and tugs at his jacket and he shivers violently and knows this American life he is planning for himself is as improbable and ridiculous as the Morningside wife, three sons, fur coat and gilded sugar bowl he'd sketched out when he first caught sight of Jack's house.

And he's no doubt, even now, that if he asked Jack and Netty for The Sycamores, everything in it, the rights to their daughter and the contents of their diminishing, if not already emptied bank accounts, they would give it to him. Probably thank him for taking it off their hands on their way out of the door, carrying nothing, owning only the clothes they stood up in. He could do that. It was only a step away from what he was doing already, wasn't it? He rakes his eyes over the fields and scrub, limestone pavements and juniper bushes, the grey slate roofs and white houses down in Cartmel, the nobbies churning back and forth across the bay, the tractor working over the soil towards Humphrey Head, and beyond it all, Howgill Fells, Bowland Fells, Clougha Pike and, if he squinted and let his mind and eye wander, the uneven hazy shapes of Walney and Piel. He could ask for this and that and that and he'd probably get it all, eventually.

Tim lifts his hands from the railing at the edge of the hospice and stares at them. He is not, he decides, fully human at all. There's something missing in him if this unpredictable and entirely ungovernable talent of his can rise up in him at a moment's notice, and then ebb away without warning. Jack's wife is dying in front of him — she has days, if that — and because of that, Tim has no right to fret about how frightening it is to be able to put your hands on someone and fix them. He can still feel Gregson's rabbits squirming in his fists after he'd doosht the crate they were lying in. The loose click of their necks

287

breaking before their hot, oily-smelling bodies fell limp and dropped from his hands into the bucket.

If he were any sort of real man he'd be in charge of this — able to deploy the thing as and when he wanted. He wants to do something for them. He even likes them. In spite of himself, he does. He'd like to be able to click his fingers and sort it out — any half-decent human being would. But (he wipes his eyes) he's been stupid. As if a suit of clothes, even if it was a Brioni three-piece in dove-grey mohair (which was what he always wore in these fantasies of his) could ever cover up what is wrong with him. For the first time in his entire life, Timothy Richardson wants to do the right thing by himself and these people. The most honest and decent thing. And he has no idea what that thing might be.

★ ★ ★

It takes Tim another two hours to pick his way slowly down from the fell and back into town. He walks slowly, wearily. But with purpose. The haberdasher's shop is open and the bell on the door rattles as he enters. He's muddy: his Daks damp nearly to the knee and his Barkers ruined. His hair is greasy and he stinks, he knows, of stale sweat. But he waits at the counter smiling until the old man appears from the back room. It will be all right. This will work.

'I'll need suiting, please. The best you have. Charcoal, or navy blue. Wool, I think — worsted or twill. Let me have a look at them unrolled first. Trim and buttons — horn, if you have them. Thread. And lining for the jacket.' What was that Jack had said about the tie? He said a blue one was most useful, didn't he? 'If you have silk, I'll have four yard of it, eggshell blue. Make it five, actually — I'll need a bit for the pockets and waistband, won't I?'

The haberdasher is writing all this down in a little notebook, his eyebrows rising a bit with each new order. Canvas and horsehair for the lining in the front of the jacket, more buttons for the trousers — button fly, they are going to be, with even more little black buttons on the waist-band for braces. Blue ribbon to edge the inside pockets with. Something subtle, in the same shade as the lining. The haberdasher lays the things out on the counter, pointing out differences in qual-ity, recommending certain threads and chalks, offering to throw in two best thimbles and a packet of Singer needles for free. Twelve guineas, it comes to. Tim takes a breath and turns a violent smile on the man, a smile so brilliant that the poor gadge stops in the middle of his calcula-tions, his mind quite emptied. The pencil falls from his hands and rolls over the counter to come to rest against the package of neatly wrapped material.

'I won't be paying for this right now, you understand. What I'll do is write down an address to which you'll send the bill. I'll do it now.' Tim sees a flash of doubt in the old man's misted eyes. He picks up the pencil from the counter and takes an empty paper bag from the pile next to the till. 'You'll let me take all these things away and get started, and you'll make out the bill, with a little extra in respect of your trouble and service, and you'll send it here.'

Tim leans over the counter and makes a show of writing extravagantly on the paper bag with the pencil, really flourishing. He writes like a child who can't form the letters yet but has seen others do so and is curious about the magic trick — a line of loops and spirals, some jagged marks that look like teeth, or birds flying in formation. Nonsense. It's just pretend. He hands the bag to the old man, who turns it over and inspects it curiously, with no sign that what he sees is anything other than a respectable local address. Tim collects his parcels. Nods his thanks and waits for the man to come out from behind the counter and open the door for him.

'It'll get there all right?' the man says. He speaks quietly, as if in a dream. 'The bill will arrive safely?'

'Safe as houses,' Tim says. 'I guarantee it.'

He goes back to The Sycamores to start on the new suit. Whistling.

25

Today Eve and Maddy take Tom out to do the Christmas food shop and when the house is empty, Annette comes down from her room and sits in the armchair near the fire with the view of the front garden. She is sitting there with her damaged hands in her lap, watching the snowfall and thinking about nothing, when the van draws up and they're home. Where did the time go? She stands up quickly, gathers her newspaper and teacup and turns to plump the cushion she has been leaning against. They have been nothing but welcoming to her, yet she likes to leave their rooms (the phrase *the communal areas* bubbles up from nowhere) without a trace of herself left behind in them.

She looks back out of the window: before the van has fully come to a stop Maddy opens the passenger door and leaps out. Eve parks, opens her door and helps Tom to climb down. He jumps out and skids on the gravel, sliding about in it until Maddy turns and instructs him — Annette can tell — to stop arsing around and get into the house before he freezes to death. Maddy is gesticulating at Eve too: pointing at the house, and at herself, and at the house again, her mouth going ten to the dozen. Annette can't hear what she's saying, but she knows enough to tell that the pair are having a blazing row. She takes a step back. Not quite hiding, but allowing the curtain to obscure her shape in the window.

In the middle of her tirade Maddy stops to take a breath and Eve steps forward and grasps Maddy gently by the shoulders, looks into her face, and kisses her. A proper kiss, and sod the neighbours, and sod Tom too, who is looking at Annette through the window, utterly disgusted by his parents. He raises one eyebrow. She smiles at him. Waves, now he's seen her. He shakes his head and pretends to stick one finger down his throat, providing what is to Annette's mind an Oscar-worthy performance of a boy lavishly vomiting into the flower beds. It is some kiss, and when it ends, Maddy is still frowning, but soon bursts into laughter before resuming the pointing — continuing to talk about whatever has upset her, but with less energy now. Annette smiles at Tom then quickly moves away from the window so they won't come in and see her pressed against it, peeping at their private moments. Tom comes into the house first, shouts hello to her then, before she can reply, thunders up the stairs, tracking mud and grit through the hallway. Annette can't blame him for making himself scarce.

Once, after they'd moved into the glass and brick bungalow, Candy had remarked on something or other on the news about a change in the law concerning men who lived together as if they were married. That's how she phrased it — mindful of Annette's impressionable ears, no doubt. She was old-fashioned about it. Candy and her dad had been sitting on the settee, her father with a glass of whisky balancing on the arm, Candy's stockinged feet in his lap. Annette can't remember Candy's exact words, but she remembers her father's response. He hardly ever shouted, but that day, he did, and tipped his glass and spilled his whisky on the wall-to-wall and said he wouldn't have name-calling in the house, wouldn't have her casting aspersions on people who weren't any different from them, and even if they were, well whose business was it anyway, so long as everyone was happy and no one was being harmed, and didn't she think lads of that persuasion had things hard enough without someone like her, someone who'd faced criticism herself, pitching in and chucking oil onto the fire? It had been quite a showing. Annette had been shocked — bent over her homework at the kitchen table, pretending not to listen — and Candy even more so.

Something strange had happened then. She'd been working on maths homework. She doesn't remember what the task was — something that involved a compass and a protractor and a row of black-and-yellow-striped pencils she'd sharpened and lined up next to her exercise book. Candy had a rule — she had to do her homework the very night it was set. No leaving things to the last minute in *this* house, she said. Annette had stared at the pencils and tried to pretend that the argument wasn't happening, and they had slowly rolled away from her and dropped off the edge of the table. It was a new table, with chrome tubes for legs and a smoky glass top, and it probably wasn't level, and she wouldn't have thought about the pencils at all

— hadn't thought about them from then to now, not really — except that Jack had looked at her sharply, then at the pencils on the carpet, and Annette had caught something in his expression. She wanted to say, 'They're only pencils. I didn't do it on purpose,' but she understood, for the first time, that saying that wouldn't exactly be the truth. She kneeled to pick up the pencils, letting her hair swing over her face and hide her from Jack's gaze.

Candy didn't notice. She had removed her feet from his lap, tucked them under her and touched her lips with her knuckles. She huffed and tutted and said something about her not being able to predict the day when she wasn't even able to express an opinion in her own house, and if Jack wanted a mindless housewife to wash his socks and look pretty and go about with soap bubbles between her ears, he should have married one, but seeing as he hadn't he should take a good long look at what he did have, and consider himself bloody lucky to have it, because if he didn't, other men would. Then Jack had gone to get a tea towel for the carpet and refilled his glass and brought Candy in a little glass of her own, and sat back down, and she'd put her feet back in his lap and he'd curled his hand around her calf and they'd changed the channel to watch something less inflaming, Jack still glancing at Annette now and again, as if the set-to was her fault and he was scared of her.

The conversation had never come up again. It was something and nothing. All couples argue, Candy had said later. It doesn't mean anything.

Doesn't mean that they don't love each other, and didn't love her. Annette only thinks of it now because she sees her teenage self at the table letting her hair fall around her face like a shield while the brief argument flared around her, and remembers that in the seconds before the pencils had started to roll, very slowly, across the table and then off its edge, she'd silently wished for Mister Richardson to amble in, hands in his pockets. He'd make a joke, and Candy and her father would laugh, and once he had them laughing he'd start in with one of his tall stories, or engage them all in some ridiculously complicated game that of course he would win.

Maddy comes into the house first, a loaded carrier bag in each hand. Annette has been in the habit of keeping to her room when the family is home, not wanting to get in the way, but as she edges towards the bottom of the stairs Eve appears right behind her, carrying a box and closing the door with her foot.

'Let me take some of these,' Annette says, without planning to. Eve tries to wave her away, but she insists. The box is heavy and awkward, filled with things from the supermarket, but it is easier on her hands than the carrier bags would be, and she manages it as far as the kitchen table. Maddy fills the kettle and urges her to sit. They've been arguing about me, Annette thinks. And now they're going to say it's time for me to get back to my own house, and that my hands are in good enough nick now for me to start looking after myself, and this was never supposed to be a long-term arrangement and isn't it about time I started thinking about what my next move is going to be?

'I know what you're going to say,' Annette begins, folding her hands together and hiding them in her lap.

'You can settle something for us,' Eve starts, and Maddy sighs and starts unloading tins and packets. 'We're still not fixed about this school trip he's going on. I've had a bit of a change of heart. He's not far off thirteen. That's not too young. But Maddy says — '

'Maddy says nothing!' she breaks in. 'Maddy can speak for herself!'

'It's not like we can't afford it.' Eve has a packet of dates in one hand, and a bag of satsumas in the other. 'Look at this lot. Disgusting amount of food. And just for the four of us.'

The four of us. Annette grins in relief. Can't help it.

'We don't have to decide for ages,' Maddy says. 'They don't want it paid until March. There's bags of time to — '

'To ruin Christmas arguing about it?'

They turn to Annette, exasperated, searching for a referee.

'We can't compromise. He either goes, or he doesn't.'

'Well,' Annette begins slowly. 'There's no need to ruin Christmas. I knew someone who always thought a disagreement should be solved in one of two ways. The first,' she has their attention now, 'well, the first would be a card game. Ladies' choice. And in this case . . . '

Eve is laughing. 'I'm not playing cards with her. She cheats!'

'I do not.'

'Well, if cards are no good, there's only one thing for it.'

Eve and Maddy smile. 'What?'

'You're going to have to get out there and settle it the old-fashioned way. Three rounds each. I'll hold your coats.' Annette remembers the way he had — Richardson — of raising one eyebrow in a way that meant you were never quite sure if he was joking or not. She tries it. 'Off you go. Out in the garden. I've heard some people find the method very effective. I'll ask Tom to fetch the first aid kit.'

Eve and Maddy are laughing now, Eve's arm around her waist. 'God, are we that bad? Sorry, Annette. You must think we're awful.'

Annette nods sadly. Tries a Richardson-style voice, which comes out sounding a little like Maggie Smith's Brodie.

'Absolutely terrible. In fact, I've a good mind to contact the authorities.' She stands to leave — to clear out and get out of their way. It must be no fun for them, having her cluttering up the place when they're trying to get the shopping unpacked. But then she remembers *the four of us*, and because they have the kettle on, and are making a whole pot of tea, she stays.

26

We're there where we shouldn't be, or where we should always have been, watching the little girl who is sitting up in bed quietly listening even though it is past midnight. We see now she is used to being woken in the night by her mother's wails and moans. She rocks gently, imagining she's in a boat and the boatman is silent, but kind, and ferries her wherever she wants to go and where she wants to go tonight is backwards, to being three, and not having to go to school and being allowed to suck your thumb. She screws her feet into fists so tightly she gives herself cramp. Once Mum told Dad that the pain she felt on nights like this was like the worst cramp she'd ever experienced, worse than childbirth, even, which meant her, because there weren't any other children.

(Henet! Henet!)

There's a racket in the next room. Is Mum trying to say something? A chair is pushed across the floor. Dad has started sleeping, not in the bed, not on the floor next to the bed, not in a bed in a different room, but in a chair next to Mum's side of the bed. He keeps a bowl on his knee and strokes her head when the cramps that her body has make her be sick.

It isn't the mumps she's got because her face hasn't gone big.

(Henet!)

The door opens and closes. Dad's footsteps hurry down the stairs. We watch as Annette bites her thumb and imagines the blood running away and her fingernail turning white in the dark. On nights like this Dad often goes to get Mister Richardson. She's seen him pull Mum's nightie right up, looking where he should not look, and push his hands on her belly as if he is trying to put his fingers right through her skin. Dad must think it is going to help her stop making so much noise. Why else would he wake him up in the middle of the night? Dad will kneel by the side of the bed and Mister Richardson will put his hands on Mum and the three of them will stay there like that, Mum's hairy legs writhing around on the bed, until she falls asleep, sometimes with a bit of sick leaking out of the side of her mouth and blood on the bed sheets. Mister Richardson is not a doctor and Annette knows, because they almost always close the door tightly behind them (there is a crack though — she has seen so many things through that lighted gap!), that in watching these things she has looked where she should not look too.

We wait with her, gathered in the bedclothes, patting her arms and hands uselessly in the dark. We examine her entirely, noting the bruise on her shin and her unbrushed teeth and the dirt under her fingernails. And still we wait with her, pushing our fingers through the knots in her hair and laying our hands against her rib cage as she holds her breath. She listens. And we wait with her, listening to the whole house shudder as Dad thumps his way up the stairs and sure enough

Mister Richardson is with him. They are muttering. Mister Richardson is in a bad mood. Maybe he has to get up especially early tomorrow or maybe he was in a very deep sleep having a nice dream about riding a horse or going on holiday to a hot place, with a beach and lemon trees. She waits, sitting up with the blankets gathered around her shoulders like a cape, and listens to Dad usher him into the bedroom.

There are no more sounds for a while. She doesn't think the pelican is going to come back tonight but she reaches under her pillow and brings out her special things anyway. They are, one: a thimble, two: a scrap of white cotton, three: a worn triangle of blue dressmaker's chalk. She has lots of things from the other lodgers tucked inside an old jumper at the back of her dresser but none of those things are as powerful as these are. She puts the thimble on her thumb and wraps the scrap of material around her fingers and rubs the chalk gently against her top lip. It smells powdery and dry; it tastes like nothing. She rubs and smells and thinks about Mister Richardson until she feels better, then she uncurls the material from around her fingers and places all three special things under her pillow.

Tonight is much worse than the nights before it. Mum keeps making these noises. The bottles and glasses on the nightstand clatter as if they are being knocked over, maybe by Dad who is trying to rearrange her pillows or take away the dirty sheets (one of the most amazing things Annette has seen recently is the nurse changing

Mum's bed linen with Mum still in the bed!) or perhaps Mum was moving about and knocked it over herself.

Dad and Mister Richardson forget to whisper, and start to argue. Dad shouts at Mister Richardson to do something, do it right now, before the morning! And Mister Richardson tells him it's too late, that he's tried already, over and over again he's tried, and he's asking Dad to call the doctor, or the night nurses, or to do something. It's not too late to call the doctor. It's not. You're allowed to call the doctor in the middle of the night. That noise Mum is making is going on and on and on, her voice going in and out, up and down, just like the sea, and they argue over the noise of it, sometimes in their normal voices, and sometimes in funny loud whispers that aren't really quiet at all.

Maybe she should get up and call the doctor. And the doctor should come very quickly and bring his bag and his stethoscope and also bring a barley sugar in his inside pocket and give it to her, when no one is looking, with a wink and tell her to be good. And after she's unwrapped the barley sugar and stored it inside her cheek the doctor should say that no doubt they'd be seeing improvements soon enough, which is what he said last time and was a very good thing to hear. She'd stroked the barley sugar with her tongue where it lay inside her cheek for a whole hour and felt better.

But she can't ring the doctor. She's not allowed to touch the telephone and even if she was, once she has been put in bed she is not allowed back up for any reason at all. No messing about on the landing, no asking for glasses of water, no turning the light on, no nothing.

We see her hand creeping back under her pillow to find the thimble.

She doesn't know what this disease is called that Mum has got or how she caught it. Maybe from the water in the lido. Or from walking barefoot in the park. Or drinking milk after it's been left out of the refrigerator. There are thousands of ways for a disease to get into your body and start wreaking havoc and most of them Do Not Bear Thinking About.

The illness itself is a creeping illness and its main symptom has been to make Mum's skin stop working. Everything that belongs inside: blood and sick and wee and number two and spit and some strange green-yellow stuff Mum leaves on the bed and on the back of her nightdresses sometimes, is coming out through her skin to the world outside where it should not be. And things that belong outside Mum's body, like thunderstorms, and heat waves, and holes full of soil, and the noise of boughs breaking, and the voices of neighbours who have died, and visits from distant relatives (overcoats and weekend cases and all!) who live miles away in Scarborough, all end up (Mum swears to it!) broadcasting as loud as a cinema inside her head when she's quite awake and definitely not dreaming. She hopes it is not catching. Candy says not but Candy does not know everything.

We press the blankets around her closely but she will not sleep and eventually she gets up. We watch as she swings her feet out of bed. She pads over the carpet to her bedroom door, and, without touching it, listens intently. Satisfied that Dad is not going to come out into the narrow landing at the stop of the stairs between their rooms or, even worse, open her door to check she is still sleeping, she goes back to the bed and kneels. We see that there is a brown paper bag under there and we notice her smile a little when her scrabbling fingertips find it. The half-loaf inside is still all right for eating, just about, she thinks. So she stands under the dormer window and in the light from the streetlamp outside we watch her as she picks the mould spots off the hunk of bread and eats the good parts. We learn now that she has a particular method for this. She ignores the crust and digs the fluffy soft innards out of the centre with her finger and thumb. This she rolls into a ball, then puts in her mouth to chew, slowly. Her stomach contracts with pleasure and she uses her tongue to press the gluey paste against the roof of her mouth. Then she leans her forehead against the coolness of the window, looks down at the garden, and waits for the bread to dissolve and the noises from next door to stop.

★　★　★

We don't want to irritate Tim or to disturb him while he is working. This is so important. We do understand that it is too late now. But all the same we wait and hope as the heat gathers in his hands — thank Christ! — but before he can

303

touch her she writhes away from him again and brings up the syrup Jack's just tried to force down her throat. His fingers are stinging — tiny electric shocks all over the skin — and he plants them on her but feels nothing. He may as well be up to his elbows in a bath full of tepid water and with all the noise and moving about going on he can feel it lifting off him.

Jack knocks over the bottle in his haste to get some more of the poppy juice down her throat and when Tim takes his hands off her to retrieve it before the whole lot decants onto the carpet Jack starts shouting and bawling at him as if all this that's happening is his fault. Not fucking working. Tim ignores him and lifts the bottle. The lid is away somewhere and the carpet where the bottle's been lying is sticky but when he holds it up to the light he sees what's left sloshing around in the bottom. It's thick. He moves the bottle from one hand to the other and licks his fingers. Three inches of the stuff. Maybe more.

'What are you doing?' Jack asks.

But Netty sees what he's doing. She sees it, right enough, and opens her eyes wide and reaches towards him for the bottle.

'What dose does she normally have?'

Jack throws himself into the chair beside the bed and shakes his head.

'She can't have it. She can't keep it down.'

'Do you no' think I've seen? How much does she normally have?'

Jack won't or can't answer so Tim looks at the various spoons and needleless syringes on the bedside table and finds no clue. Netty is starting to pant and wail again, snotters all over her face, her eyes flitting around the room as if she sees things that they don't. The noise she's making! The poor bitch can't help it, he knows that, but he has to breathe deeply and count to ten before he can focus on the bottle. It should have the dosage on the typed label from the chemist's but this bottle has been on the go for ages and the wear of handling and the stickiness from the spilled syrup has made the paper translucent, the writing invisible. She twists and turns and mutters through her dreams about birds and black mud. The room fills with the smell of the sea, as strong as music. It's us. Jack opens one of the windows.

'Help her,' he says.

The boy puts his hands in his hair and screws his eyes shut. Opens them, as if he's suddenly had an idea. Gropes in his pockets.

'Have you any money?' he asks.

Jack doesn't even think to argue, to ask why. Between them they have a small handful of change. The boy takes Netty's hand, pours the coins into it, closes his fingers over hers. 'Pay your sand pilot, Mrs C.,' he says.

We hold her hands. We pull. But she sticks fast. The Sycamores is a detached house, so there are no neighbours sharing a party wall to worry about. But all the same it's embarrassing to be making such a racket. She never made a fuss like this, not even when she was having Annette and swore blind to herself that if the midwife turned her back she'd get up and throw herself right out of the window. We pull again. We know in one more moment Netty will be past worrying about hypothetical neighbours and school cardigans (her knitting lies abandoned in her armchair — Candy will see to it in the spring) and where the money will come from and how Jack will manage if she isn't able to get back on her feet and fill the house up with lodgers again. And in the moment after that, the world and everything in it will shrink to this room, the edges made hazy with pain. She lies in her bed, twisting the damp sheets around her and hearing Jack shush her, as if from very far away.

Even in the — in the dark.

In the middle of the longest moments.

Noises —

— her own mouth and embarrassed.

She can — ?

Wet.

She's wet.

Hands turn her.

And when the moment passes she can open her eyes and there's the fringed shade on the bedside lamp. Needs dusting. And the roses all dancing up the walls and Jack — where's Jack? — there's Jack's hands on her head smoothing her hair back over and over again, too hard, and she's wet and there's someone else here — someone who? It's the boy. The good boy. His shirt is buttoned up wrong. Jack must have pulled him out of bed. The poor. The pain has a shape and here's the start of it. Jack holds her head steady. What's he doing? Fingers hooked into the corner of her mouth. Fish. Flukes for tea. And he's pulling until she opens wide and he forces her jaw. The boy's hands are rough and cool on her skin. He's saying something but the words don't reach her — something floats across her vision — the bird? No — the bottle — the syrup in the back of her throat makes her gag — that noise. She is making it — sick on the bed — the pain has a shape. With the fear of its arrival her feet scrabble the bed sheets. Little rabbit digging for a way out — rabbit pie? Got to get away — go home — Jack is not stroking her head. Holding her down — her hands.

The beautiful boy. Wet — she's wet. His face over hers — look at her — no — looking at her eyes.
Pulls up her nightie. And. Here it is.
He rubs his hands together. Spits.
It's not working. Push.
A ringing in the room.
It's not working. It
still hurts — it hurts
until it stops.
It stops.
Pull.
Stop.

★   ★   ★

She opens her hands and the coins fly away from her, glittering like stars.

27

Annette stirs in her bed and we go to her. Lean against the walls, waiting. She stays in bed for ages after it gets light but nobody is getting up so she gets herself up on her own. She goes down the stairs in her bare feet and checks the kitchen but there is no breakfast lying out like there sometimes is when Candy has been round. Candy does sometimes come early and brings porridge and sausages and reads bits out of the Bible while Annette is eating. She reads about a man who has a devil in him whose name is Legion. Enough of a devil to fill up a whole herd of pigs when it was cast out. A shoal or a flock of devils, moving from the poor man (who gets better as soon as Jesus touches him and says the words) into the pigs who know they have nothing better to do now than go and drown themselves.

We go with Annette as she opens the front door, which she is not normally allowed to do on her own. But Dad and Mister Richardson must be asleep and she wants to be ready and wait for Nurse. If Annette is ready at the front door she can let her in when she comes and she won't ring the bell and that means Dad and Mister Richardson won't wake up. She is being considerate. We watch as she waits on the front step between their two big nice trees. It is not too cold except on her feet and if she stands on one foot and then the other it isn't too bad.

Mum said to Aunty Candy once that the only way they've managed to get by these past few months is because Annette is good at entertaining herself. She is no real bother. She entertains herself now by counting people passing on their way to work and school, pushing prams and walking dogs, and spots the postman but he's not got anything for them today. We see her give him a big wave but he doesn't notice her. Like she's a ghost. She knows today is not going to be a school day. So she will carry on counting and make a wish and we will wait with her now for as long as it takes.

She has the thimble on the end of her thumb, tucked tight inside her fist where it can't roll away and get lost. She wishes that the very next person she counts is going to be Nurse. It's Dad's job to look after Mum during the day and during the night, which is very tiring even though Mister Richardson has been helping a little bit. It is so tiring it makes Dad want to have sleeps in the day so when he is sleeping in the day it is important not to make a noise and not to be a pain and wake him up. The hospital sends different nurses, not the same one every day, and seeing as she is wishing, she wishes for the best nurse, the one she likes the most, the coloured one. She likes her the best out of all the nurses that come because she's got an accent and she sometimes gives Annette mint imperials and saves the funny pages from her Sunday paper for her. She says: Annette girl don't hang around me or I will trip over you! but she doesn't mean it. She always laughs and gives her things to carry and lets her take away the little metal dish of cotton-wool balls after she's finished cleaning Mum's eyes.

Yesterday there was a sore place on Mum's leg from being in the bed for so long and the nurse did something amazing. She opened her brown bag and took out a bandage and a big pad and asked Annette to go and turn the oven on and find her a biscuit tin. Annette's not allowed to touch the cooker but if the nurse told her to then it must be all right; must be in the rules. So she did, and when the nurse came into the kitchen she opened the biscuit tin and put the broken ends of the biscuits in the bin and washed out the tin and dried it and then (Annette still can't quite believe this, even though she saw it with her own eyes) she put the bandage and the pad inside the biscuit tin and put the lid on and put the tin in the oven! When it came out it was boiling hot and the nurse had to hold the tin with an oven glove to get the lid off. But it meant all the dirt on the bandage had been killed and it was safe to use.

She doesn't know what the nurse's name is because everyone just calls her Nurse so Annette can't do a proper wish, one of the strong-working and long-lasting ones. Instead she goes out into the garden and collects all the spinning jennies from the path and the lawn and then throws them up in the air all at once. She blows them as they come down, making a sound like pattering rain and she says to herself please send the nice coloured nurse to come and wake my dad and Mr Richardson and also wake my mum up and get them all ready for a day out. It's a really long wish and she's got to say it exactly right seven times and if she makes a mistake, start again. She scoops up more spinning jennies and throws them, then while she is still wishing for Mum to get out of bed and be better and it not be a school day, the gate makes a noise and she looks up and there she is: the nurse that she wished for! She is wheeling her bike up the path and frowning like there is going to be trouble.

'What are you doing playing out here in your nightdress, Annette Clifford?'

We see her fasten the gate closed behind her and lean her bike against the house. Annette takes her hand and pulls her along the path and inside. We should wait in the garden. Should we wait in the garden? We don't know what else to do other than to follow, to come along and see the nurse stop to wipe her feet and put down her bag but — look — Annette keeps on pulling her until they get to the bottom of the stairs.

'Where is your father? Is he upstairs?'

Nurse undoes her blue coat and drapes it over the banister and goes into the kitchen, like she always does, to scrub her hands. When she's finished she doesn't let Annette hold her hand because they are clean now. Nothing else is allowed to touch them and she has to open the doors with her elbows or get someone else to do it, which is sometimes Annette's job when she is around and making herself useful.

'No one's thought to put the pan on, I see?' Nurse says, and clicks her tongue. One of the morning jobs is to get a big pan of hot water

311

ready because there are pipes going under the bed covers that help Mum not have to get up for a wee all the time and every day the pipes come out and get boiled in a big pan on the cooker so they are extra clean. It was the soup pan for when they had a houseful but they've no houseful now and they wouldn't want to use the pan for anything else now it's had the pipes in it anyway. We see Annette catch hold of one of the strings on the nurse's apron very gently and she doesn't tug so the nurse doesn't know she is hanging on. The nurse goes slowly, puffing a bit even though she's not fat like the other one, so Annette goes slow too and puts both feet together on the same step. It's a special walk as if she is a bridesmaid holding up the back of a bride's dress like at Princess Margaret's wedding with her lovely white head thing. She hangs on and follows her up the stairs past Mister Richardson's bedroom and up the second stairs to the attic rooms where they live.

'When did you last go to school, miss?'

Annette puts her fingers in her mouth and doesn't answer. We clutter the landing. Mum and Dad's bedroom door is open and Nurse sees Mum unmoving in the bed, no one helping her sit up or bringing the morning medicine, no one bringing bowls of hot water for washing and clean sheets for the making-the-bed-trick, no one even opening the curtains and saying hello to Nurse and asking her if she would like a cup of tea and maybe a piece of toast and marmalade. Mister Richardson is sitting in Dad's chair, his legs stretched out, fast asleep. His shirt is

312

buttoned up wrong and he's just got his pyjama trousers on. Dad is sitting on the floor leaning against Mum's bedside cabinet. He's fallen asleep too, which sometimes happens. They stay up too late talking or playing games and they have bad heads in the morning and Annette has to try and not be a pain. They're all sleeping and when people are asleep you're supposed to be quiet and not wake them up, especially if it is Sunday morning or very early any other morning. You're not supposed to clatter about and you're really not supposed to go into people's rooms and bang doors and swipe the curtains open and say,

'Mr Clifford. Mr Clifford! Why did you not call the doctor? Are you aware your daughter was playing in the street unsupervised!'

That is a lie! Annette was not playing in the street, she was wishing in the garden. She knows she is allowed in the garden, on the path and up to the gate but not beyond and not to swing on the gate or hang over it like a hussy! Even though it is not true, Nurse says that Annette has been left out on her own in the garden in her nightclothes and Mister Richardson stands up and finally Dad opens his eyes and gets up from the floor and Nurse turns around and quickly closes the door. Annette knows she is going to be in trouble so she goes down and into the back garden.

We go with her. The house is no place to be, today. The grass is cold and tickly under her toes. You've got to be careful because of the slugs and snails; you really don't want to stand on

313

them. There are no spinning jennies out there at the back so she blows a dandelion, which she is not allowed to do because blowing dandelion clocks makes more dandelions grow in the lawn and Mum doesn't like them and Dad doesn't like them and at school they don't even call them dandelions, they call them piss-the-beds because that is what happens to you if you pick them. But Annette hasn't peed in the bed for ages. No one is around to see what she is doing and there are no spinning jennies so she picks a dandelion clock and blows all the fluff off in one big go and the seeds all come apart and whizz about the garden and over the hedge and into next door and she chases them a bit and makes her wish out loud because the magic is bigger that way.

28

Annette shouldn't have woken us. The dark-time, the no-time, before she came back, was not like being asleep. There were no dreams. No sense of time passing, either slowly or fast. No events, desired or otherwise. No breath, no words, no laughter. No drip of the broken tap, or the upstairs indoor ivy shedding old leaves in faint brown whispers onto the floor. No frost, no bird's nests in the chimney, no creaking and doors opening and closing, and no waiting. Nothing at all until she came back and woke us. And this is a different morning, some time later. A key in the lock. We do know that sound. The key; the door opening; the creak of the boards in the hallway. We know it. We've been waiting for it.

But it's not. It's not. What's the word?

A woman — not our daughter, she's too quick, too brisk and heavy-footed to be Annette — bustles in, kicking through the fresh tide of free papers and flyers in the hall, slamming the door and frowning at the dust and mess around her. She pushes her glasses up her nose. A habit.

Christ. The state of the place. She said she'd cleaned.

This is Maddy, who in spite of her workload, the time of year and the unexpected imposition of the houseguest that no one asked her or even properly warned her about, has been the one to

315

make the time. To take action. To get the ball rolling. She moves through the downstairs rooms, clucking at the rotting net curtains and the dusty dining table. Coughs and sniffs: the damp. Is embarrassed (she will keep this fact to herself) to feel the tears start in her eyes at the sight of an old pink armchair Annette has obviously tried to clean with a scrubbing brush and a bucket of water. The fabric has torn itself into rags.

The woman puts her hands in her pockets and climbs the stairs, into the attic rooms, pulling open wardrobes and drawers and searching under beds for suitcases and boxes. We've no hidden treasure — we'd tell her, if only we could. We've given up trying to use our voices. Our new words are worthless here. Maddy is rough and quick, old envelopes tearing under her fingers, a pile of papers growing next to her where she kneels. She's not quite angry, but something like it. We catch it. The taste of it. *Not a hotel. Not tenable as a long-term solution. Practicalities to think of.*

She's glad Eve didn't bring Tom here. There'd been something nagging at her, she said. Something disturbing her sleep. Thank God Tom hadn't seen what Eve had: the dishevelled woman with blood on her skirts lying wet and shivering in her own front garden like a broken umbrella — no, like a sodden bird dropped out of its nest. How would she have explained this to him?

★ ★ ★

Maddy searches for an hour, not an ounce of guilt in her. Upstairs in the bedroom that used to be ours she finds another shoebox, jammed into the very back of a divan drawer along with a red blanket and a yellowed christening dress that falls into dust when she shakes it. The lid of the shoebox is tied down with red string and she works at the knot, feeling the pins and needles start to chew at her feet where they are tucked up beneath her. It's not prying. It isn't rooting into someone else's business. It's taking action. She's all for helping those less fortunate but there's the long term to think of. This is a bloody great house sitting here rotting and when you think about it in some lights it's immoral, is what it is. Their own spare room was meant for guests but destined for all kinds of junk. It's not as if they're overcrowded, but it wasn't what they were set up for.

The string is knotted in a few places and Maddy tugs at it, pulls at the lid, then finally slips it free. Inside there are letters. More of the same? She sighs. Most of what she's found so far has been useless. Photograph albums, old postcards, invitations, bills from grocers and butchers, records and rent books from when the place was a going concern. Names and amounts in old money, all noted down in smudged pencil. Jackson. Gravesend. Richardson. A right museum piece. There are birthday cards and Christmas cards too and even a set of old school exercise books filled with red pen and childish handwriting. These people weren't quite hoarders, the things were kept neatly and packed away in drawers and wardrobes, but

317

there was a bloody lot of it. She opens the envelopes. Typed letters. The old-fashioned logos of building societies and insurance companies. Account numbers and policy numbers, beneficiaries and — There's a sound at the window, a rap like a stone being thrown; she drops the letter and looks up. Nothing. Stands, looks out. The dormer is narrow. Black with damp in the corners. Bad for your chest. She holds her breath and looks through the glass and down along the crooked tiles to the clotted gutters. Birds, probably. She turns back to the letter. Sits on the sagging bed to read it, her thumb between her teeth.

Bingo.

★ ★ ★

We follow her back to her own house, where she lays out the letters on the kitchen table and starts with a confession.

'I didn't think you'd mind. You're not in a state to do it yourself, are you?'

She hands Annette her house keys and shrugs. Eve raises her eyebrows. Murmurs something to Tom — who obligingly disappears.

'You're still not fit yet, is all I mean.'

Annette's hands aren't bandaged, but her skin is still raw — she wears plasters around her exposed nail beds for the sake of Tom not having to see that sort of thing at teatime, even though what her wounds need (according to Eve) is a bit of fresh air and salt water.

'It did need doing. And I had the afternoon. So.'

318

Annette nods at this. The imposition. The violation. The Sycamores isn't her house, not really. Not in the way that this house belongs to Maddy and Eve. And Tom. There is nothing private in there. So. She can't get upset about it. Especially in the circumstances — put up by strangers, you've no rights at all. And she couldn't — though it might be fun to try — even pretend to be angry or surprised.

Maddy bites her lip. Smooths the letters out with her hands. They're old. Done with a typewriter and not a computer.

'I found these. They were in a shoebox. Could easily have been thrown out. Eaten up by mice. But here they are. The room at the front. It looked like it had been nice, once. Roses on the wallpaper. Books, everywhere, and foreign postcards stuck up around the dressing-table mirror.'

Annette nods. Doesn't need the place describing to her — but Maddy carries on, for Eve's benefit. Nothing in there had been touched in years, by the looks of it. But in the drawer, inside the shoebox, she found just what she'd been looking for. The practicalities. She gestures towards the envelopes that Annette has not touched. Ta da.

'Some stuff for you to look at. I've been through it. Put it in order. They're old, these policies. But with a bit of luck . . . How long ago was it your dad went?'

'Maddy.' Eve tugs at her shirt cuffs. This is a mannerism that appears whenever she's feeling upset, or stressed, or unsure. Annette's been here

319

long enough to learn these things and the familiarity, and the sudden recognition of it, isn't entirely uncomfortable.

'Passed on, I mean. How long since you were . . . bereaved?'

Annette smiles. She can't help it. Maddy is trying so hard.

'Six years. And then Candy — his wife — a few months ago. The summer. That's when it all came to me.'

'Well then, there you go. Nothing's out of date. You can claim.'

Annette looks at the papers. She's done office work. She has been a typist and an administrator and a general assistant at an accountancy firm. She has temped everywhere there is to temp in all the major cities of the British Isles. To sum up: she has typed more official letters than these two will ever receive and the details about the wills and the life insurance and the other documents make easy sense to her.

'It's called probate,' Maddy explains. 'Me and Eve had to do it last year for her mum. It's worse than it sounds — you wouldn't believe the forms — but once it's done and dusted, there'll be money to do up the house. Or get somewhere for yourself, if you want. Somewhere else. World's your oyster.'

The three of them sit there with the letters in the yellow glow of the overhead light. The kitchen smells like coffee and garlic. Annette predicts Eve will be the one to jump first and she does — off to the cupboard for a bottle and three glasses. The whisky is good, but Maddy can't

320

resist observing that they were supposed to be saving it for Christmas. Annette sips.

'I could buy somewhere. That's what it looks like,' she says. She turns the letters over.

'Looks like they had it all planned out for you,' says Maddy. 'Couldn't find a will for your dad. But if he let everything go to Candy automatically, and she left everything for you, then . . .'

'She gets it,' Eve says. 'Give her a minute.'

There are other things to look at besides letters — Maddy has collected anything official or financial looking and brought it home with her. There are a few old rent books in a brown envelope. Annette tips them out, opens them. Runs a figure down their columns. The sums look pitiful now — pounds and pennies, odd amounts, here and there.

'This is how they used to make their money, my parents,' Annette says. 'Before my mum died and Candy and my dad got the new house together. That was the business they ran. Lodgers.'

'I guessed as much,' Maddy says. She's read everything. 'And you three slept up in the attic.'

Annette nods. 'It was good fun, sometimes.' She takes a coin out of her pocket and holds it on her palm. 'Look.' Makes it trip and trickle over her knuckles, backwards and forwards, then disappear into her palm. She opens her hand, spreads her fingers wide. Nothing. 'One of them taught me that. Card tricks too. I'm always handy at a party.'

Maddy watches Annette closely, but there's

very little to see. She gathers up the rent books, stacks them together, holds them close. The woman is maddening. No relief, no thanks, she just folds up the letters, still nursing hands she's clearly afraid to flex and stretch in case the skin splits, and takes the whole folder up to the blue room. Says she'll look it over. Use the phone in the morning to get things started, if that's all right. Be out as soon as she can. Later, they'll find a coin under the salt pot and she'll refuse to tell them how she slipped it there.

29

We can't bear to be in our house right now. We can't be in the kitchen or the dining room or in any of the old lodgers' rooms. We are not wanted in the garden. We know things need to be done but we are not the ones to do them. We have no responsibilities here. We have nothing to do but wait with Candy, who is a young woman again — looks younger than she is, on account of not having children of her own — and at home in her bedsitter, remembering that Fiona at the Women's Union doesn't need to work although she is a fully trained hairdresser and will pop to the house to do a bleach, trim and perm for her friends. Candy hennas her own hair but she does like Fiona to come and give her a wash and set or put her hair up for special occasions. Though special occasions are few and far between at the moment. Anyway, this Fiona has a little saying that Candy has picked up on and made her own. Payment is not required but to offer expenses is polite. She likes the fact that it isn't a question; the fussiness of the grammar, the way it would take a person a second or two to work out what you meant, and so put them on the back foot.

To offer expenses is polite. It won't have occurred to Jack, the state the poor bastard is in, but Candy is spending most of her wages on meals for him and Annette now and while she doesn't begrudge them the expense — bread cast on water always finds a way of coming back to you, she's learned that lesson often enough — the nights are drawing in and she realises, as she roots down the side of the armchair in her bedsitter for any dropped coins she can find, she isn't exactly looking forward to coppering up for the gas for the rest of the winter. She'll be damned if she's feeding that ghoul of a lodger that's hanging around them all, eating his head off and lying around, neither use nor ornament. He'll get nothing from her. She wouldn't give him the steam off of her tea if he curtseyed while he asked her for it. She finds a few pennies and a handful of fluff, deposits the haul on her nightstand and goes to wash her hands.

Jack's going to have to work out what he'll do for money. There's no work on the sands any more. Candy's brother went out, first for the fluke and cockles, and made a decent enough living from that. Then the hard winter came last year and the frosts were so bad the sands froze rock hard, no cramb could get near, and all the little wheat froze in their shells. The water bailiffs banned the use of jumbos to give what was left a fighting chance of replenishing itself, but those who still went out with horse and cart, and there were plenty of them, just started using the tail boards and that was that. There was no work now for anyone. Some of the men moved on to the mussel beds but they were on their last legs too and her brother, poor bastard, had resorted to plucking starfish out of the defunct cockle beds by hand and taking them back to his boiling shed where he drowned them in buckets of formalin. Once they were dry and stiff he packaged them up and sent them off to American research laboratories. There were scientists, he'd told her, who would pay good (enough) money to study an English starfish that could grow its broken legs back just in case it told them something useful about cancer. You couldn't credit it. But none of that was Jack's scene.

We watch Candy rinse her hands and carefully prop the soap up against the taps to dry so it'll last longer. She should worry about herself and never mind Jack and his financial situation, that's what she should do. She used to be able to spend a little bit of money on herself now and again. Not lavishly, but there's no harm in treating yourself nicely, not if your rent is paid up and you don't owe on the catalogue. No point waiting for someone else to do what you can do yourself. That's her motto. She's about to pull the chair out and see if there's any joy to be found in looking down the back of it — she found a crumpled five-bob note the last time — when a loud banging at the door interrupts her.

Her heart sinks.

A pounding like that, and at this time in the morning, can only mean one sort of news and it isn't likely to be good.

Oh, love.

Candy crosses herself, like a child. Spectacles, testicles, wallet and watch. That's what the boys used to say. It's sacrilegious, she supposes, but if there is a God he'll be a damn sight bigger than children's jokes, and letting Netty go off without

325

putting a good word in for her feels wrong, somehow. It's better she's gone, though, the poor, poor bitch. She's out of her suffering and off to a better place now. Candy has seen some linger for months and months until they were no more than yellow skeletons in their beds, their breath rattling in their chests like pebbles down a drainpipe. Better for Netty to have avoided all that. If Candy had to pick a way, it would be the way Netty's done it. With her man next to her, her own things around her. It would have been peaceful. Slipping away in her sleep. Calm. And (the banging at the door becomes more frantic but she doesn't move) it isn't wrong of her to think, to hope — no, to know — that her own intervention, direction and support (she's a nurturer, that's her gift — everyone has one and putting herself out for the sake of others is hers) made things easier on poor Netty than it would have been otherwise. It let her keep a bit of hope, right up to the end. She never promised Netty anything more than comfort. An easy mind. And Jack will be all right. He has that big house. He's young enough to find someone else to mother the little one. The world turns and everything changes. You may as well cry over the tide going out.

We are watching Candy still standing at the sink, the bar of soap in her hand. Her feet won't carry her towards the door. If no one says it, it won't be true, she thinks. She's surprised to find tears in her eyes and pulls her handkerchief from her sleeve and wipes them before uprooting herself and hurrying down the stairs, skidding on piles of unopened letters and catalogues addressed to tenants who moved on years since. She's expecting Jack but when she opens the door to her flat it's only his bloody lodger there, white as a sheet and holding Annette's hand in his. The three of them stand for a moment and Candy is unable to speak, her hand patting at her throat. Annette is wearing a good party dress that is too small for her and isn't fastened properly at the back. Her legs are bare.

'You'd better come up to the flat,' Candy says. She turns and they follow her up the stairs. 'Wipe your feet properly. Close the door behind you. Pick your feet up, Annette, Mrs Seabourne won't be awake yet and she'll complain if she hears you clattering.'

Candy's never had two guests in her sitter at the same time before. Tim has to stand pressed flat against the wall, the stockings and under-skirts dangling from the pulley brushing the top of his head. She heats her last half-pint of milk on the two-ring stove and makes toast and jam for Annette, who sits at the card table eating pear drops out of a paper bag.

'Look at her. She's starving. What did she have for her tea last night? Was there some of my stew left? Did you warm a bit up for her?'

Tim shrugs. He's unshaven.

'When did she last have a bath?'

'I don't know, Candy.' He sounds irritated, and Candy clicks her tongue at him.

'You won't speak to me like that in my own house, Mister. You won't dare.' She pours warm milk from the pan into two small matching

327

mugs. 'Sit. You look terrible.' She points to one of the mugs. 'Get that down you. Then you better get back to the house. Are there arrangements that need attending to?' She looks at Annette meaningfully.

Tim lifts the cup and drinks. She waits. 'I don't know,' he says, stands, and wipes his mouth. 'I'd better get back to him.'

He leaves, closing the door quietly without saying goodbye to Annette.

★ ★ ★

What can we do? What can we do now? Candy and the girl wait in all day for news, but there isn't any. After tea, she runs a deep bath in the shared bathroom and pours in a half-bottle of her lavender and camomile foaming oil, which is supposed to be relaxing, was probably expensive and was a gift from one of the bosses in the office that she wanted to try and make last. The landlady has drawn a line around the inside of the bath, about six inches from the bottom, in black marker — it is supposed to indicate the maximum depth of water allowed to tenants, but Candy ignores it. The tight-fisted bitch can shell out on some hot water for once; the circumstances today are exceptional, after all.

Annette still isn't saying much, but she complies when Candy slips her dress up and over her head and helps her take her socks and shoes off. She holds Candy's hand as she steps into the bath and Candy notices the filth under her fingernails, the knots in the back of her hair, and goes to fetch her comb and nail brush. The little get looks like she's been dragged up in a slum, Candy thinks, and tuts. Soap costs pennies, if that. There's no excuse.

'When I was little,' she says, lifting water out of the bath with the giant pink and white scallop shell they use for a soap dish and letting it run over Annette's shoulders, 'I used to go and stay at my aunty's house every summer for a few weeks. My mam was working, and she couldn't look after us in the school holidays. My aunty lived right out in the countryside and she didn't have a bath, lots of people didn't then, but when it was hot she used to make us stand in the horse trough and pour buckets of water over our heads. Or we went in the sea and made do. There were no fancy bubbles and fluffy towels like this.'

She examines Annette carefully. The girl is staring at the taps, the sponge, the chain of the plug, as if she is trying to commit the whole room to memory, or maybe as if she isn't quite sure whether any of this is real, or a dream. If someone's told her what has just happened, she'll be in shock. Shock can be medical. She's read about it.

'We didn't mind, though,' Candy carries on, thinking this dead-ended tale about baths that was only half true was a poor substitute for a bedtime story, but she's no experience and she is doing her best.

'All right. You're done. Out.' She holds up the towel and Annette pouts and has to have the plug pulled before she'll agree to get out.

Once the girl is dried Candy wraps her up in a

red kimono that was a present from a man she used to see, just casually, and even though it was perfectly clean and kept the girl warm and decent, was stupidly too big for her. But what else could she do? She'd come with nothing. The lodger was about as much use as a chocolate teapot and hadn't even thought to bring the girl a change of clothes. Candy might not know anything about children but she knew that much. She knew they needed washing and feeding, that someone had to have a conversation with them now and again, to make sure they weren't scared, or bored, or sickening for something. It was just basic common sense. Looking after Annette couldn't be substantially different from looking after herself, and she'd managed that all right all this time, hadn't she?

Annette won't let Candy dry her hair with the hair-dryer. She says her mother always plaits it when it's wet and lets it dry like that, overnight, so that in the morning when her hair is brushed out, it waves like a mermaid's. It's the first thing she's asked for. Candy turns Annette around in the chair and reaches for her comb.

'My mother used to comb my hair over the side of the bath,' she says. 'Every Sunday night before school we'd get scrubbed and she'd put paraffin on our heads and comb our hair through to get rid of the nits.' A thought occurs to her. Enough to make her blood run cold. 'You've not got nits, have you?' She pokes Annette's scalp with the comb and examines it dubiously. 'I can't see anything. But we'd best get it all plaited up tight and tidy like you want it, eh?'

Annette nods. Candy puts her two armchairs face to face and tucks a pillow and two blankets into the hollow for Annette to sleep in. Good job she's not any bigger. It isn't perfect, not by anyone's standards, but it will have to do. When Annette's breathing is soft and regular she creeps downstairs, out onto the street and along to the public telephone. She rings the house she will always think of as Netty's, hoping that Jack or that idle lodger of theirs will answer, but no one does, and she allows herself a brief, brisk cry in the phone box before blowing her nose and hurrying home to hand-wash Annette's clothes in her sink so she'll have something clean to wear in the morning.

30

This is full winter. The dead of it, the dark of it. The first we have known together in years. It gets so cold that it starts to freeze inside the house as well as out. This, to the best of our knowledge (which isn't much — we understand that) has never happened before. The pipe that leads to the outside tap — the one we let Timothy Richardson tie his rabbits to — should have been lagged and wasn't. The water inside it freezes and swells and for hours there's an invisible build-up of pressure until the pipe splits around the joint. Water oozes slowly, forming an extra knuckle of ice around the fault. We try, but our breath cannot warm it. So we go back to the house on the outskirts of the city that straddles the Lune on the south side of the bay. The house with the little lights in the window — because where else is there, for us?

It's the school holidays now. The place is full. Tom is frantic with anticipation and needs constant entertaining. Today, Eve comes into the sitting room to find him and Annette on the living-room loveseat, looking through furniture catalogues, their heads bowed together. Like a pair of kids. Like thieves.

'You'll want tellies,' Tom is saying. 'Massive tellies.'

'Will I?' Annette is neutral. Curious.

He nods. Eve waits by the door, fearing to tread.

'People won't come and pay to stay unless they have their own telly in their own bedroom. And little kettles too. It's just how it is.'

'Is that right?'

Tom nods seriously. 'And you'll have to get a giant washing machine, like they have in launderettes, and you'll have to get little round soaps and tiny bottles of shampoo and conditioner, and in some places you get miniature envelopes with shower caps and sewing kits inside, for people who've forgotten their own, or who want to mend something. We always have them when we go away, don't we, Mum?'

Eve comes into the room fully now, nodding. Remembering weekends away to Scarborough — and pleased, somehow, that they're so prominent in Tom's memory too. But her attention is snagged by the catalogue Tom and Annette are holding between them. Where the hell have they got that from?

'What are you up to? He's not bothering you, is he?'

Annette looks up. 'He brought me these, to look at. Very useful.' She lifts the catalogue, some thin, glossy thing that looks like it's been rescued from a Sunday newspaper. Left over from his paper round, no doubt. 'He thought I'd want to take a look at it.'

'You'll want to make it nice, won't you?' Tom insists. Oblivious to the sensitivity needed — Annette was still touchy about the house. They couldn't mention it. Couldn't ask her about her plans for it, even now. Not without the strange silences and the going off to her room, or sitting in the garden on her own for hours on end, in all weathers. But Tom — Tom doesn't know this. Eve tugs at her cuffs.

'Tom — '

'He's all right, Eve. In fact, he's more than all right.' She turns to Tom. 'I've stayed in some grim places in my time. You wouldn't believe it if I told you. What some landlords get away with. It's nice to have a home from home. That's what they say, isn't it?' She ducks her head and turns a page.

'You're thinking about staying in the place?'

Annette shrugs.

'I can't see myself there. Can't imagine it. The place feels . . . ' She looks at the ceiling. Scrapes back her hair. 'I don't know. Full. I've never had a proper house before. Of my own. All that space and I still felt — when I was there — that it wasn't mine. That it didn't belong to me. That it had a life of its own and there was no room for me in it.'

'You must have felt at home somewhere.'

'I stayed places. I drifted. One rental is the same as the other. Six months here, six there. House shares. Bedsits. They suited me. I think I was too — ' she breaks off. 'My dad and Candy used to say I was too erratic to settle down. They wanted me to. Candy would have liked grandchildren. She hinted at them. I think she'd have liked to look after a baby. But,' Annette shakes her head, 'I couldn't ever get myself in the mood to do it.'

'Nothing wrong with erratic,' Eve says. 'No one says you have to settle down, just because most people do. You don't have to do anything.'

'I wasn't glad to have been left the house,' Annette says. 'I'd rather have had the money. But now I've had some time. To mull it over.' Annette turns a page in the catalogue, and laughs. 'And now there's the money *and* the house. Well.'

Eve waits and does not pretend to understand.

'Do you know what Maddy said to me the other day?' Annette asks.

'I dread to think.'

Annette chuckles gently.

'She said there was no point being sentimental about the place if there was money to sort it out properly. She said I'd feel differently if I got builders in. Got it cleared out properly. Gutted from top to bottom. That's what she said. Gut the place.'

Tom answers before Eve can.

'Mum says you could turn it into a boutique hotel and rake it in. I heard her. You could print your own money, she said.' He laughs. Eve imagines him with a swag bag, the little mercenary — Maddy through and through. 'And,' he ducks his head, suddenly shy, 'I think we could come and stay with you. When you get it all up and running. For a holiday.'

Eve coughs even though she doesn't need to, instead of having to find something to say. *Bloody Maddy.* Subtle as a brick. But Annette just laughs again. Genuinely. Whether at Tom's plain speaking, or Eve's awkwardness, she doesn't know. But Eve hasn't heard that from her before — not a proper laugh, like that.

'A holiday just to come and stay with me?

You'll want to go further than that, won't you? Somewhere a bit more exotic than just up the road.'

'I'm going to France in the summer,' Tom says. 'On my own. We're going to go in a coach, through the tunnel. I'll have to take a travel sickness pill because last time — '

'We've not said you can go,' Eve warns.

Yes. This is what they've been arguing about. Annette closes the catalogue quickly. Tom frowns.

'Well, maybe home is best,' Annette says quickly, winking at Eve. 'No place like it. And they do say the Kent is on the move again. I heard something about it on the radio. That salt marsh might be a beach, like it used to be, before too long. People will want somewhere to stay. You won't remember it being all sandy, Tom, but it was, and people used to build castles on it. There were even donkey rides, sometimes. My dad bought me candyfloss once and it melted in my hair and my mum had to wash it out with green dish soap.'

Eve tries not to stare. In the time Annette has been staying with them, this is the longest sentence she's ever spoken. And about herself, too. She'll have to tell Maddy. Couldn't get a word in edgeways. She was practically chatting.

'Did you go to the beach all the time when you lived there?' Tom has been distracted, the inevitable argument averted, and Eve smiles her thanks at Annette — gets a nod in return.

That tiny gesture of acknowledgement between them — that was new too. Maybe it was the right thing to go in and find those papers. Help her sort out the finances a bit. It wasn't okay, just to break in like that, but maybe Maddy had been right about it after all. Eve sighs. Smiles. She'll never tell her, though.

31

We should act or leave but the way forward is not clear and what else can we do now but watch? The nurse has used the telephone and left on her bicycle. The men loiter in the house all day. And now Jack leans against the banisters and waits on the landing. A while ago he had reason to pull out and consult Netty's little dictionary. Collins *Gem* said that metastasis meant both 'beyond' and 'still', and at the time it made no sense. But now, with the house so emptied it nearly hums with absence, he remembers the word again and winces, dry-eyed. The undertakers move up and down the stairs, sliding the stretcher around the neck of the landing like they're doing a house clearance. It's draped with a sheet. Not one of theirs. Jack cries out, his hand outstretched, as they tilt the stretcher downwards.

'Don't hurt her,' he says.

Tim pulls at his elbow.

'Come on. Outside. We'll get some fresh air.'

They go out the back and smoke. Jack regards the withered stumps of the begonias, the moss and leaves clogging the lawn, and wonders numbly where the summer has gone. The brassicas have had it — either slime mould or black-rot and he can't tell which and it probably doesn't matter. The sky is grey. Early morning or late afternoon. He'd thought it was nighttime — it was dark, wasn't it, when Netty was taken so badly? — but now it's light and though he's not hungry, he suspects hours and hours have slid past without him. Jack forgets the cigarette in his hand. The long column of ash burns undisturbed. He closes his eyes and hears it fall onto the grass.

'You should go to bed.'

'It's daytime. What time is it?'

'You need a kip. There'll be things for you to do. You'll need your energy.'

The boy does not head to his bedroom, but slinks into the dining room and as Jack mounts the stairs the Singer starts its buzz and rattle. It's been going near constantly, at all hours of the day and night, this past fortnight. Nothing touches that boy. Imagine him being so desperate to make himself a fancy set of clothes at a time like this.

It must be nice to be like that. To drift through life unworried by grief. The bed appears before him so Jack lies down. It must be night after all, despite the light. The house has never been much good for sleeping in: too draughty, too creaky, too many bumps in the night. He does usually manage but without the steady dry rattle of Netty's laboured breathing, so slow, and the sickly sweet and chemical smell of her medications filling the room, he won't be able to settle. He reckons he's not had a single wink in days. He's been spending hours (how many have there been?) hunched in front of the television, smoking, drinking and staring balefully at the test-card. He closes his eyes.

Maybe he does sleep, because the next thing

he knows, it is dark. He rises and goes barefoot down the narrow staircase from his attic bedroom down to the lodgers' floor of the house, not fully awake until he feels the smooth coolness of the painted banister under his palm. The house is silent. In times past you'd hear the muffled sound of a radio playing, a late-night game of cards or even, occasionally, the creak and whisper of one of the boys smuggling a woman into or out of his room. The doors of the emptied rooms stand ajar, drifting slowly closed or open as the house breathes out the warmth of the day and settles into its nighttime chill. Behind the doors are only empty fireplaces, stripped single beds and tallboys with their drawers sagging open. He walks softly, missing the last step (the one that always groans like it's in pain whenever it is stepped on) and tiptoes across the flattened, worn-out strip of carpet on the landing. There are shirts hanging over the banisters to dry. The place smells damp and fusty.

Only one of the rooms is occupied — the one at the front with the damp under the bay window that they always have trouble letting. The door is closed; Jack grasps the handle and turns it quickly. It clicks and cries a little as it opens but the sleeping figure in the bed does not move and soon Jack is standing above Timothy Richardson who is shirtless, lying on his back and snoring softly with his mouth half open. The quality of the faint, greyish light (it must be near dawn now) perfects his skin in some strange way: the boy looks like he's been carved out of marble, and if it wasn't for the snoring he'd look like a statue, or a corpse.

Jack glances around the room. The pile of magazines stacked on top of the tallboy. The cardboard suitcase protruding from under the bed. The jackets hanging in the wardrobe, a towel slung over the open door to dry, ties dangling from the doorknob. His bloody books and manuals, full of pictures of men posing in fancy outfits. There's a cake of soap and a badger shaving brush on the bedside table, and the sight of the cracked and curved soap triggers something in him. He returns to the bed and then in a lithe little leap he neither anticipated nor knew he was capable of, straddles Richardson and fits his hands around the boy's pale bastard throat. Our hands — our useless hands — go to Jack, but we know already that he only gets to enjoy the feeling of Tim's warm, slightly damp skin against his palms for a few seconds. The boy wakes immediately, of course. The whites of his eyes pick up the dim glow from the streetlight coming in between the curtains and flash in the dark. He isn't able to make a sound. The boy's windpipe, the thick rolling gristle of it, is under his thumbs. He squeezes harder. Tim's hands are batting at the bed, his feet kicking, and Jack is moving, up and down, as the boy tries to buck him off. Even in the dim light Jack can see the boy's complexion darkening and now the air sucks and rasps in the boy's throat as he tries to choke back his last mouthful. In a matter of seconds, maybe less, Timothy Richardson has brought up his hands to Jack's face, pressed his thumbs into his eye-sockets and pushed.

There's pressure, then pain and although he's determined to hold on to the end no matter what it costs him, Jack is forced to release his grip and falls backwards onto the bed. His legs are bent beneath him and it hurts. The back of his head catches the brass rail at the end of the bed and that hurts too. Tim leaps up and across the room, and stands, doubled over and coughing, in front of the window. Jack slowly rights himself and sits on the edge of the bed, rubbing his eyes.

'Get out of here!' Jack is still blinded. 'Pack your things and get out. Out.'

Tim is coughing. He staggers over to the sink in the corner of his bedroom and turns on the taps. The water chugs into the bowl, the pipes popping and banging, and Jack, still nursing his eyes, wonders about Annette. He'd forgotten about her. Was she awake now? Had the clatter of the struggle and his raised voice woken her up? He'd thought of her so little in the past few days. Had he managed to sit her down yet, to speak to her properly about what had happened? It was hard to tell, hard to remember. He needed to make a list. Consider what his duties were and how best to execute them. No good her coming down in the night (was she in bed? Had he put her to bed?) and catching the boy and him with their hands around each other's necks.

The boy. He needed clearing out. Out of the house, out of their lives. And then things could go back to normal.

His mind skitters painfully away from what

342

normal might consist of now. Netty's frenzied preparations for Christmas. The boys up on ladders hanging paper chains and tinsel from the light fittings. Sherry in front of the telly, and the electric blanket on an hour before bed. Her Christmas card book, and the yearly ritual of crossing out the dead and those who didn't send a card last year and so may as well be. None of those things. The coming weeks loom at him like a black hole and, shamefully, a whine escapes from him. A childish noise he is unable to bite back or control. There are still no tears.

Tim clears his throat, spits into the sink and splashes water on his face and neck. When he is finished he crosses the room, pulls the cord and snaps on the overhead light. Jack covers his tender eyes, but in the moment before he's restored himself to darkness, he sees Tim, chest bare, advancing on him.

'What the hell do you think you're playing at? Trying to kill me in my sleep? What sort of cowardly trick is that?'

Jack lowers his hands. He isn't blinded, thank God. It would serve him right if he was. Just the kind of luck a stupid bastard like him should have learned to expect by now. Tim stands over him; blurry, certainly, but there. The thin, high noise is still emanating from him. He listens to it curiously, as if it is coming from somewhere else. A broken radio, perhaps, or the wind howling down the chimney. He holds his breath. Perhaps that will make it go away.

'You must go,' he says, finally.

'Right now?'

Jack laces his fingers together and puts his hands on top of his head. Tim has his breath back now and is only panting slightly as he stares, enraged. But Jack is suffocating. Tim waits another second and, perhaps realising Jack is unable, or unwilling to answer, kicks the suitcase out from under the bed, opens it, and starts to dump jackets and shirts into it. The badger brush and soap are swept off into it, the magazines, the ties. He leaves the towel. Netty issues all the boys with their own brown striped towel once they arrive; she says it makes the laundry easier — less sorting to do. He must remember that.

'Don't start greeting now, pal. I'm the one who's been woken up with your fucking hands round my throat!'

A great tiredness overcomes Jack as he watches Tim pack. He lies on the bed, on top of the sheets and blankets that hold the curious smell of the boy — part salt, part smoke — and turns away. The clasps on the suitcase fasten with a dull click. He'll close his eyes and in the morning the boy will be gone. He'll wash the pots then do a proper cooked breakfast for himself and see what's what. Tomorrow. The overhead light goes out and Jack, his eyes still closed, waits for the sound of the boy's tread on the stair, the final slam of the front door. He holds his breath. Should he arrange for the locks to be changed? Ask Peter Jackson to come and fix some shutters to the downstairs windows?

'I spoke to Gregson,' Jack says, not knowing why. 'Those rabbits.'

344

Tim grunts. 'He told you about that?'

Jack, still facing away from the boy, nods in the dark.

'He did. I went to see him.'

'You were checking up on me. What did you want?'

'I didn't want anything. Only to know. What was going on. It was quite a story.'

He hears Tim breathing. Calmer now.

'I couldn't help it.'

'No. I can see that.'

'It was horrible,' Tim says.

The silence lies between them, the boy waiting for Jack to say something. He's nothing left in him. The wardrobe door opens and closes. Something else is put into the suitcase.

'It sounds it. But you did your best, didn't you, son?' Jack says.

No reply. The bed moves, and Jack stiffens as he realises Tim is getting into it. His muscles are like water, as if he's got the flu. He makes a small sound of protest, but the boy says nothing, only tucks his knees behind Jack's and loops an arm around his belly, like he is a woman. They are pressed together — the warmth of Tim's chest is against his spine, his breath hot and wet on the back of his neck. Jack's chest heaves and shudders and Tim holds him firmly, his elbow against his hip, their feet touching. Jack tries to shrug him off, but Tim grasps him, refusing to move or to make a sound, to give full space in the room to the noises that Jack continues to make, his shoulders shaking, his head about to burst, the muscles in his abdomen spasming against the boy's hand. Eventually the storm passes and Jack finally allows himself to sleep.

★ ★ ★

We sit in the stairwell all night. In the morning the boy and his suitcase are gone. The room is cleaned out: the only sign Timothy Richardson was ever there is a new white shirt and navy suit on a hanger in the doorway, drifting gently with the movement of the air like a ghost. And when he wakes Jack will search the house for Annette and discover that Tim has written the number of the bakery next door to Candy's flat on the hall mirror in Netty's lipstick. He'll dial the number. She and Annette will arrive at six o'clock that same evening with a casserole, a steamed syrup sponge and an overnight bag. She will feed them, put Annette to bed, berate Jack over the state of the house, himself and the arrangements not yet made. And she will insist he sleeps while she stays up all night laundering bed linen and scrubbing floors. Outfits will need to be arranged, she'll say. Annette can wear her Sunday dress and the school shoes from last year will do. There's a new suit and shirt for Jack — sober enough for the occasion, though a bit more modern than Candy would have chosen herself. The cut of the lapel is almost jaunty — who knows where he got that from — but it was his only smart set of clothes and needs must. Beggars can't be choosers. There are arrangements to make and if nobody else is stepping in to make them, she'll have to do it herself. There are the practicalities to think of. The no-good boy they've had staying with them is gone. She makes up her mind to be annoyed about that — about him abandoning Jack at his lowest moment. But the feeling won't stick. Instead she decides him clearing out like that was something more like kindness. In his own way, perhaps. After all, when there's nothing to do but get in the way, you might as well clear out and make room for those that can help.

32

There's no thaw. The freeze lasts until Christmas and will take us beyond it; we're sure of that. We take to waiting in the sycamores for the view it gives us over the glittering bay and the narrow streets. Some of the cafes start to offer speciality drinks — fripperies like ginger lattes and salted caramel mochas. Nothing like that in our day. We're out of touch. Someone puts fairy lights in the bare branches of the cherry trees along the promenade, and there's a one-off performance in the old bandstand — not one of the old brass bands that used to play there, proper music, but a church choir singing carols shakily, children clapping coconut shells together, and a bucket full of dirty coppers passed around afterwards. We're drawn back to Eve and Maddy's house. Where else could we go?

It's taken much longer than anyone thought for Annette's hands to heal. Her skin scabs over, cracks, becomes infected and scabs over again. It's Christmas Day itself before Annette can stand at the kitchen sink and marvel at the softness of the water against the pink, shiny new skin that has appeared on her palms. The water is too hot. Her hands are sensitive now. Maybe they'll always be that way.

'You don't have to do that, Annette,' Maddy says.

'Of course I do. The pair of you have been

348

stood in this kitchen for two days. Least I can do.'

She enjoys it too. The ordinary task. Being part of things. The fact she knows her way around the kitchen, doesn't have to ask where things are any more. Is welcome to take things out of the cupboards. To help herself. Tom stands beside her, his elbow butting her hip. They're friends now, these two, especially since they started looking through the catalogues together. Choosing furniture, speculating about paint colours. Every room a different shade of blue and grey, Tom says, to remind people of the bay even when the weather's too bad (because it will be — nothing changes that much) to get out on it.

Annette rinses wine glasses, chasing all the bubbles away. She's telling him about her dad's vegetable garden; the scarecrow they made to keep the starlings away from the peas, the time her mother came running out of the kitchen swishing a tea towel because the birds had started perching on the broom handle which formed the outstretched arms of the scarecrow. She swipes the tea towel at Tom, to show him what she means, and the both of them are laughing too much to notice that the conversation at the kitchen table has fallen silent, that the others are watching and listening to this story too. Even Maddy is smiling, amused at the sight of Annette in her shabby cardigan and too-big borrowed trousers chasing Tom around the kitchen.

And afterwards, once Annette has been

persuaded to leave the bloody washing-up and come back to the table and have her pudding and whisky and wear her party hat, the others, overfed and a little groggy with booze, will start to ask her questions. They skirt around the topic of the night that brought her here — that uncharacteristic bout of madness, of grief and anger, that even Annette herself will never understand. She's more careful about the wine bottles now, and pays attention to the special luck she seems to have when it comes to things lasting longer than they should. The knack isn't always a blessing in disguise. She will have whisky though, and she sips it while they ask her about the house. About why such a big handsome place would stand empty so long.

'I grew up there. And after my mother died, my dad and me stayed, with Candy.'

'Your stepmother?'

She nods. Her silence fills with stories of wicked stepmothers, of Cinderellas and Snow Whites and all kinds of other nonsense, and she feels the questions gather, and laughs them off.

'She was a good woman. But she couldn't live there. Not with my mum in every room. No competing with a dead woman, she said. So we all went to a little bungalow in Ulverston. My dad got a job in an office. Candy cooked in an old people's home. I had to change schools.'

'Was it all right?'

Annette pauses. Was it all right? Were they all right? She thinks about Jack in his fancy suit, Candy in her red dress, sparkly jewellery. Off out to the Roxy. To the bingo. Laughter on the stairs

350

late at night. Full Sunday dinners, and the pair of them in their best clothes in the front row for all the school plays. Later, going by the postcards they used to send, there were cruises, the two of them working themselves stupid looking after other people all year long just so they could spend a few weeks of each summer on a big white boat, going slowly over the water from place to place. But it hadn't always been so easy. She sips her whisky and thinks about that first Christmas — only six weeks after her mother died — with Candy using her own key in the small hours to put up her tree and put a ham in the oven, to leave something for her to open at the bottom of her bed, because she knew Jack wouldn't think of it. What was it? Annette can't remember. A portable record player? Yes. Expensive, and she already had one, and wasn't allowed to tell Candy that — so the old one (red, it was, with silver writing on the side) had to be hidden away so she'd never see it and be upset. And what else? Candy had carved the ham and brought crackers and helped Annette set the table and her dad — well, he'd done his best, and shaved, and came down the stairs wearing his good shirt and a light blue tie he kept touching as if he'd never seen it before. Candy had read all the jokes from the crackers and laughed at the punchlines herself and it was so tiring that Annette remembers she was almost glad when she went home again. Almost. Better a pretend Christmas than no Christmas at all.

'They were happy, I think. Happy enough. They argued sometimes. But she was good to us.

I had a better life with her in it than I would have done otherwise.'

Annette realises, in the saying of it, that it is true. She should have made some time to tell Candy that. Should have visited. Been kinder. Made more time for them.

'But none of you ever went back to the house?' Maddy asks. 'Not until your dad went?' Eve nudges her under the table. Not today. Annette pretends not to notice.

'He wouldn't sell it. It belonged to his parents. His dad was something to do with cotton, but the money all went during the war and there was nothing left to leave him but bricks and mortar. Now and again he and Candy would talk about fixing it up and renting it out to someone but he always said he didn't have time. I don't think he could bear to go back to it. My mum's clothes were still in the wardrobes. They were there waiting for me when I got back.'

She's thinking of the skip. They murmur. Appropriate sympathy. Not intrusive. No one is asking questions now — it's not the day for it, not really — but Annette tells them anyway.

'Candy once said she thought my dad left the best part of himself back in that house. That she was living with the leftovers; a shadow. She was right. But she looked after us anyway. It wasn't the same, though. People did things differently then. We weren't allowed to talk about my mother. And because I couldn't talk about her, I started to forget. I suppose there'll be photographs in the house. What they looked like. If the damp hasn't got to them. It was strange: living your whole life with a story you weren't allowed to tell, then forgetting what it was you wanted to say in the first place. Like there was a gap,' she pats her chest, 'here. With nothing to go inside it.'

Annette gazes into the candlelight. Tom fidgets, wanting to be let down from the table to play with his new toys. Maddy discreetly waves him away to his PlayStation.

'I left Ulverston as soon as I was finished with school. I suppose it was the same for me as it was for my dad. We belonged to that house.'

She's remembering something else now. That first Christmas, she'd asked if the lodgers were coming back. She'd asked for Richardson. There'd been a toy in one of the crackers — a little matchbox with a secret drawer for making money and paperclips disappear. She'd tried to tell Candy and her dad about the trick he'd done with the bird — the way he could bring things back to life (she wasn't a baby — she knew it was just a game, like seaside fortune-telling and people getting cut in half at the circus and rabbits coming out of hats on the television, but it was a really good trick) and the matchbox reminded her of him, and she tried to tell the story to cheer everyone up and make them laugh and Candy shushed her and took her plate away and Jack would not answer, but only slipped off his tie and put it next to his plate, looked out of the window, and drank. Annette knows his name now — Timothy — from the old rent book she's keeping in the top drawer of her bedside table. He'd been the one to take her to Candy's house

353

that morning. He'd kissed her hand at the bottom of the stairs before taking her up and leaving her there.

Maddy touches the back of Annette's hand. Looks into her face, expecting to see her upset, and instead she finds her smiling.

'It's all right,' she says, surprising herself. She looks around at the fairy lights strung over the doorway, the mess of the turkey carcass on the table, the candles guttering. 'I've been sorting out the paperwork. It's all coming through. The money. And in the spring — you'll help me?'

'What with, love?'

'With the trees? Make a proper job of it. With the structural engineers and the people for the drains. And getting builders in. All of that stuff.'

'Course we will,' Maddy answers before Eve gets a chance. 'She's been itching to get her chainsaw on the go since she saw the place.'

'Good. Well, I'll be all right then. Won't I?'

She sounds like a child again — that pleading, trembling tone Eve had first heard from her the afternoon they'd met.

'You're going to be fine,' Eve says.

One of the others coughs. They'll chase the awkwardness with another bottle of wine. And they'll drink to that — to being all right, and when Tom comes back, bored already by his new game, they'll turn on the overhead light and urge Annette to show him the trick with the coin until the table is covered with spare change and everyone is laughing.

★ ★ ★

Our house falls back into darkness and silence. Frost blooms along the insides of the windows. There are mice in the kitchen, twittering and squeaking as they run along the skirting boards. When it rains, it drips through the roof and onto one of the beds in the attic. We can only look in on the feast through windows that don't belong to us. Like Tim, staring into bedrooms that weren't his, that should have remained dark to him, insinuating himself into places he was uninvited. Mostly we sleep and wait. And slowly it comes: we're the guests now. We see things that we should not see, that shouldn't be our business any more. Why did she wake us? She didn't mean to. Didn't want to.

The house is too full, she says. We left the best parts of ourselves behind in it, she says. Is that what she thinks? Is that why she won't come home? We touch the walls and curve our palms around the chill of the cut-glass doorknobs. We press our cheeks against the windows and listen. We run our fingertips along the cracks in the floorboards and inspect the secret places where the dust gathers.

We know what to do now.

LAST

They had to wait until the spring and the danger of frost and snow was properly over. Until Eve had a quiet week and could convince Alec and a few friends to join her at the house. Until someone from the council could confirm that the trees weren't special nor subject to any order that would prevent her from felling them. Our trees. It took a long time. But today is the day that the sycamore trees come down.

The garden is full of noise because Eve has a stump grinder on loan and they've arranged a permit to close the road. The neighbours — faces we do not recognise, eyes that stare right through us, as if our welcome and our hospitality are no longer wanted — are out in force. There's laughter, and gasps as branches fall from the denuded, humiliated trees. Eve tells Annette that when she gets back to the house (and she is coming back to the house: this is some comfort to us — not much, not enough, but some comfort all the same) she will have to face their tea and sympathy, their thirst for gossip, their casseroles and homemade cakes and jams and invitations to beetle drives and choir practices for weeks. There's a scaffold being erected in the back garden because these industrious women have even roped in a builder acquaintance of theirs to patch up the ridge tiles on the roof. It won't last forever, they've said, but it will do for

359

now. The place will be liveable, if not palatial.

It is kind of them. She owes them. But they're not doing too badly out of her, either. This is an opportunity for Eve and Alec to put a brightly coloured hoarding advertising their tree and garden services in the front garden and to talk to the local radio station about their good deed. They ask Annette if she will go and have her photograph taken with the sad, branchless trees. The photograph will be for their website. Annette tells them to fuck off and they laugh. Alec claps her on the shoulder. She goes back to the van with Maddy and Tom and watches through the windows.

They have festooned the trees with ropes. The noise of the chainsaw is deafening and the sawdust hails downwards. Alec is up high like a spider, scrambling around and cutting off the branches one by one until all that is left is a pair of miserable spikes that can come down in hefty chunks. The air stinks of sap. Maddy worries that this will be upsetting to Annette, to see the home of her childhood desecrated so callously, even if the work is necessary, and Maddy even presents Annette with lavender bushes in pots (pots — is that the right word?) which she promises won't hurt the house, and which she and Tom will plant in the bare ground as soon as Eve gives the all-clear. Annette frowns at the pots. Raises an eyebrow. She is thinking that only old ladies get lavender.

Because Annette is not grateful enough, Maddy is irritated. She rolls her eyes, tuts and gets out of the van. She stands in the garden, complaining to Eve. Months of effort and though she leaves her muddy boots at the back door these days they haven't managed to house-train her yet. This work had better be done by the end of this week because Maddy wants her house back.

'It's a simple enough job,' Eve says. 'None of the birds were protected.'

She points. The starlings have left the branches and are perched on the ridge tiles and the telephone lines, cluttering gutters and chimney pots up and down the street. There are hundreds of them. More than we thought possible. They can't all have roosted in the trees but it seems that they did and they are homeless now.

We wait with Annette in the van. Tom is there too. He is looking carefully at her. He is shaking his head slowly, like an adult. In a moment he will roll his eyes.

'You could just play along now and again,' he says. 'For their sake. And lavender isn't only for old ladies.'

Annette just smiles.

'Show me your hand,' she says. 'Dexter and sinister. One for the past, one for the future.'

He holds out his right hand. Of course he does. It's soft and unlined and slightly grubby, just as it should be. Annette traces a line with her finger and it tickles him: his fingers curl.

'You'll travel,' she says. 'You'll turn out to be a right little globetrotter.'

'Did you talk to them?'

Annette nods. 'She's going to write the cheque today.'

Tom punches the air and whoops. 'How did you manage that?' He has a lopsided smile. 'Did you put a spell on them?'

Annette winks. We think she is going to say something else now, but there's a sharp crack — like the report of a gun: is it a gun, is that the thing we mean? — and they both look up in time to see the final bough separate itself from the trunk of the second tree and fall downwards. The noise it makes is tremendous — it startles Annette and Tom and they clutch at each other then laugh at themselves, and it startles us. It lifts the starlings from their perches and up they come from the roof things — from the tiles and the . . . the cables for the telephone . . . the wires, that's it — and from the hedges and shed roofs and bird tables, all along the street, up they come, flocking into the grey sky in a great throbbing murmuration, homeless now, but on their way, up over the town, seeing the Kent (is that its name? We used to know, we're sure we used to know but the word feels like a stranger now, and now we try to think of it again, it's gone), seeing the river disgorge into the bay, the main road hug the edge of the . . . what is the word for that? The green and brown of the . . . what is it called? What have we done? We have loved her and each other incompletely and imperfectly. But we have . . . we have. What's the word? The sun. Yellow. And the. The thing. That. Here are the. Birds. All of the.

We go with them.

Acknowledgements

With grateful thanks to Richard Anderson and Brian Lishak at Richard Anderson Limited, Savile Row, Audrey Ardern-Jones, Nurse Specialist in Cancer Genetics at The Royal Marsden NHS Hospital Trust, Mark Clowes at the Health Sciences Library at the University of Leeds, Gill Hutchinson, Lead Cancer Care Nurse (retired), Tony Kirkham, Head of Arboretum and Horticultural Services at the Royal Botanical Gardens, Kew, Elizabeth Toon at the Centre for the History of Science, Technology and Medicine at Manchester University, Jo Carruthers and the Placing Morecambe project at Lancaster University, Hilary Hinds at Lancaster University and Jon McGregor. Thanks also to Anthony Goff and Carole Welch.

HOMEGOING

Yaa Gyasi

In eighteenth-century Ghana, two half-sisters, Effia and Esi, are born into different villages. Effia is eventually married to an Englishman and lives in comfort in the palatial rooms of Cape Coast Castle. Unbeknownst to her, Esi is imprisoned beneath in the castle's dungeons, sold with thousands of others into the Gold Coast's booming slave trade, and then shipped off to America, where her children and grandchildren will be raised in slavery. The consequences of the sisters' fates reverberate through the generations that follow. From the Gold Coast to the cotton-picking plantations of Mississippi; from the missionary schools of Ghana to the dive bars of Harlem, spanning three continents and seven generations, this is the story of how the memory of captivity came to be inscribed in the soul of a nation.